I0522613

CONFIDENTIALITY

JESSICA AIKEN-HALL

MOONLIT MADNESS
PRESS

Copyright © 2020 Jessica Aiken-Hall

First Edition.

All rights reserved. No part of this publication may be reproduced, stored in any retrieval system, or transmitted, in any form or by any means, electronic, mechanical, photocopying, recording or otherwise, without the prior written permission of the author. If you would like permission to use material from the book (other than for review purposes), please contact http://jessicaaikenhall.com/contact

This is a work of fiction. Names, characters, businesses, organizations, products, places, and events portrayed in this novel are either products of the author's imagination or used fictitiously. Any resemblance to actual persons, living or dead, events or locales is entirely coincidental.

ISBN-13: 978-0-9993656-3-2 (paper)

ISBN-13: 978-0-9993656-6-3(e-book)

Library of Congress Control Number: 2020910499

Moonlit Madness Press

Cover Design © Victoria Cooper Art

Editor: Proofreading by the Page

*Warning- Contains sensitive subject matter including, but not limited to domestic violence, rape, and murder.

jessicaaikenhall.com

CONFIDENTIALITY

ALSO BY JESSICA AIKEN-HALL

The Monster That Ate My Mommy- A Memoir

Boundaries: Scope of Practice- Book One

For all of the survivors of domestic violence. I hear you. I see you. I believe you.
In memory of all of the victims of domestic violence. With brave wings they fly.

CHAPTER ONE

Outside of the church, I took Tim's hand and walked into the building. He gave it a tight squeeze before he opened the enormous mahogany door. I filled my lungs with fresh air before my black slides hit the stone entryway. The click of Tim's dress shoes echoed through the building as we followed the red carpet to find a seat in the pews. "You doing alright?"

Tim's concern helped chase away some of the nausea. "Yeah, I'm fine." I pushed up a fake smile as I crossed my ankles and straightened my black dress. The pounding of my heartbeat echoed in my head, drowning out the background noises. My attention was drawn to the woman with bleach blonde hair dabbing at her eyes in the front row. The silver casket was open and the outline of Jane's body was all I could focus on.

Tim tapped my knee and whispered, "Do you think that's her mom?"

"I don't know, she said she didn't have any family." I

looked around the church as I saw a few people scattered around in different benches.

"Do you think all these people knew her?" His whisper increased in volume with each word.

A woman, two rows in front of us, turned and smiled. I recognized the familiar face as a nurse from the hospital. "I think so." A few more people arrived and found seats in the empty spaces. Seth was not one of them. That wasn't a big surprise, though.

The priest walked to the front of the church and began the service. The thoughts circling my head washed out his words. The more I looked around; the more guilt ate at me. I hadn't considered this many people being affected by Jane's death before today. The woman in the front was the biggest surprise of all. Who was she and why hadn't Jane mentioned her?

The woman in question was welcomed to the front by the priest. "And, now, let us hear from Mrs. Brooks, Jane's mother."

Her long, elegant, black dress rested just above her designer high heels. A dainty black hat rested on her head, with a square of black lace covering her eyes and a pair of long, satin black gloves covered her hands and most of her arms. "Jane was a good girl. My heart is broken." She paused as she dabbed at her eyes with her white handkerchief. "A mother should never have to bury her child." She turned around to face Jane and wept. "I won't rest until I find the monster who did this to you."

The priest put his arm around Mrs. Brooks and helped her back to her seat. Tim elbowed me in the side and raised his eyebrows. The room around me started to spin. I closed my eyes and held on to the seat in front of me. "Val... are you alright?"

I swallowed to try to get moisture back in my mouth. "I just need some air." Tim took my hand and led me out of the building. The cool air hit my face and helped ground me.

"Are you okay?"

"Yeah, I'm... fine... it's just a lot to take in. I can feel her pain, you know?"

"I get it. It's intense." He put his hand on my back and pulled me into him.

"I had no idea she had a mom... I thought she was just a lost soul out on her own. So... that means, Carmen had a grandma."

"Val, most people have moms."

"Ha, ha. But I'm serious. Did you know about Mrs. Brooks?"

"No, I didn't know about her and I did look for next of kin to notify."

"And... who was it? Who was her next of kin?"

"Seth. He was the only one listed on any of her paper-work." Tim pulled me closer and hugged me. "Are you okay, Val? You're acting... umm... well... I'm just worried about you."

I pulled away from him. "How am I acting?" I crossed my arms as I waited for him to answer.

"I'm just worried about you, that's all." He put his hands into the pockets of his dress slacks.

"I'm fine." I turned my head as the door behind us opened. The priest held it as the guests left the building.

Jennifer, the nurse from Lawrenceville Regional Hospital, stopped and put her hand on my arm. "So sad, isn't it? She was doing so good... we thought she was going to beat it."

"Yeah, it's unfortunate. Addiction is unpredictable... you just never know." My body rose and fell under her hand.

"She really admired you, Val. You should be proud of the work you did with her." The pity behind her smile stung as she walked down the stone stairs.

I took Tim's hand and went down the stairs with the other guests. We stood under the tall maple tree, the sun shining down on us through the bare branches. The warmth of the sun on my face helped ease some of the uneasy feelings swimming inside of me. I closed my eyes and soaked up as much as I could. Sunshine in Vermont in March was a luxury.

The clack of heels hitting the stone stairs jolted me out of the calm I had been channeling. Mrs. Brooks stopped in front of us. "I'm sorry for your loss, ma'am." Tim extended his hand to her.

She stared back at him. "And who are you?" She peered at him through the lace on her hat.

"I'm Detective Tim Phillips."

"Oh my, you're a handsome young man." She bit her bottom lip as her eyes undressed him. "Please, call me Ginger."

Tim's cheeks darkened with her compliment. "Well, Ginger, if there is anything we can help you with, please let us know."

I forced a smile. "Yes, if there is anything at all."

"And you are?" Ginger lifted her penciled on eyebrows.

"I'm Valerie. I worked with Jane in the hospital."

"Oh, then, you're both the people I need to speak with." She took off her long, satin glove and pulled out her iPhone. "When will you be available?" Her eyes focused on the screen.

"We have some time now if you're up for it." Tim squeezed my hand in his. "We could go grab a coffee or something."

"I guess that would work. I'm headed back to Boston tomorrow and I want this all squared away before then."

"Well, Val and I will be glad to help in any way we can."

"I don't think I want to go to a coffee shop around here." Ginger turned up her nose as she looked around. "How about we meet at your office?"

"Yeah, sure, we can go back to the hospital." I looked up at Tim, who nodded his head in agreement.

"I was thinking more on the lines of the Detective's office." Ginger's focus went back to Tim.

"Well, I think it'd be best to go to the hospital. We'll have more room and privacy there." He ran his hand through his hair.

"I guess that'll do." Ginger slipped her phone back into her Louis Vuitton purse and pulled out her car keys. She hit the button and lights on a black BMW X5 flashed. "I'll follow you."

Tim and I got into his Volkswagen Touareg to lead the way. "She seems to like you."

"Oh, her? No, I don't..."

"Oh, please. She was practically in your pants out there."

"Is someone jealous?" He gave me a smirk. "It's kinda

cute, but you have nothing to worry about. You're the only woman for me."

"I better be." I crossed my arms and squinted my eyes. "What do you think she wants?"

"I don't know, I guess we'll find out soon."

I turned on Tom Petty Radio just as *You Don't Know How It Feels* started playing. I let Tom Petty's voice ease the turmoil in my head. The song ended as we pulled into the hospital parking lot, Ginger was right behind us. "Here we go." A sigh followed my words.

"Val, relax. There's nothing to worry about. It's just a mother that's having a hard time with the loss of her child. You deal with this stuff all the time."

"I know... but they're not all after my man." My joke left even me with a smile.

I'm so sorry for your loss." Tiffany stood up and held her hand out to Ginger.

Ginger nodded her head and as her eyes rolled, she said, "Yeah, it's been a real pleasure."

"Thanks, Tiff." I waited for her to leave the room. Was it really breaking confidentiality when the patient was dead? Could I risk an attorney getting involved? But, could I risk Ginger meeting Seth? The obvious answer won. "Jane lived at 156 Wildflower Avenue, apartment 3."

"And that's where Seth will be?"

"As far as I know. Is there anything else I can help you with?"

"Not yet. I'll be in touch." Ginger pushed her chair away from the table and stood up. "You know, I'm not usually a bitch."

"Funny, that sounds like something Jane would have said."

"You're a smartass. That must've been why Jane liked you." She nodded her head before walking down the hall.

"Ginger." She turned to look at me. "I'm sorry... for your loss."

"Thank you for your help... and for helping Jane. It's comforting to know she had someone like you."

Her words hit me like a slap in the face. There was nothing left for me to say. All I can do is wait, and hope Seth cooperates enough to make Ginger go away. For this all to go away.

CHAPTER THREE

In all the time I knew Jane, she never once talked about her mom. Her story was always the same... once Carmen died, she was on her own. Where was Ginger when Jane was in the hospital or when she returned from rehab? And, what made her say Carmen was a devil child? Even Jane appeared to love Carmen in her own twisted way. I had thought once Jane was gone, she would be out of my mind. Why was this woman haunting me? Justice for Carmen came on that park bench when Jane lost her life. That was when this was supposed to end. Nothing goes as planned. Murphy's Law should be the title of my memoir.

A knock on my door, followed by Tim's voice took me out of the rabbit hole. "Coming."

Tim's clean-shaven face was still shaded red. I had never seen him angry before. It wasn't becoming. "Sorry I took off before. That woman is a real..."

"Witch?"

"Not what I was thinking, but I guess it works." His smile softened his face.

"Why did you let her get to you so much?"

"Val, she's trying to blame you, me, anyone she can. I can't stand people like her. Where was she when Jane needed her? She doesn't know how much you tried to help Jane. I just hate it when people are such assholes."

A weight settled on my chest as I heard his words. "Ginger is a piece of work... but her daughter is dead."

"I know, but it's not like she even cared. Come on, who calls their grandchild the devil? You have to admit it was over the top."

"I get it. I guess Jane didn't fall too far from the tree." Nervous laughter made its way out of my mouth.

Tim raised his eyebrows at me. "Ouch. Let them bury the lady before you start cracking jokes."

I cleared my throat. "Sorry, ... I... ah..."

"I get it, Val. It's easier to crack jokes than it is to feel."

"Simmer down, Dr. Phil."

"What? We haven't even talked about Jane's death. It's like you don't want to face it. Are you feeling guilty?"

He knew. How could I have been so stupid? Of course, he knew. He is a detective. There was no way to pull something like this over on him.

"Val." His voice pulled me out of my thoughts. "It's not your fault."

"Yes, it is." My heart was beating so fast I was sure he could hear the echo in the tiny, windowless room.

"No, it's not. Jane's death. It's not your fault. Even if you wished for her to pay for what she did to Carmen. You are not responsible for her death."

He didn't know. Relief washed over me, but the guilt lingered. Tears stained my cheeks as my lies put a distance between us. "I guess I do feel guilty for wishing she was held accountable for Carmen's death. I didn't know she had anyone that gave a shit about her."

"It's normal to feel like that. I doubt Ginger really gives a shit, she's just looking for someone to blame."

"I guess you're right." A heavy sigh expelled from my lungs. "I've got to get upstairs to group, want to walk me up?"

"I'd love to." He took my hand and pulled me into a hug. "Don't let her get to you, okay? It's not worth it. I love you, Val."

"I love you, too. Thanks for being so amazing."

"I do my best." He squeezed my hand and winked.

Norma and Maggie were waiting for me in the conference room. "Hey ladies, how are you holding up?"

Maggie and Norma remained silent. Norma had Maggie's hand in hers, their eyes in direct contact. Sonya entered the room and shut the door behind her before anyone could break the silence.

"Whoa, who died?" Sonya looked around the room when no one laughed. "Oh, yeah... poor choice of words... but, really, what's going on?"

Seconds felt like an eternity before Norma spoke. "Do you want me to tell them, dear?"

Maggie nodded her head, tears ran down her cheeks. The bags under her eyes told me she had not slept in a few days.

Her hair was a mess, and what looked like breakfast was on the front of her sweatshirt.

"Maggie found drugs in Lexi's room." Norma paused while Maggie blew her nose.

"She's been acting strange, so Maggie and I did a little investigating and..."

"Wait a minute." Sonya butted in. "You invaded her space and snooped through her things? That's not cool." She sat back against her chair and crossed her arms. "You can say goodbye to her ever trusting you again."

"Sonya, that's enough." I fought back the urge to roll my eyes.

"No, she's right." That was all Maggie could push out through the tears.

Sonya shook her head. "I'm sorry, I didn't mean to come off like a bitch... I just remember being Lexi's age... and I would've been so pissed at my mom if she snooped through my stuff."

"Have you talked with Lexi about it yet?" I picked up the box of tissues and held it out for Maggie.

"No, not yet. She's so angry lately... she's lost so much... so I haven't pushed her, but I had to know what was going on. I wish I never looked."

"No, it's a good thing you know now. Maybe you can help her stop before she gets addicted."

"Yeah, Val's right, you don't want her to end up like Jane." Sonya covered her open mouth. "I didn't mean..."

"My God, Sonya. You're full of help today." I closed my eyes as I shook my head. "What did you find?"

"I'm not sure what it was, just a bottle of pills and a little baggie of marijuana."

A flashback to Seth's apartment took over the room. There was no way they came from him. Lawrenceville's a small place, but that's way too small.

Maggie reached into her pocket and pulled out the amber colored bottle and handed it to me. "There is part of a label on here, but I couldn't make out enough to be helpful."

Only a small white portion of the label remained. The only letters I could make out were *Ja*, the rest was missing. The room went black as I tried to push out what was happening. The bastard was at it again. What were the odds there were multiple drug dealers in town with access to pill bottles with a first name that starts with J? I steadied my breathing to calm myself enough to come back to the conversation. "Do you know where Lexi could have gotten these?"

"No. She hasn't been coming home right after school lately. I was just happy she had made some new friends, I didn't get after her about it. I had no idea she was doing anything she shouldn't."

"Does she have a boyfriend?" I let a sigh out through my pursed lips.

"I didn't think so, but I noticed she had a hickey on her neck last night. I didn't dare ask any questions. Mostly because I don't want to know the answer."

"I know it's hard, Maggie, but you need to take some control over her. Norma, will you be able to offer her some support?"

"Of course, I'll do anything she needs." Norma turned

her head to face Maggie. "How about a good old fashion family meeting?"

"A family meeting? What is this, the Brady Bunch?" Sonya rolled her eyes. "How about you follow her around? Put a tracking device on her phone?"

"That's not a bad idea. What do you think?" I turned my attention to Maggie.

Sonya interrupted me. "I was kidding. She's sixteen, right? How about you trust her to make up her own mind? She's a smart girl, right?"

My frustration grew with every word she spoke. "She's a child. If Maggie wants our help, how about we give it to her?"

"I am trying to help. It wasn't that long ago I was Lexi's age, and if my mom started having family meetings and spying on me, I would have been..."

"This isn't about you, Sonya, this is about Lexi and Maggie. They need our help."

"Whoa, calm down, Val." Sonya held her hands up.

"Thank you, Val, for caring so much about Lexi." Norma let go of Maggie's hand to take mine. "Let's work together and figure this out."

She was right, they both were. I needed to take a step back. The thought of Seth being involved was ludicrous. It couldn't be him. There would be no way they could have met. She is a child and he's a grown man. And, last I knew, he wasn't using anymore. "That sounds like a good plan. What can we do to help?"

"I do like the idea of a family meeting." Maggie patted

her nose with her tissue. "Do you think we should do it tonight?"

"I think that's a good idea." Norma smiled.

"I know I don't live there, but how about you make it something casual, over dinner? And, maybe start off by asking questions to both girls? Like, how's school? Who are your new friends? Where do you buy your weed? You know, just slip it in there?" Sonya shrugged her shoulders.

I nodded in agreement. "Aside from the last question, I think Sonya has a great idea. Just do something casual and ask Sammy questions, too. So Lexi won't feel attacked. You want her to be able to talk to you if something happens."

"We could order pizza or something she'd like. Make it fun. Maybe it's not as bad as we're thinking." Norma pat the top of Maggie's knee.

"I don't want her to hate me. I could try to be the fun mom."

"Yes. See, I knew these ladies would help." Norma turned to face Maggie and smiled.

"So, tell us, how was the funeral?" Sonya leaned forward, her elbows on her knees.

"It was... interesting."

"How is a funeral interesting?" Sonya raised her eyebrows.

"Her mom was there and her boyfriend was not."

"Wait... she had a boyfriend?"

"I guess you could call him that."

"Okay... so... tell us more. So far, this doesn't sound very interesting." Sonya sat back in her chair with her arms crossed.

"Well, her mom thinks someone killed Jane."

"Yeah, they did... it's called the drug dealer," Sonya said.

"But, anyway, that was all really."

"How are you doing, dear?" Norma's eyes glistened under her glasses.

"I'm fine. How are you?"

"I'm fine, too. I just feel bad. I should have been nicer to her. I keep thinking about that last meeting, and how quickly we all left when she arrived." Norma shook her head. "I keep thinking if we had stayed, maybe she wouldn't have wanted to..."

"Jane's death wasn't your fault. She was sick. Please, don't blame yourself." I watched as the weight of guilt weighed on Norma.

"It's just such a sad story." Norma hung her head.

"It is. But none of you are responsible for Jane's death." A heaviness pushed me into my chair. I hadn't considered they would feel responsible, or even feel anything. Jane was a nuisance, I hadn't imagined she would be missed by anyone.

CHAPTER FOUR

Gabriel met me at the door in his usual spot. It wasn't close to dinner time today, so I knew it was just me he was missing. Some days I wondered if he loved me as much as I do him, but there was no question in times like this. "Hey, buddy. How was your day? As long and as grueling as mine? No? I didn't think so." I scooped him up and pressed my forehead to his. The vibration of his purring calmed my nerves.

"So, the saga of Jane continues... even in death. I'll never be rid of that lady." I scratched behind his ear before setting him on the floor. "Now, a new pain in the ass... her mom, Ginger. What kind of name is that, anyway?" I took out a can of Fancy Feast and put it in his dish. "She's from Boston... that's only a three-hour drive... but she never came to visit her daughter? What kind of mother does that?" My laugh filled the kitchen. "Yeah, good point. But she comes here to make a scene... and now she wants to find out who killed her baby. I hope she goes back to Boston and stays there."

"Hey, am I interrupting something?" Tim's voice took me by surprise.

"Jesus, you scared the shit out of me. How long have you been here?"

"I just got here. Should I come back, you know, after you and Gabe are done with your conversation?" His laugh made me smile.

"Very funny. You know I talk with Gabe when I need expert advice."

"Oh, that kind of stung."

"No, I was just telling him about Ginger."

"About that... she came by my office. She said you gave her Seth's address."

"Yeah, I wanted to get rid of her, I didn't think it was a big deal."

"I guess it wasn't, really. She said Seth was an asshole, so she didn't get anything out of the visit. She did say she wanted to offer a reward to get any information about Jane's death."

"A reward? What for? She just can't accept her daughter was an addict?"

"It's hard for her. She said she hadn't seen Jane in years and she wants to make it up to her."

"She does realize this won't do anything?" Frustration built as I thought about this new thorn in my side.

"Maybe it will. It might give her closure to be able to find the person who sold her the drugs. At least it'll keep her busy while she looks."

"I thought she was going back to Boston."

"She is. Why is this so upsetting to you?"

"I don't know. I just thought this was over." My shoulders rose and fell with a heavy sigh. "Can we talk about something else now? Anything?"

"I thought you'd never ask." Tim cleared his throat. "My mom called today, she wants to know if we set a date yet."

"Oh, God."

"Wow, not the response I was hoping for."

"Sorry. It's not that I don't want to think about the wedding, it's just that... you just asked me... can't we just enjoy this for now?"

Tim pulled me into a hug. "We can, but wouldn't it be nice to have an idea of when? I just can't wait to wake up every morning next to you."

"I know, that does sound nice. It's just hard for me... you know... I don't have family I can share it with. It makes me realize how alone I really am."

"How about we elope? Hop on a plane to Vegas and let Elvis work his magic."

"Hmmm... that could work... but why the hurry? I mean, you just asked me."

"I think Mom wants a timeline for the grandkids."

My hand went to my necklace and rubbed the warm metal. The edges from the broken heart smooth from wear. Thoughts about the son I missed out on crept in. The anguish pushed out tears I held onto for so many years. Unable to tame the rush of unleashed emotions, the pain oozed out of me. Tim held me closer to help ease the suffering.

"Oh, Val, I'm sorry. I didn't think. I'm so thoughtless sometimes."

With a big sniffle in, I was able to compose myself. "No,

it's not that... it's just... I never imagined I'd ever be a mom. I always thought I missed my chance."

"You know that wasn't your fault, right? I know you would have been... will be a great mom. But we can slow things down. There's no need to hurry."

"Does she know?"

"My mom? No, I didn't tell her. I didn't think it was my place to share. It's not her business. When you're ready... when we're ready. No pressure."

"So, about Elvis. I think I like that plan." The idea put a smile on my face.

"We don't have to hurry with that, either. When we're both ready, we can set a date and make a plan."

"I'm a lucky girl." I reached up and kissed him. The warmth of his lips intensified my gratitude of having him in my life. "Thank you for being so patient... and kind... and, well, awesome."

"I'm the lucky one, Val. You're one of a kind, and I'm never letting you go."

"I really like the sound of waking up with you every morning. Do you think we should test drive this marriage thing? You know, make sure you're really sure?"

"Hmmm... you mean live in sin?" A boyish laugh escaped from his mouth.

"What do you think we're doing? I mean unless you want to stop..."

"Oh, no... no, I like living a life of sin." He cleared his throat to mask the remaining laughter. "I think that's a great idea. Are you thinking of me moving in here? Or you coming to live with me?"

"What if we find a new place? New to both of us?"

"That's not a bad idea. Maybe we can find a house to rent. I'm so sick of hearing my neighbors live in their own life of sin. How much sex can one horny college guy have?"

"I don't know, you tell me... you've been a horny college boy, I haven't. It can't be that bad, it's got to be like free entertainment."

"You're a perv. I can't believe you'd think that about me." Tim placed his hand on his chest and batted his eyes.

"Oh, geez, I'm sorry. I love that you're so pure and innocent."

"That's more like it." His smile took some of my apprehension away. "Do you want to stay in Lawrenceville or look around?"

"I don't know, I kind of like it here. I never thought about leaving before. Where do you want to live?"

"Well, I do like my job, so I guess I'd like to stay in the area, but my heart isn't in Lawrenceville. If we find something outside of town, I'd be open."

We sat together on the couch and scrolled through our phones, looking on Craigslist at available houses for rent. For the past sixteen years, I had lived alone, with only Gabriel as my companion for the last twelve years. As much as I love Tim, I wasn't sure I was ready for this step. There are days where I just want to sit in the dark and not interact with anyone. What if he doesn't let me have the space I need, or what if he decides he doesn't love me? What if I'm too much for him? He has never seen the days I don't want to get out of bed, or the nights I stay awake thinking about everything that has ever gone wrong.

Looking around my apartment, years' worth of stuff began to suffocate me. What is worth keeping? Will I have to give up everything, again? My heart shot into my throat as the thoughts overtook me. I tried to imagine holding my baby, the one Tim spoke of, but I couldn't see past the little boy I was forced to give away.

"I want to find Gabriel." My voice broke as I spoke.

Without looking away from his phone, Tim pointed to the kitchen. "He's in there, on the table."

I brushed the tears off my cheeks with the sleeve of my sweater. "No, not him... my son. I want to find him."

"Oh, Val. I'm sorry... I just... I was so excited to find our new place, I wasn't really listening." He took my hand. "I'll find him."

"How can you be certain? What if we can't find him? I'm not sure I'll be able to have another baby until I do."

"Now that I have your permission, I won't give up until I find him. There's so much technology these days, I'm sure we'll find him."

"You think so?" I wiped my nose on my sleeve before realizing what I was doing. "Oh, gross. See, this is what you want to live with?" Laughter helped change the mood.

"Yes, I'm sure." He smiled. "To both questions."

Having Gabriel in my life was not something I thought possible. Since the day I found out I was pregnant, he never left my mind. Every year on his birthday, I would imagine him blowing out the candles on his cake and opening his presents surrounded by people who love him. The pain only intensified with every passing year as it was that much more time without him in my life. I would think about everything I missed out on. I knew I would never be able to give my love to another child until I knew Gabriel was safe and loved. Excitement replaced the years of hollowness. I *knew* Tim would grant me this wish. That was one of the reasons why I loved him.

CHAPTER FIVE

nside the lobby of the hospital, a man lingered, pacing the hall. From a distance, his build looked familiar. It wasn't until I walked past him that I knew. Unsure if I should be seen talking with him or not, I kept walking. "Are you here to see me?"

"Who the fuck else would I be here to see?"

I stopped a few feet away from him and looked back only long enough to respond. "Meet me outside by the oak tree in a couple minutes." Not giving him time to respond, I continued to my office and put my tote bag and coffee mug on my desk. Locking the door behind me, I made my way back out to the parking lot. The list of reasons he might be here played out in my head. I hadn't seen him since the afternoon I purchased the pills from him.

Seth had his hands in the front pockets of his navy blue sweatshirt. His jeans looked stiff from the dirt they were covered in. As I got closer to him, I noticed the bags under his bloodshot eyes. Any thought he had stayed clean went out the window.

"What can I do for you?"

"That's all you've got to say? I know what you did. I know you killed Jane. You're fucken sick... to kill her with her own pills."

"Excuse me?" The heat from my face spread to my neck.

"Don't act dumb. I know why you needed those pills. You killed Jane... and I really didn't care... I mean, you got the bitch outta my hair."

"Then, why are you here?" I pulled my cardigan tight against me and crossed my arms.

"So, you admit it. I didn't think it'd be this easy." Seth pulled his cell phone out of the pocket of his sweatshirt.

"I didn't admit anything. I simply asked you why you are here."

"You didn't deny it. You know damn well you bought those pills and you gave them to Jane."

"I have no idea what you're talking about. Is that still recording?" I pointed to his phone.

"Yeah, why?"

"I just wanted to make sure there was a record of me asking you about Lexi. You do know her, don't you? She's sixteen... I think there's plenty of trouble with your name on it."

"I don't know who the fuck you're talking about. I just need you to tell me you did it." He held his phone in front of my face. "Here, just say it into this."

I pushed his arm away from my face. "Get away from me, or I'll call security."

"Go ahead. I can tell them you're a murderer."

"What do you want from me, Seth?"

"You sent that cra—" He caught himself as he looked down at his phone. "Ginger, to my place. She was up in my shit about her daughter... I told her to get the fuck out. But, you know what she said before she left? She told me if I helped her figure out what happened to Jane, she'd give me $5,000."

"Oh, so you're bribing me to confess so you can make a few bucks? Do you know how much trouble you can get in for supplying drugs used in a murder? If what you are alluding to is true, that would make you an accessory. You'd be just as guilty."

He took a step back. "The fuck it would. You're the only murderer here. My hands are clean."

"Yeah." I laughed. "But you're not. You're high as a kite. You start with these threats, and I'll turn you in myself. One look at you, and there is no way they'd believe a word you're saying."

He shook his phone in the air. "You seem to be forgetting about this."

"That? Take a look, it stopped recording the first time you held it up to my face, you dumbass."

"Fuck." His fingers swiped up the screen to turn it back on. "Hang on."

"You know what else? Supplying drugs to children is a pretty big offense, too. I have a bottle you sold to Lexi... I'm sure your prints are all over it."

"I don't know who the fuck you're talking about. I'm not a drug dealer."

"Oh, really?"

"I don't know what you're fucking talking about. Just confess. I need that fucken money."

"Seth, you're delusional. I'm not admitting to anything, and think about what you're saying. You're going to get yourself in trouble."

He took a step toward me and I took one back. "Fuck you, you stupid whore."

I put my hands up. "Whoa. Calm down."

"You have a fucken choice. You confess, or you give me the money."

"What money?"

"The fucken reward money. You have one week, or I'm going to the police."

"That's not a smart plan, Seth."

"Shut the fuck up." He put his hand into his pocket and pointed something at me. "Do what I fucken say, or you'll end up like Jane."

My hand went to my necklace. As I rubbed the metal under my fingers, I thought about dying before getting the chance to meet Gabriel or getting married or having a family. My body stiffened with tension. "Where should I bring the money?"

"Bring cash, all large bills, to my apartment." His hand still pointing at me through his sweatshirt. "One week... or you're dead."

Still standing under the oak tree, I unclenched my jaw as I watched him walk away. My legs trembled as I walked back to my office. I made sure to lock the door behind me and sat at my desk. A migraine crept in as the room began to spin. This was the reason for things like confidentiality. If I hadn't broken it, Ginger would never have found him. And, why did I ever tell Seth who I really was? I kicked myself in the ass for being so careless.

I picked up my phone and started writing a text to Tim. When I looked down, I deleted all the words I wrote. This was not something he could help me with. This was a mess I had made myself.

I logged onto my bank account and checked my balance. There was plenty of money in my account. It wasn't about money, not for me. There was no proof of what happened to Jane. The only person who *thinks* they know what happened is a junkie. There would be no way anyone would believe him over me. Jane's death couldn't be linked to me. I was careful.

Jane's last day replayed in front of me. There was surveillance footage at the hospital, and probably the pizza place that would show us together. How long do they keep those things for? Would they still have it? Jane met with the staff on med-surge before we left. Did she tell them she was having lunch with me? No one had mentioned anything before. But, what if this triggered their memory?

I had to pay him. It was the only way to ensure he didn't talk. But, what if it didn't? What if it didn't keep him quiet? What if he took my money and still went to the cops? To Tim. Would Tim believe me? My obsession with Jane was a little... strange... and even he noticed I stopped talking about her as soon as she died.

I rubbed the bridge of my nose to try to knock out the migraine, but it wouldn't budge. I hadn't thought this through, not entirely. Nausea swept over me, leaving my skin clammy. Reaching for the garbage can, lightheadedness caused the room to spin. I tilted my head back, resting against my chair as I tried to refocus. I'd have to get rid of Seth; that was the only way out of this.

If the pills Lexi had were from Seth, I wasn't doing this just for myself, but for her, too. I couldn't take his life to protect mine, but she is a child. Certainly, taking his life to make sure she is safe was a good enough reason. As I talked through the scenarios, I knew it had to happen. He was a dangerous man. My first impression of him was right. Always trust your gut, a lesson I often forget. When a person shows their true character, it's only our fault when we don't listen. Well, I'm all ears.

On a scratch piece of paper, I wrote down methods to kill someone from some of the past *Snapped* episodes Tim and I had watched. Stabbing- can't do that, don't like blood. Shooting- can't do that, don't own a gun. Poisoning- would he even eat or drink anything from me? Murder for hire- can't do that, don't want anyone else involved. My mind was blank. How would I kill him? What if he tried to kill me first?

I pulled out my phone to search "ways to get away with murder," and erased it as quickly as I wrote it. How do murderers come up with their ideas? From all of the shows I've watched, I knew I couldn't leave a trail of clues behind. This was not worth going to prison for. It wasn't worth dying for, either. I was in over my head, but there was no way out, only in deeper.

Pushing aside all of these thoughts, I listened to my voicemail. A message from Jeanine asking me to come see her as soon as I got in. Looking at my clock, I realized how much time I had wasted. Two hours. I picked up the phone and called Jeanine, there was no way I wanted to see her or anyone.

"Nice of you to arrive." Jeanine's voice beamed through the receiver.

"I've been here all morning, just hadn't gotten around to my messages. What do you need?"

"I asked you to come up, so we could talk."

"I know... I'm just not feeling very well. What can I do for you?"

"You haven't been feeling well a lot lately. Is everything okay?"

"Thanks for your concern... yeah, I'm fine... maybe all the mold down here."

A long sigh escaped. "I need you to go visit someone for me. She came in last night."

My sigh echoed hers. "Really? Jesus. Can't more people die so I can do my own job?"

"Wow, Val, sounds like you need a vacation." She waited for my sarcastic response and continued when there wasn't one. "Room 207, she came in last night after her husband beat her. He broke a couple of her ribs, her nose and gave her a black eye."

"Why are you sending me to her room?"

"I was hoping she could go to your support group. If she met you before she left, she'd probably be more likely to show up, don't you think?"

"You're right. I'll go see her before I leave."

"Thanks, Val. I'm serious though, maybe think about some time off."

She was right. I hadn't taken any time off in a while. There was never a reason to, I usually just cashed the hours in at the end of the year to pad my savings account. At this point, a break was worth way more than the money.

CHAPTER SIX

When I reached room 207, I wasn't sure what to expect. A woman, alone in her room, was asleep in her bed. Her brunette bob framed her face which was bandaged, but I could see the bruises that were not covered. Her arms matched the color of her face with blotches of red and purple. In the dark, I sat in the chair in the corner of the room. My problems drifted away as I watched her sleep.

When her eyes opened, I noticed her body flinch when she saw me. "Hi there, I'm Valerie, from social services." My voice was just louder than a whisper.

"Hi." She lifted her arm to wave, only getting it a few inches off the bed before gritting her teeth.

"I just wanted to introduce myself and see if you needed anything."

A tear rolled out of her eye. "Could you... call my mom? I don't think she knows I'm here."

"Sure, I'll look in your file for her number."

"Thanks. Could you tell her I'm fine? I don't want her to know how bad it was."

"Does she live close by?"

"No, she's in Florida. I just don't want to worry her when she tries to call the house and I'm not there."

"Do you want to call her? So you two can talk?"

"No... I don't want her to hear me cry. Will you tell her Lily says she loves her and will call as soon as she can?"

"Okay... who's Lily?"

"That's what she calls me... what my friends call me."

"Sure, I'll pass the message along. Do you have any friends or family close by, that you want me to call?"

"No. I really don't want anyone to see me like this."

"Is there anything else I can do for you?"

"Can I have the TV remote?"

I found the remote on the bedside table and handed it to her. "I know you're probably not up to this yet, but there's a support group here at the hospital on Tuesdays, and I'd love it if you joined us."

Lily's eyes met mine and she nodded her head. "You know, he's never hurt me like this before. It's never been this bad before."

I pushed up a half smile. "It's okay, Lily. You don't have to explain anything to me. It's a small group, just four of us. We've all been through our own stuff. No judgment. You don't even have to talk if you're not ready."

Lily blinked her eyes to push away the tears. "Thanks."

"I'll stop by tomorrow, too, if that's alright with you."

"Yeah, that'd be nice." She held the remote in her hand. "Do you know when they're going to let me go home?"

"No, I'm not sure. Your doctor will let you know when you're ready. Do you want me to see if I can find out for you?"

"Nah, I'll ask him tomorrow when he comes in. He probably thinks I'm stupid."

"Why would you think that?"

"Look at me. I let this happen... I..."

"You stop right there. You did not do this. What happened to you is not your fault. No one is blaming you for what happened." I put my hand down on hers, above the IV. "I'm just glad you're here."

Lily closed her eyes. "Thanks."

When I left Lily's room, I went back to my office and pulled up her file. I found her mother's phone number and read the nurse's notes. According to their documentation, Lily's husband was arrested after she was brought in. It was noted the police wanted to talk with her, but she hasn't been up to meeting with them. It didn't make sense that she wouldn't want to talk to them to make sure he wasn't released. I also knew there was always a reason behind a person's actions and it wasn't my place to question her.

Like Lily said, this appeared to be the first time it got this bad or at least the first time it sent her to the hospital. Typically, the first violent incident doesn't get reported. Most likely, she has been living in this hell for years. The notes stated she didn't have any children but did mention a miscarriage. It would be hard not to assume he had something to do with it.

I picked up the phone and dialed Lily's mom's number. She answered right away. "Hi, Mrs. Stevens? This is Valerie

Williamson. I'm a social worker at Lawrenceville Regional Hospital. I'm just calling to let you know your daughter Lily has been admitted."

"What happened? Is she okay? Can I talk to her?"

Her questions fired off at me faster than I could respond. "She is going to be fine. She's resting now. She wanted me to tell you she will call you when she's feeling up to it and she loves you."

"Was it Earl? Did he do this to her?"

"I'm sorry, Mrs. Stevens, I really can't release any other information at this time. But, just know Lily is safe, and she is going to be okay." I imagined receiving such a phone call about my child, and I wished I could give her more. Being so far away must be difficult and then to not have any answers. "If you'd like, you can try calling her later, she's on the med-surge unit."

After hanging up the phone, I dug deeper into Lily's chart to see if there was anything I could find. It didn't look like she had lived in the area for long, because her records only went back three years. There were no forwarded notes or remarks as to when she arrived in Lawrenceville. It did seem suspicious the first thing her mother thought was if it had something to do with Earl. I guess a mother would know these things. A mother who gave a damn, anyway.

On my phone, I logged into my Stephanie Mills Facebook account and searched for Lily, first by the name in the chart, *Laura Knight*, and then Lily. Nothing came up for either name. When I entered Earl Knight in the search bar, one fatheaded man's picture popped up. His picture resembled Larry the Cable Guy, a plaid wife-beater to boot. When

I clicked on his profile, I wasn't surprised to see forwarded posts of half-naked young women, Bud-light, and the second amendment. Your stereotypical redneck.

When I scrolled through his page, I noticed he said he was single. There were no pictures of Lily and no mention of her. He was no prize and should be grateful any woman would want to be married to him. Most of his friends were young women with semi-exposed chests. The more I dug, the more I saw just what a piece of shit he was. I didn't need any more evidence after seeing Lily bandaged up in her bed, but there was now no room for any doubt.

He would be easy to bait. Just send him a picture of my breasts, and I'm sure he'd meet me in any back alley... well, after he's released from jail. Men like him were a dime a dozen around here. Lawrenceville is known for its Bud-light drinking, plaid wearing, wife-beating men who think any woman who walks past them is their eye candy. That was why I was so surprised Tim was none of those things. It was apparent he was a Lawrenceville transplant.

CHAPTER SEVEN

When I walked into Lily's room, I was surprised to see her sitting up in bed. She already looked like she was feeling better. "Hi Lily, how was your night?"

"It was okay... it's hard to sleep when people are always coming in checking on me, but it's nice to be feeling better. Thanks for calling my mom."

"No problem. She's really worried about you. I didn't give her any information, though."

"I know, she called me and we talked. Thank you for respecting my privacy."

"You deserve at least that. I'm glad you two had a chance to talk."

"Yeah, me, too. She knew it was Earl. She said she's always wondered when he was going to hurt me. I had no idea it was that obvious."

"Moms just know sometimes. You're lucky to have her. Is she coming to visit?"

"No, I asked her not to. I told her I don't want her to see me like this." Lily's eyes looked down. "I told her I was going to start going to a support group. She was happy to hear that."

"Oh, I'm glad you'll be joining us. I think you'll love the other ladies. We've become our own little family."

"That sounds like just what I need. Thanks for letting me know about it, and thanks for checking in on me."

"We meet in a few minutes, do you want to try to come?"

"I don't think I'm up for it just yet, but maybe next week. I think I'll be getting out of here pretty soon."

"Do you want me to stop by later and help get anything lined up for your discharge?"

"Yeah, that might be a good idea. I'm not sure how it is all going to work, being home alone."

"Lots to think about. I don't want to overwhelm you. One step at a time. It sounds cliché, but it's true."

"I'm not sure I have many more in me right now." Lily laughed as her hazel eyes caught mine.

As I walked to the conference room to meet the ladies for group, I couldn't stop thinking about what Earl did to Lily. I can't imagine being hurt like that by someone who was supposed to love me. I guess I was, but the pain inflicted on me just didn't leave any scars... at least on the outside.

Maggie, Norma and Sonya were already talking when I arrived. I looked down at my watch and saw I was five minutes late. "Sorry, ladies, it seems I'm not able to tell time these days." I found an open seat and slid into it.

"Oh, don't be so hard on yourself, dear. We were just chatting, you didn't miss anything." Norma's smile helped me believe her words.

"So, how did the family meeting go?" I turned my attention to Maggie.

Maggie pushed up a smile. "It was good. Lexi told me she has a boyfriend. She said he's a good boy."

I felt my right eyebrow raise. "Okay... I'm glad to hear that." I looked over at Norma to gauge the reality of Maggie's report, and her expressionless face stared straight ahead. "Did you ask her about the drugs you found?"

"Oh, yes. She's holding them for her boyfriend, who was holding them for a friend. Lexi told me she has no interest in drugs. She's a good girl, she's just been through a lot."

I felt my eyes widen as I pushed up a fake smile and nodded my head. "Okay."

Maggie lost her smile. "What? Why are you looking at me like that?"

"Oh, no... it's nothing... it's just..."

"It's bullshit." Sonya turned her head to look at me. "That's the word you were looking for, right?"

"No... not exactly. I just find it hard to believe. I mean, I remember hearing something similar in some movie I've seen."

"Because it's bullshit. You really believe her, Maggie?" Sonya shook her head in disgust.

"What? You told me to give her some slack, and now you act like she's a liar. I don't get it, Sonya." Maggie crossed her arms.

"Well, yeah, give her some slack, let her be a teenager, but don't let her walk all over you. Norma, what are your thoughts?" Sonya spun around in her chair to look at Norma.

"Oh... I don't know. I guess Lexi's story was hard to

believe, but Maggie is doing her best." Norma put on her best fake smile and patted Maggie on the knee.

"You didn't believe her?" Maggie turned to Norma. "You think she was lying to me? Why didn't you say something?"

"Oh honey, I didn't want to butt in. She was talking to you, you two... you three have been through so much, I didn't want to get in the middle of anything."

"No, I don't have any idea what I'm doing. I need your help. I... I just want to do what's best for the girls. I've already screwed so much up." Maggie began to cry.

"That's nonsense. You're doing a great job. Lexi is just testing you. I know you're doing your best." Norma put her arm around Maggie and pulled her close.

"Norma's right, Maggie. You are doing a great job, but you don't have to do it alone. You have all of us. I'm glad Lexi opened up to you. Maybe she was lying, but some of it was the truth. She trusted you enough to tell you about her boyfriend." I gave her a sympathetic smile.

"Val's right. We are all here for you. I'm the closest to Lexi's age, so I can give you some inside tips." Sonya winked. "Have you thought about inviting her boyfriend to dinner? Maybe you could get some info that way."

"I tried that. She said he wouldn't come, but I can ask again." Maggie looked down at her fingernails.

"Did she tell you his name?" I leaned forward in my chair to get closer to the group.

"Yeah. She said his name was Seth. Right, Norma?"

"Seth?" The words punctured my lungs as it robbed my oxygen. "You're sure?"

"Pretty sure." Maggie nodded.

"Did she tell you how old he was?" The room went dark as I waited for her answer.

"No, just that he's a little older than her."

"Oh my God, Maggie, you can't let her see him."

"What's the matter? Do you know him?" Maggie asked.

"Yes, ...he's... he's... he was Jane's boyfriend."

"Wait... you think Lexi hooked up with Jane's man? That's totally messed up." Sonya leaned back in her chair and crossed her arms. "I think you're losing it, Val... there is probably more than one Seth in this town."

"I know... but... I know it's him. He's dangerous." I pushed the hair out of my face.

"How can you be sure?" Sonya tilted her head.

"The bottle you showed me last week... the one you found in Lexi's bag... the letters on the bottle were Ja... as in Jane." My mouth went dry as I tried to swallow the panic brewing inside of me.

"Still could be a coincidence." Sonya looked around the circle.

Maggie's hand was on her mouth. "You think it's him?"

"I don't know." I shook my head. "But what are the chances? He's not safe. You have to do everything you can to keep her away from him."

Norma let out a sigh. "Oh, dear. This complicates things. Don't worry Maggie, I'll take care of it."

"How? How are you going to stop her?" Maggie asked.

"Let me just talk to her, maybe she'll listen to me. I'm an old lady... maybe she'll take me seriously."

"I think it's a good idea. Let Norma talk to her, maybe

she'll listen. Or, I can talk to her. You know, I'm the cool one." Sonya joked in an attempt to lighten the mood in the room.

"I don't know. I'm scared now. What if he hurts her? What if they're having sex?" The color drained from Maggie's face.

"Don't let your mind go there, Maggie. We are here to help. We're all behind you." I knew I had to come up with a way to kill Seth even sooner. Maggie was right, what if they were having sex and he gets Lexi pregnant? That's way more than either she or Maggie can handle right now.

My thoughts raced as I tried to focus on a murder method. The voices in the room turned to a hum as I closed my eyes and tried to pull up the different ways used on the episodes of *Snapped* I've watched. Like the list from earlier, all that came were stabbings and shooting. Over and over guns and knives. I wasn't ready for either.

And then it hit me. I knew what I could do. It would be the perfect murder, with no trail of evidence back to me. I felt my lips curl up into a smile as my eyes popped open. "Don't worry, Maggie. Lexi will be just fine."

CHAPTER EIGHT

The adrenaline ran through my body as the stones crunched under my tires. It was just warm enough to have my windows down. The melody of chickadees and robins brought a familiarity with them. It felt like any other early spring day in Vermont, except it wasn't. Today would be anything but ordinary.

When I arrived at my destination, I put my Toyota Corolla in park. I turned the key in the ignition, my keychains and keys jingled as I pulled them out. A deep breath expelled from my lungs as I looked at my reflection in the rearview mirror. *This is for Lexi.* It was the only way I would be able to go through with it. Saving myself was just an added bonus.

With my tote bag full of supplies over my shoulder, I closed the car door behind me and walked the same path I had just weeks before. A quick scan around the yard didn't yield any potential witnesses. It appeared the building's occupants were out enjoying one of the first beautiful days of the season. April 5th was a day close to my heart, the day I brought life into this world, now it would be the day I took one out. I hadn't planned it this way.

The urgency to finish the job intensified as soon as I knew *he* was the one hurting Lexi. At sixteen, she had her whole life ahead of her. I couldn't stand by and watch him turn her into another Carmen. No, he had to be stopped once and for all. My first impressions were usually always right, I knew there was something off about him, and now I knew what it was. He was a predator. Latching on to vulnerable, young girls and victimizing them. Done with one and on to the next. Now was the time to extinguish him. Put an end to his relentless abuse of power.

My knuckles hit the door and I stood back to wait for him to let me in. My heart raced as I waited for him. When he didn't answer, I knocked again, harder this time. "Seth, it's Val. I have something for you."

Still, no answer. My nerve was wavering as the seconds passed. With a balled fist, I pounded on the door. "Seth, come on, I have your money, let me in." I turned the flaking metal knob in my hand. The door creaked opened. "Seth?"

I kicked it open the rest of the way, my hand holding my tote bag tight against me. Once in, I shut the door behind me. "Seth, it's Val. I have your money. Seth?" Each step led me further into his apartment, for the first time, past the kitchen. I turned the corner to enter the living room. A gasp stung my throat. "Oh my god." Frozen in my tracks, I knew I needed to get out of there.

Seth was in the recliner facing the TV, his feet up, and his head slumped down. "Seth?" Careful not to touch anything, I kicked his chair. He was dead. Someone had beat me to it. A mix of relief and panic swirled around in my stomach. *What if they were still here?* I took a step backward, with my hand over my mouth, and surveyed the area. Nothing looked out of place, no more than usual. The volume on the TV drowned out any outside sounds.

Once my thoughts slowed down, I walked back through the apartment. With the sleeve of my cardigan, I opened the door and shut it behind me. I rubbed my sweater over the outside knob and used my shoulder to brush off any marks the knocking might have left. Back in my car, I pulled my cell phone out of my purse and dialed Tim. After the first ring, I ended the call. He can't know I was here.

With my car back on the dirt road, I tried to figure out who might have done the dirty work for me. I was surprised by the lingering tinge of disappointment. I was also grateful the job was completed without getting his blood on my hands.

The list of potential killers grew as I thought about the number of people Seth had probably wronged in his lifetime. How long before someone noticed he was missing from society? A heavy weight settled on my shoulders when I pictured Lexi finding him. I hit my hand on the steering wheel. "Fuck." What if she loved him, and this was how she would always remember him? I couldn't be held responsible for causing her any more pain.

I pulled my car on to the side of the road to think about my options. I knew calling the police wasn't one of them. I didn't kill him, but I had planned on it. I didn't want to risk anything tracing me back to him, or Jane.

I closed my eyes as I tried to develop a plan. All I could

picture was Lexi. I'd have to call it in. A payphone would be the safest way. I remember seeing one in town, but I couldn't place it for my life. I pulled back on the road and began my search. The days of having a payphone on every corner were over, it was just pure luck; there was still one left in town. As I got closer to the center of town, it came back to me. It was at Lawrenceville Pizza. *Perfect.*

With a roll of my eyes, I turned my car around at the convenience store and headed back down Main Street. As I drove past the park bench where I last saw Jane, I thought about her last moments, and Carmen, and now Seth. An overwhelming sadness filled me as I imagined who they could have been, had things been different. So many wasted lives, and for what?

I dialed 911, cleared my throat, and tried to disguise my voice. "I'd like to request a welfare check at 156 Wildflower Avenue, apartment 3. My uh... friend didn't show up for work, and no one has been able to reach him. He has a history of depression." The last piece added to express urgency.

The woman on the other end of the line asked for my information. I've made plenty of these calls before for work and almost slipped as I fell back into the social worker role. I considered giving a false name but decided to remain anonymous. After hanging up, I wasn't confident they took me seriously, but there was nothing left to do except wait.

Back in my car, I heard the ringing as I opened the door. I bent down and picked up my phone before getting in. "Hey, Tim."

"Hi. I saw I missed a call from you."

"Oh, I... ah... just wanted to tell you how much I love you."

"Well, that's a nice surprise. I love you, too. It's been a crazy day."

"Yeah, same here." Nervous laughter slipped out.

"Must be the full moon. Oh, I got to go, just got a call on the radio. I love you."

I wanted to ask more about the call but knew he wouldn't be able to tell me. Fingers crossed he was headed to Wildflower Avenue. I turned up the volume as Tom Petty's *Greatest Hits* CD played on the stereo. I was hopeful the music would wash away some of the day's stress. The image of Seth's dead body flashed before my eyes as I sat in the parking lot. If my timing was off, I could have been dead in that apartment, too.

With my car in gear, I drove around Lawrenceville. There was too much on my mind to sit at home and think. I found myself outside of Norma's house. Unsure if I should pull into the driveway, or keep driving, I felt the steering wheel turn under my hands. She always said we were welcome to stop by anytime, I was about to find out if she meant it.

As my finger found the doorbell, the door opened. "Hi dear, come on in."

"I'm sorry to bother you... I just... I was in the neighborhood and..."

"Oh, nonsense, come on in." Norma opened the door wider for me to walk past her. "I'm happy you're here, it's no bother at all."

"Really?"

"You're welcome here anytime. I've told all of you girls that."

"Thanks, Norma. I wasn't sure if it was too weird to just show up."

"Not weird at all. Do you want a cup of tea?"

"Oh, that would be lovely."

I followed Norma into the living room, where she motioned for me to sit down. "Get comfortable and I'll be back."

Framed photographs of flowers filled the walls of Norma's living room. I hadn't noticed the lack of family photos before. I let my body relax into the sofa as I waited for Norma to arrive with the tea. The house was quiet and gave me the much-needed peace I had been searching for.

"Here we are, dear." Norma set the teapot and cups on the coffee table and poured a cup and handed it to me. "Are you alright? You look like something is bothering you."

"Thank you." I held the warm cup between my hands. "I'm okay. It's just been a long day."

"Do you want to talk about it?" She picked up her cup and sat down in the chair closest to me.

"Well, I'd love to... but... it's confidential... you know, work stuff." I took a sip of the hot tea.

"I understand. You must have so much to deal with."

"I do, but I like my job. I like being able to help people."

"Yes, I bet that is nice." She took a drink. "I used to like helping people, too."

"What did you do for work?"

"Oh, you know. I guess it was kind of the same thing you do."

"You were a social worker? I can see that in you. You're so easy to talk to."

"Thank you, dear. So are you." Her smile pushed up her glasses.

"It's just that... oh, I don't know how to say it." My eyes went to the mug in my hands. "It's just hard to know about all the awful people in the world."

"Oh, honey, don't I know it." She reached over and patted my knee with her hand. "Such a sad world we live in. It's nice to have good friends." The smile on her face warmed me as much as the tea.

"It is nice, probably the only thing that helps on days like today. Speaking of friends, where are Maggie and the girls?"

"Maggie took the girls to a therapist out of town today. It was something the court asked her to do. They've been gone most of the day, and I'm not sure when they'll be back. Maggie said something about taking them to the mall and letting them get some new clothes."

"Oh, that's nice. Maggie seems like a really great mom. It's so nice that you let them move in, it must be such a relief for her."

"It's been so nice having them here. It used to get so lonely before I met you girls. I'm grateful every day when I think about our group."

"It has been nice getting to know you all. It sounds strange, but you ladies are the only friends I have." I felt my cheeks flush. "That's pretty pathetic, isn't it?"

"Not at all, not after everything you've been through. You're a strong woman, Val. It must have been so scary for you in a new town, all alone."

"It wasn't, really. It was lonely, but Gabriel helped me through some of the hardest times."

"I'm glad you found comfort in his companionship. Pets are one of the special things we often take for granted."

"That's true. I don't know what I would have done without his love." I felt a tear roll down my cheek. "Today is my son's birthday. He's twenty, no longer a boy... and I missed all of it."

"Oh, honey, I'm so sorry." She put her hand out for me to take.

"Today has always been the hardest day of the year for me. I think back to everything I missed out on and wonder if he had a good life. I wonder where I would be if I was allowed to keep him, if I would have had more kids, or if I would have found someone to spend my life with." My eyes went to my engagement ring. "I mean, I have someone wonderful now, but what would life have been like if he wasn't stolen from me?"

"I believe everything happens for a reason. I know how crass that sounds, but I think your son had an amazing life. I know it in my heart. You will find him, and you will learn about the loving parents he had, and all those years of worrying will be over."

"I hope you're right."

"Trust me. I know when you find your son, you'll be grateful he had the life he did and not the one with your mom and her awful husband. If he hadn't been taken from you, you would have never left home. He would have grown up in a toxic environment. I can't imagine the pain this caused you, but I know it was for all the right reasons. Now, when you get to see him, he will meet his incredibly smart, put-together mother. And he will love you for it."

I wiped the tears off my nose with the sleeve of my cardigan, the same one I wiped my prints off Seth's door just hours before. "Hmmm." The thought of me being well put together forced out a laugh. "Thank you, Norma. I've never talked about this with anyone before who understood my pain."

"Oh, honey, I understand more than you know."

I tilted my head waiting for her to continue.

She smiled. "I'm so glad you came by this afternoon."

"Me, too. A talk with you was just what I needed."

When I left Norma's house, I noticed a car turn onto the road. It looked like I had just missed Maggie and the girls. The time with Norma felt a lot like the time with my gram. Her calmness always seemed to ground me. Our visit was just what I needed to shake the stress from the day away. I was glad Lexi wasn't there. I'm not sure I could face her, not yet anyway.

CHAPTER NINE

"You'll never guess what happened today." Tim hadn't even shut the door before he finished talking.

I had an indication about what he was going to tell me, but he was right, I could never guess. "I have no idea."

His words came out in spurts as he caught his breath. "I was sent to do a welfare check... on Seth."

I crossed my arms as I waited for him to continue.

"You know, Jane's Seth?"

"Okay..."

"He was dead."

"Oh, no." My expression didn't change.

"Oh, no? That's all you've got? I've been waiting all day to tell you about this."

"You have? Why"

"Are you for real? Val, it's Seth... as in Jane and Carmen..."

"I know. Sorry, it's just been a crazy day. So, how did he die? Where was he?"

"He was home. I said we had to do a welfare check."

"Oh, sorry ... so, how'd he die?"

"He was shot... in the back of the head. It looks like he didn't even see it coming. The TV was on. We checked with his neighbors, but no one even heard a gunshot."

"That's strange, isn't it? How could they not hear a gunshot in the same building?"

"How do you know they are in the same building?" Tim raised his right eyebrow.

"What?" I felt my heart drop. "Oh, I just assumed... from the stories Jane told me."

"Oh, okay." He scratched his head. "He was murdered. That kind of thing never happens in Lawrenceville."

"What does that mean for you? More work? A big investigation? Longer hours?"

"All of the above. But I'm excited about it. It will be a good experience in case we ever move out of this place. Good for the old resume." He stood against the counter with his arms crossed.

"Wow... so some guy's death is good for your career?" I felt my eyebrows lift.

"Well, when you put it that way, it doesn't sound as noble."

I walked over to him and pulled him into a hug. "No, I'm messing with you. Seth was a dirtbag, so use him as a steppingstone. No judgments here."

Tim took a step back. "I'm confused. I thought he was

okay in your book? You know, since Jane came and confessed to you."

"I still don't think he was a very good person. Hey... do you think Ginger had anything to do with this? I mean, I did give her his address."

"From what I saw, I don't think a woman is behind this."

"Oh, so now you're noble and sexist."

"What? Women don't usually use guns to kill... that's all I meant. Are we fighting? What's going on here?"

"No, silly... I'm messing with you."

"Oh, alright... you just don't seem like yourself today."

"Sorry... it's a hard day for me. It's Gabriel's birthday." I bent down and picked up Gabriel and let my tears fall on to his soft, black fur. "He's twenty today. I missed all of his childhood and now all of his teen years."

"Ah, Val, I'm so sorry. I should have known what today was."

"How would you have known? It's not like I have it written on the calendar. I try to just go through the day as quiet as possible... but today was different." Gabriel jumped to the floor and circled my legs, reminding me it was dinner time.

"I know, but I love you, and I should have done something to help take your mind off things."

"No, I don't think there is anything you can do to take my mind off it. It's just one of those things. Unless..."

"Unless? Unless what?" Tim put his hand to his chin.

"Unless we find him and I get to meet him. Then, I think I could get through the day."

"I did start looking after our last talk. So far, I haven't

been able to find anything out. Do you have any idea what adoption agency your mom worked with?"

"No, they never told me anything. When I lived at home, I looked through my mom's paperwork, but I never found anything. She probably hid it at Chad's office."

"Well, we can start with the name of the home you were sent to stay at. Maybe someone there remembers the name of the adoption agency, or maybe there is only one in the area."

"Hmmm... I never thought of that. I wonder if any of the same people work there. Twenty years is a long time to work in one place."

"It is, but it's been done before." His laugh settled the butterflies in my stomach.

"The place was called Sawyer's Home for Unwed Girls. It was in Rockingdale, New Hampshire."

"Have you looked them up to see if they're still in business?"

"No." I shook my head and picked up my necklace, moving the broken heart along the chain. "I can't believe I never thought about doing that."

"Don't be so hard on yourself, Val. You weren't ready before."

"I've always wanted him with me... I just wasn't ready for the disappointment. His, not mine."

"Val, I don't think he would be disappointed by you. You can only hope for the best. It doesn't do any good to always prepare for the worst."

"Oh, my gosh... you sound like a Hallmark card."

"Ha-ha, very funny." Tim kissed the top of my head. "Want to see if we can find the place? Where's your iPad?"

"We don't have to do it now. I want to hear more about your day."

"It can wait. Today is your day. Let's try to get you closer to finding your son." He walked over to the table and picked up my iPad. "Here." He handed it to me. "Unlock this thing for Detective Phillips."

"Oh, good, I'm glad the detective is here." My tear-stained cheeks lifted with another smile as I held my finger to the home button to unlock the device.

After just seconds with the iPad, Tim's head dropped. "Oh, no."

"What?"

"They closed down five years ago." He scrolled the page. "It says here all of the records older than seven years were destroyed."

"Figures. It never comes easy."

"No, don't get discouraged. We just have to find another way. There's more than one way to skin a cat." His hand covered his mouth as his eyes widened.

"Wow, that escalated quickly." I laughed as I bent down to pet Gabe. "Don't worry, buddy, I'll save you."

"Poor choice of words. Sorry, buddy. Don't worry, you're safe with me."

"Not so fast, Detective Phillips." I took the iPad out of his hands and gave him a long, tight hug. "Thank you for trying to turn my day around."

"I'm sorry I didn't find any answers for you. Just be patient with me. I *will* find him."

"I know you will." My lips met his for a quick kiss. "Now,

let's talk about your day. I want to hear all about the investigation."

"Well, there's not a whole lot I can share." He ran his fingers through his hair. "It's still an open investigation."

"Oh, come on, who am I going to tell?"

"Val, you know the rules. I can tell you it was close to a spotless crime scene."

"Spotless? I doubt Seth's place was spotless... his hygiene... or lack of it..."

Tim tilted his head. "Hmmm."

"What?"

"You really didn't like this guy, did you?"

"No, I guess not. Sorry. Go on."

"The place wasn't spotless, it was a mess. But whoever did this knew what they were doing. They didn't leave anything behind, at least not that we were able to find."

"So, if there is no evidence at the scene, what do you do from there?"

"They sent his body to the medical examiner for an autopsy. I'll go back to his apartment and look around. Maybe find something we missed today. And then all I can really do is wait for the report and see if there are any clues."

"Clues? What kind of clues?"

"You know... like the kind of gun that was used. How long he'd been sitting there, if he had any drugs in his system. The typical crime investigation stuff."

"What about witnesses?"

"All the people we interviewed today said they didn't hear or see anything out of the ordinary. I gave them my business card, maybe they'll remember something as time passes, if not, then there are no witnesses."

"Do you know who placed the welfare call?" I felt my heart rate increase.

"No, it was an anonymous tip. Some lady, but we do know it came from the payphone outside of Lawrenceville Pizza."

I swallowed to push down the lump in my throat. "How do you know that?"

"That's the easy part. It came up on the caller ID. It's almost like she knew. We checked with the staff inside, but they said they didn't notice anyone on the phone. It is kind of hidden out of the way, so it's doubtful anyone saw her make the call."

"Why would someone who was involved call it in? That seems pretty dumb. Maybe someone genuinely was worried about him."

"Doubtful. They said he hadn't shown up for work... he hasn't worked in over a decade."

"Well, maybe it does have to do with drugs... we know he had that job."

Tim crossed his arms as he leaned back against the counter. "You think he was actively dealing drugs?"

"Don't you? You searched his apartment, didn't you find his stash or money?"

"No money, and just a couple boxes of Jane's old pills, oh, and some marijuana, probably just enough for his personal use though."

"Couldn't the killer have taken the drugs? If he owed someone money, wouldn't they have taken his stash?"

"Probably, but there was nothing out of place. It appeared he was just sitting watching TV and didn't even know anyone came inside."

"No forced entry?"

"Nope, the door was unlocked with no signs of it being tampered with. Not even a fingerprint on it. They've either done this before or watched enough crime shows to know how not to leave a trail behind."

"Have you been in contact with Ginger? I know you said it didn't look like something a woman could have done... but don't you think you should at least talk to her? I mean, she was at his place not that long ago trying to get information about Jane's death."

"Yeah, we'll be talking to her, but I really don't think it was her. We think it was probably a drug dealer or something. It would explain why no one in the building wants to talk to us."

"Look at Mr. Confidentiality, spilling the beans so easily."

His face shaded red. "Shit."

"It's alright, I won't tell anyone." I winked as I twisted my hair around my index finger.

"Maybe you should have been the detective. You've got a way of making people talk."

"Or maybe it's all those episodes of *Snapped* that make me think about things differently."

"Whatever it is, you're pretty amazing. I love you, Val."

The idea they would be looking into the case was both comforting and unsettling. I wanted to know who stole my chance at ending Seth's life, but I also hoped there were no witnesses who could place me there, or at the payphone. I had no idea how I would explain it to Tim, or anyone else. I'm just grateful Lawrenceville hadn't invested in town-wide surveillance cameras. The room started to spin and go dark when I remembered seeing the blinking red lights at Lawrenceville pizza.

CHAPTER TEN

Seth's murder was front page in the *Village News*. News around here travels as fast as gasoline ignites a fire. What wasn't whispered about in the local grocery store always found its way into our only newspaper. Murder in Lawrenceville was big news, it wasn't something that happened every day. The crime rate here kept the detectives in town asleep most of the time.

I wasn't sure if I should call Maggie to check on Lexi, or if I should ignore the whole thing. If he was the guy Lexi had been dating, this was a sure way to find out. It'd be pretty hard for her to ignore the death of a man she *loved*. I cringed at the thought.

I tossed the newspaper onto my desk and rested my head in my hands. I wasn't sure what had happened to Seth, and not knowing made my stomach feel hollow. The day played on repeat in my head. The image of his dead body sitting in his chair wouldn't leave my mind. The terror that encased me at that moment came back.

What if the person who did this to him was there? I didn't see them, but maybe they saw me. Maybe they're going to go to the police and pin this on me. I don't own a gun, but I'm sure it's an overused excuse. There are ways to get guns and dispose of them. My heart dropped to the pit of my empty stomach. *What if they took pictures of me at the crime scene?* How would I explain that?

My thoughts took me deeper into the rabbit hole of what-ifs. The worst part was there was no one I could talk to about it. Even a hypothetical conversation could backfire. The cruelest part of this whole thing was I didn't even do it. Not this time. If I'm going to be held responsible for something, I at least want the pleasure of doing it.

I shook the thought out of my head. No. I didn't want to do it. I'm grateful I didn't have to. The rush of feeling in control was more addicting than the drugs Seth was selling. It wasn't something I wanted to taste again, at least that was what I had to remind myself.

The ring of the phone brought me back to my office. Norma's name was displayed across my caller ID. "Hey, Norma."

"It's Maggie. Is this Val?"

"Oh, sorry, yeah. Hey Maggie, how are you doing?"

"Did you see the newspaper?"

"I did. Is everyone alright?"

"I... ah... I don't know."

"Is it Lexi?"

"Well, I haven't told her yet... I don't know what to say."

"Is she at school today?"

"No, I didn't wake her up. I didn't want her to find out

from friends or try to go to his apartment. She's been acting funny."

"Like how?"

"She's been glued to her phone... and agitated."

"Do you want me to stop over?"

"Really? You'd do that?"

"Of course, I'll be right over."

The thought of Lexi looking at her phone at unanswered texts left me sad and relieved. I didn't want to see her in pain, but I was glad she hadn't arrived in the middle of a crime scene. As gross as Seth was, it was still a loss for her. And, she had already lost so much. There were always so many layers... to everything.

At Norma's, Maggie greeted me at the door, her voice in a whisper. "She's still sleeping."

"Is Norma here?"

"No, she had some errands to run. She was the one who showed me the paper, though."

At the dining room table, we sat at the end furthest from the hall. "Did Sammy go to school?"

Maggie nodded her head.

"What are your plans when Lexi wakes up?"

Maggie's body trembled. "I... I'm not really sure." She picked at her fingernail. "I was hoping you could tell her."

A sigh escaped before I could pull it back in. "Me? Lexi doesn't even know me." Maggie's head dropped. "I'm sorry, Maggie. I'm just not good with kids. If you think it'd help, I'll do it."

Maggie lifted her head up, tears streaming down her face. "I just don't think I can. I can't keep it together."

"It's fine, I'll tell her." I placed my hand on Maggie's shoulder. "Should we wait for her to wake up, or do you think we should tell her now, you know, to get it over with?"

"I guess we should do it now… you probably have to get back to work." Maggie stood up and straightened her bathrobe, reaching back to the table to steady herself. She walked down the hall and went into Lexi's room. I scanned my surroundings to try and find something to focus on to channel some calmness. I knew I would be doing all of the talking. Maggie was in no shape for the conversation we were about to have.

I heard some grumbling and then saw Lexi and Maggie emerge from the darkened room. Lexi rubbed the sleep from her eyes and complained about being woken up when she saw me.

"Good morning, Lexi." I smiled as convincingly as possible.

"What is she doing here?" Lexi asked her mother.

Maggie sat back down and lifted her eyes at me, speaking without words. "Lexi, why don't you have a seat? I have something I need to talk to you about." The tension in the room was thicker than a bowl of oatmeal. I tapped my hand on the table, trying to keep a smile on my face.

Lexi crossed her arms and shot daggers at me. The upcoming news was not going to sit well. "I'd rather stand."

"Oh, I think sitting is a better idea, come on, just take a seat. Please?"

"Lexi, just sit." Maggie closed her eyes as she waited for Lexi to comply.

"This isn't one of those stupid interventions, is it?" Lexi

pulled out the chair and dropped her butt into it, keeping her arms crossed.

"No, I'm afraid it's not." I twisted my neck around to bump out any lingering tension. "Lexi... I have some hard news to share."

She rolled her eyes and stared straight ahead. "Okay."

"Your mom mentioned you are dating a boy... named Seth. Is that correct?"

Her head whipped around to face me. "Why do you want to know?"

"Well, Lexi, is she right?"

"Maybe."

"Was he... I mean... is he older than you?"

She turned her head to look at her mom. "Maybe... but only a little bit."

"And do you know where he lives?"

"Just tell me what you really want to know." She looked at her mom, then back at me.

"Lexi..." I paused while I searched for the right words. "There's been a murder in town and..."

"No... no, he's not like that. He would never hurt anyone."

"No, Lexi... a man named Seth was murdered, and we wanted to make sure it's not the same person."

"No... no... there's no way."

"Maggie, do you have the paper?"

Maggie got up and walked into the living room. She returned and handed me the paper. I placed it in front of Lexi. "Is this your Seth?"

Lexi let out a gasp and covered her mouth. "Oh my god. This can't be real." She pushed the paper away from her.

"Lexi, it's real. Seth was found dead at his apartment. When was the last time you talked to him?" I took the paper away and folded it up, hiding Seth's face.

"I don't know... it's been a few days since he answered my text."

"He was found on Wednesday."

"That explains why." She paused as tears streamed down her cheeks. "He didn't respond... I just thought he was mad at me."

"Lexi, he was thirty-two years old. Did you know that?"

"What does it matter?"

"I guess it doesn't... did he hurt you?"

"Jesus. He's fucken dead, and you want to make him into a monster? You're sick."

"Lexi, that's enough." Maggie scolded her. "He's a grown man, Lexi. What were you thinking?"

"He's dead. Why does it matter? You and your sick friend should throw a party."

"That's enough, Lexi." Maggie hit her fisted hand on the table.

"I just wanted to make sure you were okay. I know losing someone you love is never easy..."

"You want to give me a lecture about dating a grown-ass man, but where were you when dad was raping me? Huh? Why do you care now?"

"Lexi. That's not fair. Your mom did her best. She..."

"How the fuck would you know? You only know what

she told you." Lexi got up and ran down the hall, slamming her bedroom door behind her.

"Maggie... she doesn't mean what she said... she's just hurting."

"No, she's right. I didn't protect her."

"Maggie, you didn't know. You protected her as soon as you did know. Don't let her make you question yourself. If it's anyone's fault she was dating an older man, it's Hank's. Let that piece of shit take the blame."

Maggie hung her head and shook it. "No, I should have known. What kind of mother doesn't know?"

"You and I both know they're good at covering their tracks. Lexi is angry and sad. She said things she didn't mean. You know she can only talk to you like that because she feels safe with you, right? Isn't it great? You get to be her punching bag because she loves you." I elbowed Maggie's arm to try to make her smile.

She rubbed her eyes with her hands and blinked. "You think so?"

"I do, and by the sounds of things, she really loves you." I pushed Maggie's messy hair behind her ear and smiled.

Maggie laughed and leaned closer to me. "She's right about one thing... I think we should throw a party."

"Yeah. It's awful, but think about what could have happened if Seth hadn't been killed?" I closed my eyes and shook the thoughts out of my head. "I know Lexi's heart is broken right now, but this was probably the best thing that could have happened to her."

"I don't want to imagine what could have happened."

"You're right, you don't." Carmen's face flashed before my closed eyes. "She'll get through this, and so will you."

"Thanks, Val, for coming by and helping me tell her."

"I'm glad I could help, call me anytime. I mean that."

On my way back to the hospital, I thought about the damage Seth could have done to Lexi if he were still alive. It was evident Lexi was looking for an escape, and Seth had all the right stuff to get her mind off all the hard things she'd had to face over the last few months. His death made sure Lexi wouldn't be the next Carmen. I'll never understand what those girls found so attractive. He made my skin crawl.

CHAPTER ELEVEN

"I called Ginger like you suggested. She has an airtight alibi. There's no way she could have been in Lawrenceville the day Seth was murdered."

"And you confirmed this?"

"Yeah. She was at a dinner party with her husband and about a hundred other affluent people in Boston. She had no reason to kill him. She did say Seth reached out to her about Jane's death just a couple days before he died. He told her he knew who killed Jane."

I picked up my necklace and rubbed it between my fingers. "He did? Did he tell her who?"

"No, she was planning to come by next weekend and talk with him. He told her he was waiting for someone to *do the right thing*, but he didn't elaborate. So now she's not a suspect, but she is positive we dropped the ball on Jane's death. She's sure it was a murder, but without the information Seth was going to give her, that's a dead end."

"Like Jane." I covered my mouth to mute the laugh. "Sorry, I do that when I'm nervous."

"Why are you nervous?"

"Nervous? I mean, sad. I'm not even sure what I feel anymore. It's like I've been in the middle of that whole family since I walked into Carmen's room that day. You know? They've kind of consumed my whole brain the last few months. I guess I'm just tired. I'm tired of not knowing what to think or who to trust, and now Ginger is in the mix. I don't think I have it in me to get involved with one more person from that family."

"I get it, Val. It has been a lot, but this isn't about you. You don't have to get involved anymore. Carmen got the justice you wanted for her, and now, Jane got hers, too, if Seth really was abusing her. If not, well, I guess it was just his time. You're not responsible for any of it. You did so much for Jane, but your part is over now. Now, it's up to me to put Ginger's mind to rest and figure out what happened to Seth."

"That's what I'm afraid of. You taking care of Ginger." I crossed my arms.

"Hold on... I didn't say take care of Ginger, I said, put her mind to rest. You have nothing to worry about. It's strictly professional." Tim walked over and uncrossed my arms and wrapped me in a hug. "I love you, Valerie Williamson, soon to be Mrs. Phillips." His kiss erased some of my worries. But he didn't know what I knew, and he never could. If he did, there would never be a Mrs. Timothy Philips. And, orange is not my color.

"Is Ginger coming to see you? Or are you done with her?"

"No, she's not planning on coming back. She did say she'd have her attorney contact us if she changed her mind."

"Changed her mind about what?"

"If she changes her mind about having Jane's body exhumed."

"What? Are you kidding me? That lady is as crazy as her daughter. The dirt just hit the top of her coffin. The grass hasn't even had time to grow back in."

"Whoa, that's harsh. Let's change the subject. How about we talk about the wedding?"

The sigh I released said more than I could.

"I'm starting to take this personal. I know we are taking it slow, and I'm fine with that, but can we just talk about it? Share our hopes and dreams?"

"Have you picked out your dress yet?" I regretted my attempt at a joke when Tim walked into the living room. "Hey, Tim. I'm sorry. It's just hard for me. I shouldn't have said that. I didn't mean anything by it."

"It's fine. I get it."

I brought in two Sam Adams and handed him one. "I love you, Tim. I do want to marry you, I guess it's hard for me to believe you actually love me. I'm a master at sabotaging all the good things in my life." I tipped the bottle to my lips and let the cold liquid fill my stomach. "I think it's cute you're excited."

Tim picked at the label on the bottle. "Val, I do want to marry you. I want to be your husband, have a family with you, grow old with you, and get matching gravestones."

"Definitely couple goals." I took another drink of my liquid courage and let it slide down my throat. "I want that. I want to believe I deserve it. I'm just worried you'll leave me, and I'll just be old and alone."

"I don't know what I can say to make you believe me. All I can do is prove it to you. Give me that chance."

"Okay. I'll try." I took the last swig of my beer. "You know what would make our wedding perfect? If Gabriel and my gram were there."

"That seems doable." Tim set his untouched beer on the coffee table. "I wanted to tell you I think I found the adoption agency your mom worked with. I wanted to surprise you, but I wanted to get more details first."

"You did? How'd you do that?" I picked up Tim's beer and took a sip.

"Go ahead, you can drink it. I'm on call tonight."

"Shit, I'm sorry, I didn't..."

"No, it's okay, it seems like you need it more than me." Tim rubbed his hands on his pant legs. "So, I looked up Sawyer's Home for Unwed Girls again and dug a little deeper. I found a message board where other girls who stayed there reconnected."

"Wait... that's a thing?"

"Yeah, a lot of the girls who stayed there were unhappy. It seems like you weren't the only one who had your baby taken from them. The deeper I read in the thread, the more information I got. I sent a message to a few girls, and they said Love's Adoption Agency was who their parents worked with. I saw their name in the chat, too. It seems like the only one that was mentioned."

"Love's adoption agency? That's a shitty name for a place who rips babies from mother's arms. Are they still open?"

"Yeah, I looked them up, too, and they are still in business. They have great reviews, so I can only hope they do good work."

"They're probably fake. I'd never leave them a good review."

"Maybe they are, but it's not really their fault. Your mom signed the rights away. All they did was find your baby a loving home."

"Yeah, I guess you're right."

"I called them and asked them how long they keep their records."

I felt my heart do a somersault in my chest. "And?"

"And, they destroy the records when the baby turns eighteen."

"Just my luck. I'm late for everything."

"Hang on, don't get upset yet. They aren't always on top of their shredding, so there is a possibility they still have your records there. They wouldn't tell me any more information, they'll need to talk to you."

Afraid to get too excited, I didn't know how to react. "Okay."

"Aren't you happy? This could be what you need to find Gabriel."

"I'm scared. Scared they got rid of the records. Scared we'll find him, and he'll hate me. Scared he had an unhappy life. Terrified, actually."

"It's okay to be scared, Val. I'll be right by your side if you want me to be. I have a really good feeling about this."

"It's hard to believe it's so close. I just assumed it'd never happen."

"Your wish is my command." He took my hand in his. The weight and warmth made me feel safe. I had to trust him.

The two beers and being in Tim's arms helped me drift off to sleep without thinking. The reoccurring dream that usually leaves me feeling empty came. The one where my baby is crying, and he is nowhere to be found. But in this one, I found him. I felt the warmth of his little body next to mine, and I told him I loved him. My lips kissed the top of his warm, tiny head, and as I held him tight, I knew we wouldn't have to say goodbye. I rocked him to sleep and told him I would keep him safe. I wouldn't let anyone hurt him. His cries stopped, and I felt our hearts connect.

When I woke up, I was cradling a pillow. The empty parts of me felt whole. I knew we would find Gabriel, and I knew he would forgive me. I watched Tim sleep as I tried to will him awake. I didn't want to wait any longer to call the adoption agency. I didn't think I could wait one more day without my son in my life.

"Hey, buddy," I whispered to Gabe as he jumped on the bed. I was sure his purring would be enough to wake Tim. I fell back asleep with Gabe in my arms. I needed to be a mother, it was a desire I didn't know I had, but now, the urge was all I could focus on.

When Gabriel jumped off the bed, I rolled over and put my head on Tim's chest and listened to his heartbeat. I kissed his bare chest and looked up at him. When his eyes opened, he smiled when he saw me staring at him.

"Good morning, beautiful." He stretched his arms above his head and bent down to kiss me.

"Good morning. I thought you'd never wake up."

"How long have you been waiting?" He rubbed the sleep from his eyes.

"Oh, I don't know. A while."

"You should have woken me up."

"No, it's okay. I was watching you sleep and thinking."

"Oh no, should I be worried?"

"No. I want to have your baby. I want to be a mom."

"For real? What happened?"

"I had a dream about Gabriel, and I just can't wait to meet him and to get the chance to have a baby... a family... and share it all with you."

"Okay. Well, I'm glad you're so excited. I guess we have some work to do." He rolled over and hugged me.

"Let's get up and call them to see..."

"Val, it's Saturday. I think we'll have to wait until Monday."

"Oh... I guess I wasn't thinking."

"No, I get it, you're excited. And so am I. I can't wait to be a dad, especially with you. You're going to be a great mom, Val." He reached over and scratched Gabriel's head. "And, I guess, you'll be a good big brother."

"Do you want to go meet my gram? We can get that out of the way."

"I have met her."

"No, not really. She didn't know it was us then."

"Good point, but don't you think she'll recognize me when she sees me with you?"

"Maybe, but I really want her to get to know you. I know you'll love her as much as I do."

"Of course, I will. I know how special she is to you."

"Maybe she can be my maid of honor." I giggled at the thought of her walking down the aisle with one of Tim's friends.

"Yeah, that might be a sweet thing to do."

"I was kidding. Can you imagine her and one of your cop friends walking arm and arm together?"

"Sure. I think it could work. I bet she'd love you to ask her."

"I don't know. I'll think about it. I just want to make sure she's there. This is the one thing I don't want her to miss."

"I'm glad you're feeling better today. I guess all you needed was a buzz and a good night's sleep."

"That's not all I needed." I buried my head into his chest.

"Well, that never hurts anything. And think... we can start practicing."

"Practicing?"

"Yeah, you know... for baby-making."

"Oh my god, you're such a dork." I kissed his chest. "But you're my dork, and I love you."

"Thanks, I think." He laughed as he got up and dressed. "So, when do you want to go?"

"Now? Well, after coffee?"

"Okay. Sounds good to me." He yawned as he stretched his arms over his head.

I wished Gram didn't live so far away, now that she was back in my life, I wanted to see her as much as I could, but work and life got in the way. Maybe Tim and I could look for a house closer to her. The thought of living that close to my mom and Chad reminded me why it wasn't a good idea.

There was no way I wanted them near our future children. Jeanine's offer of taking time off might be just what I need to have the extra time with Gram.

"Do you remember the way?" I asked Tim as we got into the car.

"Yeah, I think so. It's in the GPS if we get lost." Tim turned on the radio as "Wildflowers" ended. "This might add to the pleasure of being in my company."

"I can think of nothing better. You and Tom Petty."

"Maybe we can get him to come play at our wedding." Tim put his sunglasses on as he turned his car onto the road.

"Can you imagine? It would be awesome."

"It would. Maybe you'd settle for a concert?"

"I've never seen him live before."

"Something told me you'd say that. He's on tour this summer, and a buddy of mine was able to score us some tickets. Front row."

"Holy shit. For real? I'll be inches away from him?"

"Well, probably not that close... feet, at least. I'm getting a little worried. Should I bring the Taser?" His laugh filled the car.

"No, I promise I'll behave. I won't do anything stupid. I can't believe you got us front row tickets."

"Only the best for my future wife."

"I think you mean fiancé."

"Nah, I don't like how that sounds. Future wife has a better ring to it."

"You can call me whatever you want. Soon, you can leave off the future."

"I can't wait."

As the sun shone in the open, blue sky on our way to Gram's, I felt like I was stuck in a dream. In such a short period, everything shifted. Life was so different from before, and it seemed like the changes were going to keep coming. This was the way life was supposed to be. "I feel like the Grinch."

"Like that little angry green guy?"

"Yeah. I feel like my heart has doubled in size since I met you. You've given me so much joy in such a short amount of time."

"All this for Tom Petty tickets?"

"No, but that doesn't hurt anything."

When we arrived at Gram's, I held Tim's hand as we walked down the path to her door. For a split second, I froze as I imagined opening the door and finding my mom with Gram. I shook the thought out of my mind and continued down the paved walkway.

"You ready to meet your grandmother-in-law?" I squeezed his hand before I rang the doorbell.

Tim smiled and nodded. "I am."

When I didn't hear Gram answer, I felt my heart rate increase. Before I allowed the negative thoughts to take over, I turned the doorknob. It was unlocked. I opened it enough to stick my head in. "Gram? Are you there?" She didn't respond, but the buzz from her TV met my ears. I pulled Tim in through the door and found Gram asleep in her recliner. I found the remote in her lap and turned the TV off. "Gram."

Her body tensed as she saw me standing over her.

"Gram, it's Val, I wanted to introduce you to someone."

"Oh, what a nice surprise. I must have fallen asleep."

"This is Tim, my fiancé I was telling you about." Tim reached his hand out for her to shake.

"It's nice to meet you, Mrs. Cooper." Tim's smile was enough to win anyone over.

"Oh, you are handsome." Gram winked at me.

"I just wanted you two to get to know each other before the wedding."

Gram smiled as she looked at us, sitting on the couch together. "When is the special day?"

"We don't have a day picked yet."

"No? What are you waiting for?"

I couldn't tell her the real reason we hadn't picked a date. She didn't know about Gabriel, and I wasn't ready to share it with her. It was too much for her to have to deal with. I imagined our wedding day with Gram and Gabriel sitting together, making up my only family. The smile was pushed off my face when I realized I would have to tell her, at least part of the story.

Tim filled the silence. "Val wanted to be sure you'd be there." He rested his hand on my knee.

"You better hurry up then, I'm not getting any younger."

"Will you be able to make it?" My question was an attempt to ignore what she had said.

"I wouldn't miss it for anything." Her smile warmed me to my core.

"I don't want Mom to know about this. Will you be able to come without her knowing?"

"I haven't told her about our visits, but the nurses might report back to her about me being gone, and she might question me about it. I can keep a secret, though." Her smile pushed up her cheeks.

"Has she been around?" I looked around the apartment to see if there was any sign of her.

"She was here just the other day. She brought some papers for me to sign." Gram ruffled through a stack of papers on the stand by her chair. "Oh, it's here, somewhere."

"Do you know what it was about?" My body temperature increased as I waited for her answer.

"It was something about... oh, I don't remember, but I think she left a copy here."

I walked over to help her look. A few menus and a brochure of a nursing home were the only things in the pile. "I don't see anything here. Are you sure she left it?"

She leaned her head back into her recliner. "I could have sworn she did... but maybe not."

"What's this for?" I held up the brochure. "You're not moving, are you?"

She squinted her eyes to look at what I was holding in front of her. "No, I don't plan on moving again. I'm not sure where that came from."

"She's not trying to put you in a home, is she?" My voice rose with the question. I knew whatever Mom made her sign couldn't have been good.

"Oh, heavens, no."

"Why do you have this then?" I shook the brochure in front of her face.

"Val." Tim's voice took me out of the rage brewing inside of me. "Why don't you and your gram talk about the wedding?"

I set the paper down and silently counted to ten as I returned to my seat next to Tim. "We're not in the planning stages just yet, but I hope you can help me when I'm ready."

Gram's smile faded. "Oh, honey, I'm afraid I'm not much help."

"Don't be silly, of course, you will be. I'll need to run some ideas by you, and you can help me just by letting me share this with you."

"Well, that does sound like something I could do." Her smile wasn't enough to hide the age that had crept up on her.

I wasn't going to let my mom ruin another day. Not today, and not our wedding. I wanted to be sure it would be a day we would always remember. I wouldn't allow her to take any more away from me. I am stronger than she ever imagined. That alone was enough to fuel the search to find Gabriel. We have a wedding to plan.

CHAPTER TWELVE

Before group, I walked down the hall to Lily's room to give her another invite. I knocked on the door and waited for an answer. "Hey, Val, who are you looking for?" I felt a hand on my shoulder. When I turned around, I noticed it was Jennifer.

"Oh, hi. I was looking for Lily. She's still here, isn't she?"

"No, I thought I left you a message when she was discharged."

I looked down at my watch. "Oh, I guess I haven't listened to my messages yet this morning."

"It was Thursday, last week."

"Oh... I guess I mustn't have gotten it. I'll have to give the IT guy a call." I felt my cheeks flush as I thought about how many other messages I probably missed. I had noticed the red light but hadn't gotten around to listening to them yet.

"Is there anything else I can help you with?"

"No, I'm running late for group."

"That's a great thing you do in there. I know so many people who could benefit from it."

"Yeah, I guess we all have some trauma to work through."

"That we do." Jennifer gave me a small smile as she looked down at her clipboard.

With a nod and smile, I turned to walk back down the hall.

"Val. How are you holding up?"

"Me?" I pointed to my chest. "I'm doing fine."

"Really? You seem like something is bothering you... and for good reason. Remember to give yourself time to grieve, too. I know I have a hard time when I lose clients."

"You forget, I'm the social worker of death." I laughed. "Thank you for your concern. It means a lot."

With a fake smile, she watched me walk down the hall. *Nice Val.* This was why I didn't have friends. I always seemed to forget not everyone had my dark sense of humor. Cracking an inappropriate joke helped assure I wouldn't have to feel. Coping mechanism 101.

In the conference room, Maggie, Norma, Sonya, and Lily were waiting for me. "Sorry, I'm late. I need to just get the t-shirt, save myself from always apologizing."

"No need to apologize. We were just getting to know each other." Norma's smile brought me back to the talk we had the other day.

"Thanks for taking such good care of our new member. I told you these ladies were great." I turned to smile at Lily. Her face was still discolored from the beating. "I was actually in your room to see if you wanted to join us. I didn't know you were released."

Lily smiled back at me. "Yeah, I've been home for a few days now."

"How's being home going?" I asked.

"It's been hard. I'm afraid of every noise. I lock my doors, and check to make sure about fifty times a day."

"Don't forget the windows." Sonya proudly added.

"Yes, those, too. I'm just so exhausted, but I can't sleep." Lily pushed her hair behind her ear.

"I remember feeling like that." Maggie turned her head to look at Lily. "It does get a little easier, but it never goes away."

"Wow, great pep talk Maggie." Sonya rolled her eyes.

"No, she's right." My response surprised me. "After all these years, I still look over my shoulder and check the locks on my doors. Now that I think about it, I guess I haven't checked the window locks in a while... but she's right, it never really goes away."

"I'm not unfamiliar with being afraid. I've been with Earl for years. This wasn't the first time he's hurt me."

"His name is Earl?" Norma smiled. "As in *Goodbye Earl?*"

"What are you even talking about?" A disgusted look planted on Sonya's face.

Lily laughed. "Yeah, just like that."

Norma nodded her head and smiled. "It's a great song."

"Yeah, it's pretty funny. I laugh every time I hear it and think about my own version of it."

"There's a song called *Goodbye Earl?*" Sonya pulled out her phone and focused her attention on the screen. "Who's it by?"

"The Dixie Chicks." Norma and Lily answered in unison, followed by laughter.

"Is this it?" Sonya held her phone up as the song played.

We sat in our circle and listened to the song together, all able to relate to the lyrics. We each had our own Earl, at least one we could imagine getting rid of. As the song filled the room, I felt our bond grow even stronger. We all wanted our abusers to pay for what they did to us. We could take our power back when we extinguished theirs.

Sonya danced in her seat as the song ended. "How have I never heard this before? It's great. Goodbye Earl... and Jimmy." She raised her hand in the air. "And Hank. Anyone else? Val's piece of shit mom and her husband. Norma, you got any names to add?"

Norma smiled. "I just loved it the first time I heard it. It's just so... I don't know... powerful."

"I didn't think you liked violence. I seem to remember you trying to talk me out of wanting to kill Hank." Sonya raised her eyebrows and looked at Norma.

"Oh, dear, it's just a song. It didn't really happen. It's just got a great beat to it."

"Norma's right, we can't go around killing everyone who ever wronged us." Maggie looked over at me for approval.

"Thanks for playing the song for us, Sonya. I'd like to use the rest of our time talking if anyone wants to start." I looked around the circle.

"You're such a buzz kill, Val." Sonya slipped her phone back into her purse.

"Oh, be nice, you girls." Norma looked around the circle.

"Remember, we have our new guest, and we want her to come back."

"Sorry, Lily, it's not usually this..."

"Fun? Sure it is. We can have a good time and talk about trauma. I think it's in the handbook." Sonya smirked after she interrupted me.

"Nice Sonya." I rolled my eyes and shook my head. "Lily, did you want to share today? No pressure."

"I wasn't going to, but you've all made me feel so welcome." She looked around the room and gave us a half smile. "Well, obviously, you can see my face is all messed up. That was courtesy of Earl." She pulled up her shirt sleeves. "These, too." She pointed to the bruises. "He wasn't always a jerk. In the beginning, he was the perfect gentleman. He'd bring me flowers, sing me songs... you know, all the stuff you see on TV."

"They all start off good. Couldn't get us where they want us if they were always assholes." Sonya crossed her arms against her chest.

"Yeah, you're probably right." Lily pulled out a tissue. "I loved him. I thought I would spend the rest of my life with him. When he started drinking, he changed. He's the meanest drunk I know. With just a few beers, he's a totally different guy. It began with him calling me names.

"First, I'm a fat ass, and when it didn't get the reaction he was looking for, he called me a whore. That one really hurt. It's my trigger word. The one that would always get a reaction out of me."

"Why that word?" Sonya tilted her head to wait for an answer.

"Because I was a virgin when we met. He was my first and only. He was the whore, the one who slept with more women than I can count. It felt like he was making fun of me for not being able to find anyone else."

"Makes sense. My word is *perfect*. He loved to rub it in my face when I screwed up. Taunt me with the word, because I could never measure up to it. I didn't know other people had trigger words." Sonya looked up at Lily.

"Me, either." Lily smiled as she and Sonya connected. "Anyway, the name-calling escalated to threats. He threatened to kill me, and all my family if I didn't bring him home beer, or if I didn't suck his... I ah... mean... wouldn't have sex with him, or if I ever told anyone about what he was doing. I didn't stop loving him, though. I just thought if I did better, he'd stop. It seemed like the harder I tried, the worse it got.

"He started choking me, just long enough to take my breath away. I think he wanted to show me he had control over me. If dinner was late or wasn't what he wanted, his hands would go straight to my throat, and he'd squeeze. Sometimes, I'd dig my nails into his arms to try to make him stop, but sometimes I didn't do anything... maybe because I wanted it to just stop, you know?"

We all nodded our heads in agreement.

"When I stopped fighting back, he upped the ante. He started kicking and punching me. In the stomach, in the back of the head, pretty much anywhere hidden by clothes. It hurt, but I took it. Until... he kicked me in the stomach and killed our unborn baby." She dabbed her eyes with the tissue. "That was the day I stopped loving him." She blew her nose. "I wanted so badly to be a mom, and he stole it from me. I hated him for it. I could barely stand to look at him."

"Oh, Lily, I'm so sorry." I pushed the tears off my face with my sleeve.

"When I stopped having sex with him, he started raping me. I didn't know it was rape until recently when I talked with the domestic violence advocate. I figured I was his wife, it couldn't be rape. But I was wrong. The bastard raped me. I got pregnant again but had a miscarriage, that one was probably due to stress. I wasn't sad about it, I was grateful I wouldn't have to try to protect my baby from such a monster. But I still didn't leave him." She closed her eyes, and her head fell as she shook it. "Nope, that wasn't enough. He maxed out all of my credit cards and drained the bank accounts, so I had no access to money. I couldn't have left if I wanted to. I depended on him for everything. Thinking about it makes me sick now.

"I got a call from some woman, telling me she was messing around with my husband. I just laughed. I told her she could have him. When he found out about my reaction, he beat me so bad, I ended up here, at the hospital. I have broken ribs, a broken nose, and broken blood vessels. He left me for dead. I think he really thought he had killed me this time. When I heard his truck pull out of the driveway, I called 911. It was the first time I ever called for help. I had always been too afraid to call before, but this time, I knew I would have died if I didn't." She blew her nose again. "And that's how I ended up here... more or less."

"Wow, I can relate to so much of your story." Sonya's eyes bugged open as she reached toward the ceiling in a stretch.

"I'm sorry to hear that. It's an awful way to live. You're so young. But I guess I was, too, when it all started."

"Do you think boyfriends can rape you?" Sonya stared straight ahead, not making eye contact with any of us.

"Yes. Just because you are in a relationship with someone, doesn't mean they are entitled to sex whenever or wherever they want it." I knew where her question was headed, and I didn't like the feeling it was leaving me with.

"Hmmm. Interesting." Sonya began rocking back and forth in her chair.

"Are you alright, Sonya?" Norma put her hand on Sonya's knee, making Sonya shoot up out of her chair.

"Yes. Of course, I am. I just got to get back to work."

"Sonya, why don't you sit back down and talk to us before you bolt out of here." I stood up to help guide her back to her seat.

"No. I.... ah... don't really feel like it right now. I just got to get to work."

She brushed past me and out the door. I took her hand in an attempt to slow her down, but she brushed me off. "Don't touch me."

As she jogged down the hall, I took a couple steps toward her. "I'm sorry, Sonya." My head hung down in defeat.

"I hope I didn't say something to upset her." Lily looked around the circle.

"Oh, no, dear, Sonya just has a lot on her mind."

My eyes met Norma's. "She does?"

"Of course, she does, dear, why else would she be here?"

"I hope you're right. I'm worried about her."

"She'll be fine, dear. Don't you worry."

But I was worried. It wasn't like Sonya to act like that. I understood she didn't want to talk about it, but for her to run off like that made me worry... a lot. And Norma? How did she seem to know all this inside information? It felt like Norma should be the one leading this group, not me. There were many days I didn't think these meetings would help anyone if it weren't for her. Norma was like a gift handed to me from God. Just her presence was enough to calm my nerves. There was no way I could have made it through the first meeting without her.

And her kindness was almost angel-like. Being with Norma reminded me of the kind of relationship I wished I had with my mom. She was who I wanted to see when things didn't go right, and who I wanted to share the exciting things with.

But why was she here? After all this time, she still hadn't shared anything about her past. Not one thing. I didn't even know if she had children. She never talked about her family or friends. It seemed as though she just existed in this little reality of ours. Whatever the reason she was here, I was grateful. She was one of the best friends I'd ever had.

"Dear, are you alright?" Norma's sweet voice shook me out of my thoughts.

"Yeah." I shot her a smile. "Sorry, I was just... thinking."

"Of course, dear. Lily shared some hard stuff."

"Yes, that's true. Lily, how are you holding up?" I turned my attention to Lily.

"I'm fine." She twisted at the tissue in her hand. "I just feel bad, like I said something to upset Sonya."

"Oh, honey, don't ever feel bad for sharing your story."

Norma turned to face Lily. "Sonya just has some things she hasn't faced yet. I bet hearing your story helped her."

I felt myself nodding my head. "Norma's right. It helps us all to hear what other people have gone through, and it helps to know we're not alone."

"That's true. These ladies have really helped me through some of the hardest times of my life. Don't be afraid to share with us. We know how it feels to have some asshole take everything away from us." Maggie showed the most animation I had ever seen her display.

"Thanks, that helps. After I shared, I felt like I kind of traumatized all of you." Lily dropped her head.

"Nah... these walls have heard a lot." Maggie smiled. "You should come by for tea and we can catch you up."

"Oh, that would be lovely. We can get to know each other. Val, you're welcome to stop by, too." Norma's face lit up with a smile.

"That's very sweet of you, Norma." And there she was again, making everyone feel welcome and connected. "This is such a great group."

"We are a pretty great group." Maggie shifted herself in her seat, still with a smile on her face. I was so glad Seth was out of the picture. I still wanted to know who got to him before I did, but some heroes go unrecognized.

CHAPTER THIRTEEN

s I walked into the hospital, I felt my phone vibrate. When I pulled it out of my jacket pocket, I saw it was Tim. We had only left each other minutes before. "Is everything alright?"

"Yeah, when I got to the office, I had an email from the adoption agency waiting for me. I couldn't wait to tell you." Enthusiasm emitted from his voice.

My heart skipped a beat as I tried to find the words. "For real?"

"Yeah, and they asked me to call them. I just didn't want to do it without you. Did you ever call them?"

"I called them first thing Monday morning but had to leave a message. I thought they'd call me, but I did give them permission to talk with you."

"I'll be right over." He hung up before I had a chance to offer to go to him.

As the minutes ticked by, all the worst-case scenarios played out before me. Why did they reach out to Tim and not me? Maybe they found him and he didn't want to be bothered. Perhaps he told them he never wanted to talk to me. Or maybe they found him and he was dead. The knock on my door helped push the thoughts out of my head.

When I opened it, Tim had his hand up to knock again. "Whoa, you surprised me. Those better be happy tears."

I pushed the tears off my face with my sleeves. "Sorry, I was just thinking."

"Don't go to those bad places, Val. I have a feeling this is good news."

I cleared out the chair in front of my desk and handed him the phone. "I hope so, I don't think I can take anything else."

Tim dialed the number as I pulled my chair over to sit next to him. "This is Detective Tim Phillips, I had a message to call Tammy Weston." As he waited to have his call transferred, he pushed my hair out of my face and smiled at me. "Hi, Tammy, I received your email about the Williamson case, and I actually have Ms. Williamson here with me. Can I put you on speakerphone?" He hit the button before hanging up the receiver.

"Hi Ms. Williamson, can you guys hear me okay?"

I nodded my head.

"Yes, we can hear you just fine," Tim answered.

"I did get your message, Ms. Williamson, and since you gave me permission to look into your case and work with Detective Philips, I went ahead and found your file. I was able to locate it."

"You found it?" I leaned forward as I talked into the speaker.

"Yes, I did, and I was able to locate your son's adoptive family."

"That's great." Tim gave me a thumbs up.

"His family said they would like to talk with him first, but they don't think it should be a problem. They said he has actually been looking for you, too."

Tim smiled and mouthed, "I told you so."

"He has? I didn't expect that."

"Yes, his adoptive family told me they kept the note and necklace you gave him when you... when they received him."

I reached up and rubbed my necklace. "So, he's not mad at me?"

"It doesn't sound like it. If it's okay with you, I'll send the contact information to Detective Phillips's email. You can reach out to the family directly."

"Thank you. That would be great." Tim looked over at me and smiled.

"You guys got lucky, these files were in the to be shredded box. It was the last box I looked in, but something told me not to give up."

"Thank you for your help and for making Val's dream come true."

"Hey, it's the least we can do. From the file, it sounds like Ms. Williamson was railroaded. I hope this is everything you have hoped for."

Tim reached over, picked up, and released the receiver to turn off the call. "I told you we'd find him."

With my necklace still between my fingers, I imagined meeting my son and learning about everything I missed out on. "I can't believe I'm going to meet him."

"Believe it, Val. How cool is it he wanted to find you, too? I'm so glad they found your file." He reached over and kissed me. "I'll let you know as soon as she emails me. It's within reach, Val. You'll have your son back before you know it."

"I love you so much, Tim. You're the best thing to ever happen to me." I scrunched up my nose to hold off the tears.

"I'm glad you gave me a chance. You've made my life so much better being in it. I want to spend the rest of my life making you happy."

"You're too good to be true. I hope I can make you as happy as you've made me."

After Tim returned to work, I thought about the lies I'd been keeping from him, and about the side of me he didn't know. Guilt poured over me as I imagined him finding out the pieces of myself I hid from him. There was no way he would love Stephanie Mills, or approve of the things she did. I'd either have to stop or learn to be more careful.

CHAPTER FOURTEEN

The front page of the *Village News* caught my attention as I walked into the grocery store. "Second Murder in less than two weeks in Lawrenceville." Intrigued and alarmed, I picked up the paper and put it in my basket. When I finished shopping and had the bags loaded in my car, I pulled out the paper to finish reading the story.

Joseph Swift, 45, was found dead in his apartment with a single gunshot wound. The rest of the article went on about how he lived alone and had just been released from jail. There was no mention of what crime had sent him to prison. The similarities made me wonder if maybe the same person had killed both men, or if it was a coincidence.

Curious as to what Mr. Swift's offense was, I typed his name into the search bar on my phone. An article published the previous week was the first to come up. When I clicked on the link, I saw he had served five years for molesting a child and was on the sex offender registry. Back in the search results was the link to his registry photo. Clicking on the link brought me to a page of information about him, including his address.

I could see why someone would want to kill him, especially if his victim's family knew he was released. Having access to his address seemed like the perfect ending to his freedom. It was only fair people were notified of his whereabouts. I couldn't see the correlation between him and Seth. A sex offender and a drug dealer. I thought about what could connect them, and what made these two men become front-page news. It couldn't have been the wrong place, the wrong time since they were both at home. I knew Tim would be eager to talk about the details, as long as I didn't make it too obvious.

I placed the newspaper on the table as I put the rest of the groceries away and waited for Tim to arrive for dinner. It was one of the few times we'd be eating a home-cooked meal and not take out, but we had a lot to celebrate. After putting the finishing touches on the lasagna, I placed it in the oven and started the salad. "Gabriel, can you believe I'm cooking?" He sat perched on the kitchen chair as he watched me slice the cucumber. "This might be a first for us, buddy. I used to love to cook in home economics. If it wasn't for Mrs. C and Gram, I would never have learned how to cook, bake, or sew or any of the important things." The memories brought a smile to my face as I dropped the cherry tomatoes onto the lettuce bed. "I guess I've got to start practicing more if I'm going to have a family."

The squeak of the door opening made me drop the knife. "Shit." I backed away as it fell between my feet.

"Whoa, easy, Val." Tim's laugh put the smile back on my face. "It smells great in here." He handed me a bouquet of pink roses and a bottle of red wine. "I wasn't sure if you even like this stuff but thought we could give it a shot... you know, since it's a special occasion."

I wiped my hands on my apron and took the flowers. "Thank you, they're beautiful." I gave him a kiss before putting them into a vase. "I'm not a wine drinker, but I'll give it a shot. I never knew what all the fuss was about. I'd rather have a few cold ones."

"That's my girl." Tim laughed. "You don't have to drink it." His eyes went to the paper as he set the bottle on the table. "Did you read this yet?"

"Oh, that? Yeah, I just skimmed it. Crazy, right?"

"Just a little. Can you believe we can go from a sleepy little town to the next Dateline episode?"

"What do you mean? Do you think they're related?"

"Ah, it's too soon to say. The cause of death is similar, both single, white guys, but that's about all. It's probably just a vigilante."

"What are your feelings about vigilantes?" I held my breath as I waited for his answer.

"That's a hard question." His hand went to his chin as he thought. "On one hand, I can understand why they do what they do, especially if they have been wronged by some dirtbag. But how does what they do make them any different than the people they are killing?"

His words stung as they hit my ears. "You honestly think that makes them the same?" My tone was harsher than I intended.

"No, not the same. It's just complicated. These guys had people who loved them, and their deaths leave people hurting. Yeah, what they did wasn't right..."

"Wasn't right?" I slammed down the pepper grinder I was holding and turned to face him. "This new guy, what's his name? Swift? He was a child molester. Do you know what that does to a kid? Because I sure as hell do."

"Whoa, hold on, Val, I didn't say..."

"No, you didn't need to. You said enough."

"Please, Val. Hear me out. I said it was complicated." He took a step closer to me and stopped. "I can understand wanting to harm someone who hurt someone you love. I get it. The minute you told me about Chad, I wanted to make him pay. All I'm saying is I don't think you can solve anything with violence."

"Well, I guess that's where we're different. If someone hurt someone I love, I don't think I'd stop until I knew they had paid their debt."

"But, this guy, he just got out of jail. He did pay..."

"You can't be serious. He did five years. Do you know how long his victim has to pay the debt they didn't even ask for?" The heat of the conversation pushed tears to the surface. "For the rest of their god damn life."

"Ah, Val. I don't want to fight. I can see your point." He finished walking to me and pulled me into a hug. "I guess I don't know what I'd do if I were put in a situation like that. It was unfair of me to..."

"No, you're entitled to your opinion. I just hate the people who think it's okay to destroy someone for their benefit. I'm sorry I got so upset. I don't want to ruin our celebration over this stupid shit."

"You're not the only one who feels this way, that's why we're leaning toward the vigilante angle. The neighborhood didn't even want him to move in, but the DOC didn't listen to what they had to say. They found him the cheapest place and dumped him there."

"They do that? Why would the DOC put him in a neighborhood of people who didn't want him?"

"The thing is, no one wants a sex offender living next to them. So no matter where he went, people would complain."

"You really think it would be enough to make someone kill him? I mean, I think about it, but I'd never act on it." Another lie added to the vault.

"The world is a crazy place. Anything is possible these days." He pulled me tighter. "Enough about work, let's talk about our new life together."

"I can't believe we found the perfect place so quickly... and then Gabriel... or... whatever his name is now."

"Things do seem to be falling into place nicely. See, you ask, and you shall receive." His eyes lifted with his smile.

"I wished I knew it was that simple ages ago, it would have saved so many problems."

"Just think of it this way, life can only improve from here." He came behind me and hugged me around my waist. "I can't wait to come home to you every day and wake up next to you every morning... for the rest of my life." He gave me a little squeeze as he kissed my neck.

"I'm looking forward to that, too. Everything is happening so fast. I don't even dare to blink."

"Just savor it. Let every ounce of joy seep in. You deserve it, more than anyone I know."

"I think I'm most nervous about tomorrow. I can't believe Gabriel wanted to meet me so soon."

"I'm excited for you, too. I can't wait to meet your son. I'm sure he's amazing."

I closed my eyes and rubbed my necklace. "I just hope he'll want me in his life."

"I'm sure he will. He's a man now, I bet he'd love to have a cool mom to run things by."

"A cool mom, huh?"

"Sure, think about it, you're only fifteen years older than him. I think it'd be rad to have a young, hot mom..."

"Rad... who are you?"

"What? I'm auditioning for the hip stepdad."

"You're such a dork." I laughed as I tried to picture how the meeting was going to go. I've rehearsed what I would say to him for the last twenty years. I hoped I wouldn't screw it up.

"Hey, I take offense to that." He winked at me. "You're going to be married to a dork... so take that."

"I can't wait."

"Mr. and Mrs. Dork. It has a nice ring to it, don't you think?"

I rolled my eyes and tapped the back of my hand against his chest. "It's a good thing you're cute."

"I can't wait to have a house full of little dorks and dorkettes running around."

"Hold on there stud, how many babies do you think I'm going to have?"

"Enough for a baseball team, with fans in the stands."

"Definitely not. I was thinking... oh... maybe two."

"Two of each? Well, maybe..."

"No. Two in total."

"Ah, where is your sense of adventure?"

"Not in the delivery room." I crossed my arms with a laugh. "You might be able to talk me into one more... but let's start with one and see how it goes."

"Fair enough."

The thought of having a baby left me equally terrified and excited. I knew I never wanted to be like my mom, but I didn't have any other example to follow. Before Chad, my mom was someone I wanted to be with. She was stern, but she also knew how to have fun. Maybe it was the drinking that changed her, or perhaps it only took Chad's attention to shake her up. Before him, I would have considered her my friend. It was almost as though a switch flipped and I became yesterday's news. She stopped spending time with me and would never listen to me. If drinking Kool-Aid is a thing, she was swimming in his.

CHAPTER FIFTEEN

Today was the day I had been waiting for since they ripped my baby boy out of my arms twenty excruciating years ago. The beat of my heart echoed in my ears as I searched my closet. "I never have anything to wear." I tossed sweaters of different shades of black, brown, and gray on to the bed. Gabriel perched on the top of the pile and tilted his head as he listened to me complain. "Don't judge me... you don't have to worry about clothes." A muffled shriek followed. "I hate that nothing ever looks good on me."

I stood in the closet with tears streaming down my cheeks when Tim walked in from the shower. "Hey, Val, relax." With the towel tied around his waist, he took my hands in his. "Take a deep breath." He mirrored my breathing, rising and falling with me. "You're beautiful in anything you wear or don't." He winked. "Your son is not going to care what you have on. I guarantee it won't be the first thing on his mind today."

"I just want this to be perfect. I've waited so long for this."

"I know, Val. And it will be." He reached into the closet and pulled out a long sleeve blouse and handed it to me. "Here, wear this with a nice pair of jeans. It's going to be too warm for a sweater today, anyway."

I held up the top he chose and wrinkled my nose. "Ugh, this thing?"

"Put it on, I bet you'll look stunning." He held his hand out with his palm facing up.

I couldn't help but laugh. "I'm so glad I get to share this with you. Thank you... for everything." The tears returned, but this time from joy.

"I'm excited for you, Val. I know how badly you've wanted this."

The place we were meeting him was an hour away. I couldn't believe he had been this close the whole time. The idea brought comfort and frustration. He was so close but lightyears away. I could have passed him on the street and not known it. I reached for my necklace and felt it at the opening of my shirt. Soon, I'd have my son and not just this necklace.

"Why don't you think they'll tell me his new name yet? They keep calling him Gabriel."

"Maybe they didn't change his name when they adopted him." Tim reached over and turned down the radio. "Could you enter the address in the GPS? I want to see the arrival time."

I entered the address and waited for it to calculate. "Only forty more minutes."

"Remember to breathe." He turned his head to give me a smile and returned his eyes to the road.

"I'm thinking about taking some time off work. Jeanine mentioned it... well, suggested it."

"She did? Why?"

"She just thinks I've been a little... off. But now is the perfect time with our move and planning a wedding."

"Oh, I like where this is going. Maybe I should take some time off, too."

"Or, maybe you should wait and we can go on an epic honeymoon."

"Epic, huh?"

I laughed. "I guess I've been spending too much time with Sonya."

"An epic honeymoon sounds like something I can't wait for. You're going to be a beautiful bride... but I'd be lying if I said I wasn't looking forward to tearing your dress off of you."

"You do have a way with words, Mr. Phillips."

"Hey, honesty is the best policy, right?" He shrugged his shoulders as a smirk spread across his face.

I pushed the comment out of my head. Today was not a day to feel guilty. Today was a day to celebrate. I didn't want anything to take away from this moment. I watched the trees pass by as we inched closer to our destination. I'd spent a lifetime of rushing through everything to just get to the next day, now it was time to slow down and savor the moments.

I took Tim's hand and laced my fingers with his. The warmth of his skin on mine chased out the lingering anxiety. I closed my eyes and focused on the rhythm of the tires against the pavement.

I felt Tim give my hand a light squeeze before he pulled out of my grip. I opened my eyes to see we had arrived at our destination. Tim had arranged to meet Gabriel and his adoptive parents in Newport. It was an hour from us, and only thirty minutes from them. As I scanned the parking lot, I noticed all of the cars. "I don't think meeting at 10:00a.m. on a Saturday at a diner was a great plan." I felt the palms of my hands start to sweat.

"You're probably right, but I wanted to accommodate them, to make it so irresistible they couldn't say no. Beth suggested this place."

"I'm sorry... I'm just nervous. I'd have gone anywhere to meet him. Thank you for coordinating everything."

"It's okay, Val, I understand." With his hand on the door handle, he looked over at me. "Are you ready?"

I closed my eyes, rubbed my necklace, and exhaled. "I am." The flutter of butterflies filled my stomach.

"Breathe," he whispered.

When we entered the restaurant, my heart dropped when I saw the back of his head. I knew right away it was *him*. I pulled Tim's hand and led him to their table.

"Hi, Beth?" Tim smiled as he waited for her reply.

"You must be Tim and Valerie." She stood up and shook my hand, her other hand holding mine as our eyes met. "It's so good to finally meet you."

While she was talking, the two men at the table stood up. "This is Paul." She pointed to the older man with thinning gray hair and a short beard to match. "And this," she pushed the younger man by his shoulders over to me, "is Gabriel."

"Gabriel?" My hand went to my necklace as I felt my eyes start to burn. "You kept his name?"

"We did." Beth smiled as she held her husband's hand.

The tall, young man standing in front of me was my son. *My Gabriel.* His blue eyes sparkled. He ran his hand through his short, clean-cut brown hair. "Hi." He reached his hand out for me to shake. "It's nice to meet you. I've been waiting for this day since Mom... ah... since they told me I was adopted."

"Oh my gosh, you're so handsome." I felt the eyes of a hundred diners pierce into my back, but I didn't care. I had my baby back. "I've been waiting for this day since they took you." I covered my mouth, not knowing what he had been told. I looked to Beth to see if I had already messed up.

We all sat down to cause less of a scene. My feet tapped under the table, vibrating the water glasses. Tim put his hand on my knee to slow it down. "Valerie, I want you to know how much your letter touched us." Beth looked over at Paul before she continued. "When we read it, I knew... we knew we would never be able to change Gabriel's name. The love you had for him seeped off those pages. It broke my heart when I noticed the words had been smudged with your tears." She placed her hand to her heart, the sparkle of her three-karat diamond ring caught my eye.

"They actually gave that to you?"

"Yes, and the necklace. I knew you must have been a sweet girl to think of something so clever." She smiled. "We told Gabe he was adopted as soon as we brought him home. We didn't want him to think it was something to be ashamed of. We read him stories about adoption as he grew up, so he would know how loved he was. When he was sixteen, we gave him your letter and the necklace you sent for him."

Gabe pulled half of a broken heart out of his t-shirt and smiled. "I've been wearing this thing ever since."

Goosebumps grew over my body as I held the other half of the broken heart between my fingers. "I've been wearing this since they took you."

"I wanted Gabe to know how much you loved him, I didn't want to keep that from him. We've been looking for you since we gave him your letter, but we kept hitting a wall."

"You've been looking for me for that long?"

"We have. The adoption agency said they had strict orders not to release any information. I figured it wasn't something you would have asked for after reading your letter so many times. I knew you would want to be found. So, we kept looking. We didn't have your last name, so we searched for all of the Valeries we could find. It was like a needle in a haystack, but I didn't want to stop until we got the two of you back together."

"That must have been something my mom did." I turned my head to look at Tim and forced a smile to bury the anger. "I can't believe you wanted to find me. I didn't even know where to start. I've thought about you every single day for the past twenty years. I was so worried you'd be mad at me." I wiped away the fallen tears off my cheek.

"Why would I be mad at you?" Gabriel tilted his head.

"Because I..."

"Honey, you were a child. We knew this wasn't something you would have done on your own." Beth dabbed at her eyes with a tissue.

"Besides, I had a great life. My parents gave me every-thing I ever wanted."

"And he was loved. By us, and our whole family. Gabriel was a gift from God."

"I named him after the archangel, Gabriel, because he's the angel of strength and protection."

"That's beautiful, Valerie."

"I'm so happy you let him keep his name. What's your middle name?" I turned my attention to my son.

"Jonathan."

"It means gift from God." Beth smiled. "I guess we were on the same wavelength."

"That's such a beautiful name." I felt my face flush. "I mean, handsome."

Gabe laughed. "It's cool, I'm manly enough to be beauti-ful." He held up the broken heart. "It does a lot for a guy to wear a BFF necklace."

Tim elbowed me. "Looks like I'm not the only comedian here."

The table erupted in laughter. "Yes, he comes by that honestly." Beth pointed at Paul.

"Guilty." Paul raised his hand. "You've got to find humor when you can, or the world will eat you alive."

"Ain't that the truth?" Tim raised his coffee cup.

We continued to get to know each other over breakfast. The longer we were together, the more comfortable I became. Twenty agonizing years of longing to see my baby were over. He was right in front of me, and I knew I would never let life take him from me again.

CHAPTER SIXTEEN

I couldn't wait to share my news with the ladies in the group. So much had happened in just a week. The spark of excitement I held was extinguished when Sonya walked through the door. She was the first to arrive.

"What's wrong, Sonya?"

"I don't even know where to start." She blew her nose and tossed the tissue into the garbage can next to the door, pulling the next one out before she sat down.

"Do you want to talk before the others get here?"

"Yeah... I really don't want to say this twice. Don't really even want to say it once... but I know I have to get it off my chest."

"Can I get you anything? Something to drink or a snack?"

She let out a sob. "I can't drink... not anymore." She blew her nose again. "And God knows I'm going to get such a fat ass."

My imagination filled in the gaps as we waited for the rest of the ladies to show up. I got up and made myself a cup of tea to kill some of the time. The peppermint hit my nose as I tore open the tea bag envelope, I let out a sigh of relief when I heard the chatter of Maggie, Norma, and Lily. Sonya blew her nose extra loud as the others settled into their seats.

"Oh, dear, what's the matter?" Norma put her purse down and reached for Sonya's hand.

"It's Jimmy. He's after me again."

"What do you mean after you?" Norma's eyes widened.

"After the last time we met, I called Jimmy and told him he raped me and I never wanted to see him again." Sonya sucked in air as the tears fell. "It turned into a screaming match. He said I was a stupid bitch and told me to tell my cunt friends to stay out of our business." She blew her nose before she continued. "The minute he started talking shit about you all, I lost my mind. I got so angry, everything turned red. Has that ever happened to you before? You just get so pissed off you can't even see straight? I just wanted to kill him." Sonya grit her teeth.

I nodded my head. "A few times."

"Well... I jumped on him and started punching him. I think I even bit him. I was so mad, it was like someone else took over."

"Has that ever happened to you before?" I regretted the question as soon as I heard it leave my mouth.

"Yeah, I have a habit of turning into a lunatic." The look of disgust covered Sonya's face.

"I'm not calling you a lunatic; I'm just asking you a question. This kind of thing happens to people sometimes, especially ones who have been through a traumatic event."

She sighed. "Hmmm. Well, anyway, he threw me off and

told me if I ever accused him of raping me again, he'd make sure there was no mistake *next time*. The motherfucker threatened to rape me after telling me he never did. What kind of bullshit is that?"

"Did you call the police?" Maggie looked over at me to avoid eye contact with Sonya.

"No. I told him if he ever came near me again, I'd blow his brains out."

"Oh my." Norma shifted in her seat.

"Do you have a gun?" Maggie turned her attention to Sonya.

"I do now." Sonya reached into her purse.

My eyes focused on her hand, and my body jumped back as she pulled her phone out. She started flipping through pictures. I looked around the circle to see if anyone had noticed. It seemed everyone else trusted Sonya a lot more than I did.

"Isn't she beautiful?" Sonya's mood shifted as she held up the photo. A small, pink handgun displayed on the screen.

"What kind of gun is it?" I asked, trying to rejoin the conversation.

"It's a nine-millimeter something or other."

"Oh, dear. That looks dangerous." Norma licked her dry lips.

"If I use it right." Sonya laughed. "This is the best I've felt in years. I actually feel in control of things for once."

"Just be safe... and don't do anything..."

Sonya's interruption saved me from saying it. "Stupid? Don't worry. I'm signed up for a self-defense class.

There is part of the lesson where we learn how to shoot and stuff. You all should join me."

"I don't really like guns. They kind of scare me." I pushed the loose hair out of my face.

"Yeah, I have to agree with Val, I wouldn't want my girls finding a gun." Maggie looked down at her dirty tennis shoes.

"You guys are no fun. You never wanted to pull the trigger? And POP?" Sonya laughed. "No, but really, there's more to the class than that."

"It's a nice offer, dear. I think this lady is too old for that, but I'd love to hear about it." Norma's smile made up for our lack of interest.

"Oh yeah, and I'm pregnant."

"Wait... you're what?" I felt my eyes squint.

"Pregnant. I took the test the other day, and then a few more... and they're all positive. I didn't want to believe it, I thought if I kept taking them, I'd get the result I wanted... turns out it doesn't work that way."

"Congratulations." Lily's voice cracked.

Norma's smile grew. "How exciting."

"Not exactly. It's not the best timing. I don't even know who the dad is."

"You don't?" Maggie raised her right eyebrow and tilted her head.

"It's either Jimmy's or my boss's. Since I've been trying to get rid of Jimmy, I've been seeing Andrew... and by seeing, I mean sleeping with."

"I figured as much... that is how babies are made." I coughed into my sleeve when no one else laughed. "So, what are you going to do."

"I don't know. But there is no way Jimmy can know about this. He'd be a horrible father, and I know he'd make my life hell if we had to share a baby."

"Have you thought about your options?" Maggie asked.

"Options? What options?" Sonya snapped her head around.

"You know... adoption or... abortion." Maggie lifted her eyes to look at Sonya.

"No, I couldn't imagine either. Besides, my mom has been after me for some grandkids. I just don't know what I'm going to do about Jimmy."

"I'm relieved to hear you're able to find something good in this." I gave her a smile.

"Yeah, it's either be happy or cry myself to sleep every night."

"Has Jimmy ever hurt you?" Lily's question made Sonya snap her head to face her.

"What do you think rape is?" Sonya crossed her arms and pursed her lips.

"Sonya." I hoped just the tone of my voice would help ease some of the tension.

"Of course, it is." Lily softened her voice to match my tone. "I mean... has he ever hit you or..."

"Just because he never left me looking like you doesn't mean he's not a piece of shit."

"Sonya, that's enough, Lily's just trying to help." I widened my eyes to keep from rolling them.

"There's no doubt in my mind he's a horrible man. I just wanted to make sure you were safe. Sorry, ... I... I don't know all of you that well yet. I didn't mean to upset you." Lily took the insult in stride.

Sonya crossed her legs and bounced her foot. "Sorry, ... it's just these crazy hormones."

"What was your excuse before?" Maggie murmured under her breath, but loud enough to be heard.

"Well, you sure have a lot on your plate, dear," Norma spoke up before Sonya could react. "We're all here for you through this. Don't you forget that."

"Thanks. You guys are the first ones I've told about the baby. I'm too ashamed to tell my mom I don't know who the dad is." Sonya dropped her head.

"Just tell her it's your boss's," Lily stated matter-of-factly. "You're in control of that piece... until a paternity test anyway."

"I thought about it... but once it's obvious I'm pregnant, Jimmy is going to start shit. He's not very good at math, but I bet he could count to nine."

The circle filled with laughter. "You have some time before you need to worry about that. Think about what Lily said, it's a good idea." I smiled as a plan was set into motion. "Things always have a way of working out."

CHAPTER SEVENTEEN

With Gabriel back in my life, I had even more reason to reach out to Ginger. I had put it off long enough. With the murder of Joseph Swift, Seth's case had fallen by the wayside. Tim did mention the camera that could have captured the caller at Lawrenceville Pizza hadn't been working for months. With that worry out of my mind, figuring out what Seth told Ginger and getting her to back off was all that was left.

I picked up the phone and dialed Ginger's number. As I waited for her to answer, I rehashed what I would say. I had rehearsed it so much at this point I wouldn't have to look at my notes. When she didn't answer the plan crashed down around me. "Hi... ah... um... Ginger, this is Valerie Williamson, from ah... Lawrenceville Regional Hospital and I just wanted to... um... see how you were. Please give me a call at 802-555-7171."

What the hell was that? That was a lame excuse. She'll never return my call. I shook off the shiver of self-loathing as I hung up the receiver. As I waited for my computer to fire up, the piercing ring echoed between my office walls. The number I had just dialed lit up the caller ID display. "Hello, Lawrenceville Regional Hospital, this is Valerie."

"Well, I should hope so, since you just called me. What is it you need?"

Thankful she hadn't had enough time to listen to the message I left I could start over. "Hello Ginger, I just wanted to touch base with you and see if you had any leads about Jane's death."

"Not one."

"No? I thought Seth had told you something?" I squeezed my eyes tight and attempted to push out a migraine by massaging my temple.

"What? Seth? He told me he knew who killed Jane... a lot of good that'll do me now."

"I have some information I think could be helpful." I glanced down at my notes.

"Well... go on... I don't have all day."

"Did you know Seth was physically abusive to Jane?"

"Yes, you've told me that before... your point?"

"He said he wanted her out of his life, and then... she's dead."

"So, your big break in the case is that Seth, the dead guy, killed my daughter?" Ginger sighed into the phone. "What am I going to do with that? Who's going to make this right? Who's going to..."

"Ginger... Jane knows you love her, and she's probably happy you cared so much about her that you offered such a nice reward. Your love for your daughter is enough. It's okay to let it go."

"How do you know any of that?"

"This is going to sound crazy, but Jane came to me in a dream the other night, and she told me." I shook my head in disbelief as I tapped my forehead. *No. No. No.* This was not what I meant to say.

"She did?" Ginger's tone softened.

"Yes. And she wanted me to tell you she loves you... and she wants you to live your life. Don't waste any more time on things that don't matter." Impressed she bought it, I was grateful my other guilty pleasure of watching Long Island Medium had come in handy.

"Thank you, Victoria. That really does put my mind to ease. I guess I just wanted to do something for Jane, I lost sight of what really matters."

"It's Val... I'm glad I could help. Have a nice day."

My ability to lie and pull stories out of nowhere was both impressive and concerning. Who had I become? I hated liars, and now I was becoming a professional. My gram always told me white lies don't hurt anyone, as long as they're done for good. This seemed like one of those situations.

Next on my list was Jimmy. He had to go, and as soon as possible. If left to her own devices, I imagined Sonya would take matters into her own hands. I didn't want to think about her baby being ripped out of her arms as she was sent back to prison.

I logged onto Facebook and typed Stephanie Mills' password in. When the page opened, I typed Jimmy into the search bar, only to realize I never found out his last name. I replaced Jimmy's name with Sonya's and clicked on her profile picture. When I opened her friends list, I scrolled through the names. Not one Jimmy on the list. I clicked back until I was on her timeline and read through her posts, looking for any clue I could find that would lead me to Jimmy.

Halfway down the page, there were two faces pressed together in a kiss. When I clicked on the photo to make it bigger, I noticed Sonya and a person named D. J. Jones were tagged in the image. Clicking on D.J.'s link brought me to his page.

D.J.'s timeline was flooded with pictures of Sonya. It had an obsessive stalker vibe to it. This had to be Jimmy. His profile listed he lived in Lawrenceville and listed some of his family members. It appeared he lived alone in a crappy little apartment. From the pictures, I wasn't able to make out where it was.

I opened a new browser and typed D.J. Jones, Lawrenceville, Vermont, in the search bar. About a dozen results populated the page. I clicked on the first one. Once there, it gave me the first three digits of his phone number, and the rest of his information was blocked out unless I wanted to pay $9.95. There was no way I wanted my credit card linked to his name on the internet. I clicked back to the search results, only to find the same thing with every click.

Frustrated, I closed all the open browsers. Why was everyone always looking to make a buck? Why couldn't you just get information like we used to? I missed the days of being able to open a real phone book and getting someone's number and address. Now, it seemed like everything else was on display for the world to see, except for the important things. I guess I'd have to figure out how to ask Sonya without raising any suspicion. As I thought about a tactic that might work, I remembered I had the information at my fingertips.

I logged into the hospital's database and pulled up Sonya's information. I was in luck. Jimmy was still listed as her emergency contact. I wrote down the address to his apartment and phone number and clicked out of her file. My heart raced as I looked down at the piece of paper in front of me. I didn't like the idea he lived in an apartment building. It was too easy for someone to spot me.

As I went to pick up my phone to call Jimmy, it sang its alarming song. I pulled my hand away from the receiver as though it was going to send a shock through me. The room began to spin as I thought about what I had almost done. It was mistakes like this that would get me caught.

When my heart rate returned to normal, my cell phone started chirping. "Hey, Tim."

"Where are you? Why didn't you answer your phone?" His voice was masked by distress.

"Oh, that was you? I'm in my office, just didn't feel like..."

"Val, I need to talk to you. It's serious. I'll be right there." Silence followed his words.

Every possibility of his urgency fell on top of me like a stack of bricks. Fear multiplied as the seconds passed. Frozen in my chair, cold sweat formed at my brow. *What if he knows? But what does he know? How? How much?* The thoughts poured in like a rushing river. I sat with my back pressed into my chair and my feet planted on the floor. With my hands on my thighs, I took a deep breath and exhaled as I counted. It was unreasonable to think this was about me. There was no way he could know anything. Donald Brice was long gone, and Jane wasn't an issue anymore.

My heart dropped when I remembered Seth. But I didn't do it. There was no way I was going to take the fall for a murder I didn't even commit. The minutes passed by like hours as I waited for Tim to arrive. My head swirled from every scenario it could possibly be. What would it take to make Tim stop loving me? The knock at my door brought me to my feet. I hoped I wouldn't find out. Not today.

Tim didn't let me open the door all the way before he rushed in past me, shutting it behind him. "Val." Tim let out a few heavy gasps before continuing. "There's been another shooting." His hands went to his knees as he hunched over to gather some air. "I just came from the scene."

I walked over to put my hand on his back. "Are you okay?"

"Yes. But they think this could be the work of a serial killer."

"Why? What makes them think that?"

He stood up and rolled his shoulders. "This guy had just been released from jail, another sex offender. This time, it was rape."

"What's his name?"

"Stephen Boulder. His release was on the front page of the *Village News*, yesterday."

"Yesterday? Holy smokes, this guy works fast."

"Yeah, that's why I'm here."

"Why?"

"A guy released from jail today was just moved into the

vacant apartment in your building."

"Oh my god, how can they do that? Just put them anywhere, and without giving us a heads up?"

"It's a friend of the family, or at least that's what they told us. His release will hit the paper tomorrow."

"Wait... isn't there enough time to make them pull it?"

"We're working on it now, but it's late. We didn't connect the dots until a few hours ago."

"I don't want you going home tonight. Come to my place, please."

"I can't..."

"Come on, Val. This could get serious."

"I can't leave Gabriel there."

"He can come, too. I just don't want anything to happen to you. We have an undercover guy covering the area, but these guys are sophisticated. They know how to go under the radar. I just don't want you in that building, especially knowing there's a sex offender living there now."

"You really think the same person killed those guys?" I paused to look at his face and matching eyes. "How can you tell?"

"It's hard to explain, and I can't leak too many details, but there were a few similarities." He ran his hand through his hair. "A few too many to be a coincidence. We just have to be on guard now and try to make sure it doesn't happen again."

"It only takes two murders to make a serial killer?" Nausea hit as I waited for his answer.

"Well, technically, it's three. We just wanted to stop this guy before we can officially give him that title, and announce we have one on the loose."

I was only one away from holding that title myself, and just hours away from adding it to my resume. The weight of those two words made me question my plans. I couldn't let it stop me. I was doing it for Sonya. I had to remember I wasn't like them. I was doing it to protect people. Can it really be murder when you look at it that way?

"Val, are you alright?"

I blinked my eyes. "Yeah. Sorry, I was just thinking."

"I know it's a lot to take in. I didn't want to scare you, but you have to promise me you won't go home without me. Call me when you leave, and we can get Gabriel together."

"I promise. I've got a few things I need to do before I leave for the day, but I'll let you know when I head out."

Tim leaned over and kissed me. "I love you, Val."

"I love you, too, Detective." I winked to try to lighten the mood. "Be careful, I need you alive."

"Will do. And... don't forget to call."

After Tim left, I thought about the possible serial killer and wondered what fueled them. What made them kill these guys? It didn't seem like what they were doing was really that bad of a thing after all. The world had too many sex offenders as it was. What's so wrong with eliminating them? Maybe we weren't that different after all. The more I thought about it, the more I realized our missions were similar.

I packed up my stuff and drove to Lawrenceville Pizza. With the cameras down, I knew it was the best place to make the call. I dug out the piece of paper with Jimmy's number and walked over to the payphone. I cleared my throat as I waited for him to answer.

"Hello?" The voice on the other end sounded like I had woken him.

"Hi, is this Jimmy?"

"Yeah?"

"Hey, this is Stephanie."

"I don't know any Stephanies, you must have the wrong number."

"Wait... Jimmy... I'm Sonya's friend."

"Sonya? What's this about?" He took the bait as I imagined he would.

"I know how you can get her back."

"You do?"

"I do, she's been talking to me. Can we meet up tomorrow?"

"Yeah. That'd be great."

"Perfect. Meet me at the park down by the river at 4:00."

"Why not just come here?"

"Sonya can't know. She'll be pissed if she knows I'm talking to you."

"Hmm... good point. See you then. I'll be in the red Toyota Takoma."

"See you then." As I hung up the phone, I felt the adrenaline rush through my body. This was going to be easier than I anticipated.

"Well, isn't this a nice surprise."

The hair on the back of my neck stood up as I turned around. I managed to smile as I stood in the parking lot, just feet from making it to my car without being noticed. "Hi Norma."

"Hi." She smiled as she lifted up the two boxes of pizza.

"Want to join us for dinner?"

"Oh, that's sweet of you to offer, but Tim is expecting me to call him."

"Oh, he's welcome, too."

"He's probably not up to it. There's a lot going on in town."

"Oh?"

"Yeah, it's crazy. He said they think there's a serial killer."

"Oh, my goodness. What a scary thought."

"I know, right? But don't worry. We're safe... just sex offenders and rapists have to worry."

"Oh, dear."

"Yeah, Tim said they just released one to my building... so he doesn't want me going there alone. They've got a detective on the scene, though, to try to catch the killer... you know... before he strikes again."

"Well, that does sound like Tim would be preoccupied. Be safe, dear. It was so nice to see you tonight."

"It was nice. Enjoy your pizza and tell Maggie and the girls I said hi."

"I will, dear."

As she walked to her car, my stomach dropped. I shouldn't have shared any of that with her. Tim would be furious if he found out. "Norma?"

"Yes, dear."

"Can we keep what I just said between us? I mean until it's released to the public?"

"Of course. Your secret is safe with me." She smiled as she got into the driver's seat.

Relief washed over me. I knew I could trust her.

CHAPTER EIGHTEEN

From searching Jimmy's Facebook profile, I knew he loved Mountain Dew, and from watching tons of episodes of *Snapped*, I learned antifreeze would mix well in a sweet drink. I also knew it wouldn't take much to do the job. A quick stop at Cumberland Farms, and I had my murder weapons in hand. A twenty-ounce bottle of soda and a jug of antifreeze. Before I left the hospital, I took a few syringes from the medical supply room, rubber gloves, and some paper towels.

I scanned the parking lot before getting to work. At the back of the lot, by the dumpsters, it seemed to be quiet. I pulled my car ahead to the spot and began the needed steps to carry out the plan. I put the gloves on before I opened the antifreeze container and stuck the syringe in, drawing up as much as it would hold. I repeated this step until all four were full. Next, I twisted off the cap of the Mountain Dew and opened my door to pour some out onto the ground. I held the bottle up to see if there was enough room to insert the antifreeze.

One by one, I emptied the syringes into the soda. I held it up to compare the level next to my unopened bottle. Just a little bit more to make it match. I opened the antifreeze one last time and drew out one more syringe full, holding the jug between my legs to keep it from spilling. With the Mountain Dew in my cup holder, I pushed the poison into the drink. I screwed the cover back onto the soda and then the antifreeze.

I pulled out the paper towels and wiped the bottle of antifreeze off before placing it back in the paper bag. I looked in my mirrors and checked my surroundings before I got out of my car and tossed it into the dumpster. Back in my car, I was finally able to exhale the air I had been holding and looked myself in the eyes in the rearview mirror. *Just a little bit longer. You can do this.*

With a quick roll of my shoulders, I turned out of the parking lot and drove to the meeting place. It had been a while since I'd been here. It was on the other side of town, the opposite direction from where I usually go. Since Gabriel had been with me, I never felt right leaving him any longer than work pulled me away. I rolled down my car window to listen to the water as I waited for Jimmy to arrive.

I reclined my seat a little, so the sun could hit my face. I hoped the serenity of the location would be enough to calm my nerves. The chirping of the birds nearby brought me to a deeper state of relaxation, one I hadn't felt in years, decades even.

Everything was going right. Everything. All of the missing pieces fell into place. I had a man I loved... and, even better... trusted. I had my gram back in my life. My son didn't hate me, maybe even loved me. I had friends, people I could share my time with, who would do anything for me, and I for them. There was a wedding to plan and a house to make a home. Everything I ever wanted was right before me.

Tim's words settled on my chest as the last of the good thoughts exited my mind. Why am I here? There was so much to lose. My loyalty to Sonya and Tim teetered in the slight, spring breeze. If I left, Sonya's life could be at risk, if not literally, definitely figuratively. And if not her, the baby. I shook off the guilt and sat back up in my seat. I needed to finish this. I couldn't let anything get in my way.

I pulled a *Woman's World* magazine out of the backseat and started flipping through the pages to keep my mind busy. I glanced at my watch; Jimmy was already twenty minutes late. I fidgeted in my seat as I scanned the parking lot. The area was secluded, but public enough for Jimmy to be found if the poison kicked in as quickly as I hoped.

Time felt like it had stopped as I waited. When I rechecked my watch, another thirty minutes were gone. Closing in on an hour late, it was becoming more apparent Jimmy wasn't going to show up. I tossed the magazine in the back seat, put my seat belt on, and gripped the steering wheel. I thought for sure he'd want to hear what I had to say. My options were to continue to wait, go to his place, or just abort the mission. Maybe Jimmy not showing up was a message from someone that I shouldn't be doing this.

As I contemplated the options, my phone rang. It was Sonya. She never called. I wasn't really in the mood to talk with her right now, so I let it go to voicemail. When the phone stopped ringing, I regretted not answering it. I stared down at my phone, debating on returning her call. I really didn't have the energy to interact with her right now and tossed the phone on the passenger seat. As soon as it landed, it started ringing again. This time curiosity won.

"Hi, Son..."

A blood-curdling scream ricocheted off my eardrum. "He's... he's... he's..."

"Sonya... are you..."

"He's dead. Oh my god." Her screams evaporated into sobs.

"Sonya, where are you."

"I... I'm at Jimmy's. Oh my god. Oh my god."

"Jimmy's dead?"

"Yes." The word extended by a howl. "He's been shot."

"Sonya, I need you to try to calm down." I waited for her to comply. "Have you called 911?"

"No... I... I can't. I can't." Rapid panting filled the empty spaces. "Can you?"

"Ah... shit." I shook my head as I bit my bottom lip. "What's the address?" I awaited her answer, even though I knew. "Sonya, I'm going to call, and I'm on my way."

"Please hurry." The desperation in her voice made me question my earlier intentions.

After hanging up the phone, I dialed 911 and requested an officer and ambulance be sent to Jimmy's apartment. I hadn't even asked Sonya enough questions to be helpful to the dispatcher, but her plea for help took logic out of the equation. All I knew was I needed to get to Sonya before the police arrived.

When I put my car in gear, I noticed the bottle of Mountain Dew still sitting in my cup holder. I needed to get rid of this before I went anywhere, but it wasn't something I could dump on the ground. It would be lethal to any curious animal. The blue porta-potty was the answer. I put my car into park, unbuckled my seatbelt and jumped out and ran to the outhouse. Holding the door open with my foot, I poured Jimmy's drink into the mixture of sewage, toilet paper, and empty beer cans. I tossed the bottle in after I dumped it, rubbed some hand sanitizer on my hands, and raced back to my car.

I sent a quick text to Tim with the address asking him to meet me there. I wasn't sure if he would be the one dispatched there, and I didn't want to chance arriving at a crime scene without him at least being aware of where I was going. The dirty work completed once more for me. I wasn't sure I was happy about it, but again, grateful I wouldn't have to carry the guilt for this one.

As my car neared the destination, an ambulance sped past me. I pulled over to get out of the way. As I pulled back onto the road, the image of Sonya's pink pistol flashed before me. *What if she did it?* I tried to imagine why she was there, and no good reason came to me. The last I heard, she didn't want anything to do with him, so why would she be the one to find him?

The serial killer crossed my mind, too, but I didn't think Jimmy had a record. Sonya had mentioned she'd gone to the domestic violence center before. I wondered if Jimmy had that on his record. For the life of me, I couldn't remember what she'd said. So far, though, the target had been sex offenders. And, Seth? Was this all related? This was quiet, boring, little Lawrenceville. What was happening?

Tim greeted me in the driveway when I got out of my car. "What the hell is going on?"

"Sonya called me, asked me to meet her here." I stopped to catch my breath. "Where is she?"

"She's over there." He nodded his head to the right.

Sonya was sitting in the ambulance being checked out by the paramedics. "Is she okay?"

"Yeah, just shaken up. They were worried about the baby... or she was. You didn't mention she was pregnant."

"Yeah, that's the newest news. What happened in there?"

"We have the area closed off, just waiting on the medical examiner. The poor guy is getting his hours in this week." Tim kicked at a stone and shook his head. "I don't know what's going on around here anymore."

"Do you have any idea? Is this related to the others?" I glanced back over at Sonya.

"It's really too early to tell." He ran his hand through his hair. "But, holy shit. I don't know how many more unsolved murders I can take."

"I love you. I know you'll figure this out." I smiled as I took his hand. "I'm glad you're here."

A tall, older man walked out of the building and waved Tim over to him. "Oh, I've gotta go." He leaned down to kiss me. He looked exhausted. I knew this had been taking a toll on him, how couldn't it?

I walked over to the ambulance to wait for them to let Sonya out. When she saw me, she sat up and swung her legs off the side of the gurney. "I'm so glad you're here. I called Norma and Maggie, too."

"Is everything okay with the baby?"

"Yeah, they just want me to get some rest." Sonya jumped out of the ambulance and latched onto me. "I've never seen anything like it before." The tears on her face were shadowed with dirt.

"I bet it was scary. I can't imagine." That was a lie I tried to feed myself. It was all I could imagine. The death of my enemy was the only thing I could think about some days.

"You have no idea." She put her head to my ear. "I can't believe I was joking about this earlier." Her eyes were wide as she took a step back.

"Shhh." I looked over her shoulder to see where the medics were. "So, you said Maggie and Norma were coming?"

"No, I called them, but I couldn't reach Norma, and Maggie's busy with the girls. I'm so glad you came, though. I thought I'd have to deal with this alone."

"Where's your..." I widened my eyes as I raised my eyebrows. "You know."

"My what?" My attempt to be subtle was not working.

"That... ah... pink thing you showed us a picture of."

Still puzzled, Sonya cocked her head. "Huh?"

"The thing you bought for your class... the one you wanted me to join with you."

"Oh... that's at home." She squinted her eyes at me and took a step back. "Why, ... you think... I did this?"

"No... I just wanted to be sure it wasn't on you."

"Why would it be?"

"I don't know... you had mentioned..."

"Jesus, Val. I thought you were my friend."

"Sonya... wait."

She stormed off toward the building, where she was stopped by police. She pulled at her hair with both hands and started screaming at the officer. "Let me in there! That's my boyfriend. Let me in." This was a side of her I'd never experienced before, but to be honest, I wasn't shocked. I started to walk in her direction when she fell to the ground. I ran the rest of the way to her.

"Sonya." I kneeled to get close to her and covered her with my body. "Shhh, it'll be okay." I rocked her in my arms as she cried, playing with her hair in an attempt to comfort her. I was confused. Did she do this? Could she have done this? Was this how a killer acted? How did I act? It was all too much to take in.

Tim walked over to us and tapped me on the shoulder. "Val, I need to ah..." He cleared his throat. "Talk to you."

I stood up, leaving Sonya on the ground, curled up in the fetal position. Tim took my hand and led me back to my car. "What's going on?"

"Ah... we're going to need to take Sonya to the station."

"Why?" I crossed my arms against my chest. "You can't think she had anything to do with this. Look at her." I turned my head in her direction. "She's in shock."

"I know, but it's part of the procedure. At the very least, we have to clear her."

"Can I go with her?"

Tim's eyes went to Sonya, still a lump on the ground.

"You can wait for her at the station if they release her, but you won't be able to be in the room with her."

When I got in my car, my body started to shake and tears spilled out of my eyes. How could things change so suddenly? If only I had met with Jimmy a day earlier, she wouldn't have to be going through this. I could have prevented this. I thought about her in jail and knew she would never last there. She has a mouth on her, but that would only get her so far. And the baby. I couldn't let them pin this on her.

I picked up my phone and dialed Norma's number. She was who I needed right now.

"Hello, dear."

Relief flooded me when I heard her voice. "Oh, Norma."

"Val, what's the matter?"

"It's Sonya... they're putting handcuffs on her right now."

"Oh, my. Where are you girls?"

"We're at Jimmy's... she found him dead... shot. We can't let them take her. We have to do something."

"Where are they taking her?" I heard Norma's keys jingle. "I'll meet you girls there."

"They're taking her to the police station. You don't think she did this, right?"

"Oh, of course not. Don't you worry, I'm on my way."

CHAPTER NINETEEN

Waking up in Tim's apartment was still taking some getting used to. I missed having the ability to hide away from everything in the privacy of my own space. The idea I wouldn't be able to return to my apartment before moving in with Tim forever was starting to weigh on me. I didn't get a chance to enjoy one last cup of hot tea, curled up on my couch with Gabriel in my lap, or one last solitary dinner at the coffee table with the TV on as background noise. Maybe what I was giving up wasn't worth missing.

I stretched before sitting on the edge of the bed, Tim was already up. When I went to find him, a yellow piece of paper caught my attention. *Val, I got called into work. Please stay here until you hear from me. I love you. Tim*

I picked up the paper and turned it over. That's all he wrote? I didn't really want to spend my day alone in his apartment. We hadn't made plans to go anywhere, but I still didn't want to sit around and wait. When I placed the note on the table, I noticed yesterday's paper, the face of the newly released sex offender staring back at me.

It looks like they were too late. Either that or the *Village News* didn't want to drop their front-page story. Now, the note he left made sense. I bet he was at my apartment building. I tried to push down the lump in my throat. If I didn't have Tim in my life, I could have been living next to this predator. I smoothed out the paper to read his name. *Bobby Green, 42, released from the Stark County Jail after serving three years for aggravated sexual assault.* Three years? That's a slap in the face to the victim. Now, I hoped Tim was at another crime scene.

I turned on my iPad and typed in Bobby Green into the search bar. The story from his arrest was top on the list, next to the sex offender registry listing. It was too early to read the details from his case, so I clicked on the second link, where the address to my apartment building came up, next to the picture used in the *Village News*. His beady little eyes stared back at me from the screen and gave me chills that ran down my spine.

I closed out of the screen and set the iPad down. I shut my eyes tight and rubbed the bridge of my nose to push out the migraine itching to take up residency in my head. The more I fought the pain, the more anger took over.

I wasn't sure if I was more upset with myself or the system that failed me. I wished I'd had what it took to turn Chad in. I ached for the world to know what a piece of shit he was, but I chose to run, not tell. I pictured Chad's limp body with a gunshot wound to the head. The desire for his life to end was something I craved the moment he started touching me. And now, there was a possible serial killer on the loose, looking for predators to kill.

A laugh was finally what pushed the tension out of my head as I pictured Chad's face on the front page of his local newspaper, with a caption that would shock his slew of fans. *Chad Ross, 63, never made it to jail for raping and impregnating his stepdaughter, once a client. He met the firing squad in the town square, instead. The perfect ending for the 'perfect' man.*

It was hard to imagine someone so wonderful came from such a hideous event. Gabriel was more than I had hoped for. He was handsome, smart, and thoughtful. I will never let my mind cloud my love for Gabriel with the hate I hold for Chad. I never equated them as being connected in any way. They may share DNA, but it stops there. It was strictly science, nothing more than a violent sperm donor.

When my phone rang, I knew it was Tim. I was waiting to hear his voice confirm my suspicions. "Hi Tim, I got your note."

"Sorry, I didn't want to wake you up, you looked so peaceful, but I wanted to make sure you didn't worry when you noticed me missing."

"Let me guess... you're at another murder scene."

"Hmm... it's getting that predictable, isn't it? I don't know how much more I can take."

"Yeah, it does seem to be the new normal."

"I'm going to be awhile, why don't you go have lunch with your friends?"

"Oh, I have permission to leave now?"

"Val..."

"Relax, I'm kidding. I know you want to keep me safe. I love you, Detective Phillips. Remember, keep your eyes open. I need you alive for a certain wedding coming up."

"That's exactly the push I need right now."

Tim and I had agreed on a wedding date, July 15th. It was only a couple months away, so the pressure was on to start planning. Norma, Maggie, and Sonya were the ones I wanted to help me. A good mixture between them to make sure every detail was covered. I gave Norma a call, and she told me she would round up the others. Getting married was not even on my bucket list, and having friends help me plan; it was not something I could have hoped for. Even in this uncertain world, where things often felt unsafe, my life was thriving.

When I arrived at Norma's, Sonya was already there. Maggie met me at the door before I even had time to knock. "I'm so glad you called." She slipped out the door and shut it behind her. "Sonya is driving us crazy. She won't stop crying. I hope making plans for your wedding will shut her up for a little while." Maggie shook her head before opening the door. "Hey guys, look who's here."

A copy of *Inside Weddings* and *The Bride Guide* were laid out on the coffee table, a pot of tea and some cookies sitting next to them. "Thanks for helping me with this... I have no idea where to start."

"Oh, it will be so much fun. You're going to be a beautiful bride." Norma poured a cup of tea and handed it to me.

Sonya's nose was red and her eyes were bloodshot. "I should be the one getting married ... but..."

"In good time, dear. Your Mr. Right will be here before you know it."

"How are you holding up, Sonya?" I looked over at her, sitting cross-legged in the chair.

Her sniffles increased to sobs. "Considering they think I'm a murderer?"

"Oh, hush. You know that's not true." Norma took a sip from her teacup. "You wouldn't be here with us if they thought that."

"It sure didn't feel like that. If it wasn't for Andrew's lawyer, I'd probably have a girlfriend in jail right now." Sonya pulled at the seam on the toe of her sock.

I couldn't help but laugh. "It's just part of their job. They have to interview everyone they think could be involved."

"Involved? Why would they even think such a thing?" Sonya dabbed at her eyes with a tissue.

"You found him. You were the only one in the apartment with him. He was your ex-boyfriend. There's plenty of reasons. It wasn't personal." Maggie took a seat next to me on the couch.

"Maggie's right. If they didn't talk to you, they wouldn't have been able to clear you..."

"I can't believe you didn't hear." Sonya sighed. "It's funny Tim wouldn't have told you."

"Told me what?"

"That I'm out on bail... or bond... or whatever the fuck they call it when they think you're guilty, but you can buy your way out of jail."

"No... how can that be? Why would they think that?

Norma and I were there with you and they let you go." I turned my head to look at Norma.

"They came to my house with a search warrant... and took my gun. How would they even know I owned a gun... unless you told him?" Sonya's tears had dried, leaving her eyes free to send daggers at me.

"Sonya, I never told Tim about your gun. He doesn't talk to me about his work. I can't tell him about what we talk about, and neither can he."

"Maybe they only knew about your gun when they found it during the search." Maggie picked up one of the magazines and started flipping through the pages.

"Why would they? What were they looking for?"

"They must have found something." Norma tilted her head to look at Sonya. "Did you call or text Jimmy before you went over?"

"Oh my god... I forgot about that..." Sonya's hand covered her mouth.

"What? What is it?" I tried to pull it out of her.

"I told him if he didn't answer his fucking phone, I was going to kill him."

"How? On his voice mail?"

"No, in a text... I sent a picture of the gun with it."

"Well, ... that might be why they were looking for your gun... holy shit, Sonya." It was worse than I thought. I wondered why Tim hadn't told me any of this. I knew he tried to be careful, but I would have thought this might have slipped out in conversation.

"But you didn't do it. They'll be able to prove it wasn't your gun that killed him." Norma set her cup on the coffee table and picked up the other magazine. "Everything will work out, don't you worry, and after we have this glorious wedding, we'll throw you a sweet little baby shower."

"I can't wait to snuggle your baby." Maggie smiled. "This is going to be so much fun... the first baby I'll get to love since my girls were little."

"But, guys... how can you be sure?" Sonya asked.

"If you didn't do it, they can't prove anything. Sure, you sent him a threat, but forensics will be able to rule out your gun. Once they do that, you'll be cleared." Norma gave Sonya a smile.

"How do you know so much about this stuff? Sounds like you know what you're talking about." I waited for her to answer.

"I'm an old lady. I've seen a lot. I know things. But don't you worry. I know Sonya didn't do it, and she'll be free to raise that precious little baby."

We spent the rest of the morning tearing out pages from the magazines Norma bought and adding them to the folder she titled "Val's Dream Wedding." After Norma was able to calm Sonya down, we had a lot of fun. It was disconcerting to think about such a joyful occasion when Tim was waist-deep in unsolved murders.

CHAPTER TWENTY

I set the folder full of my wedding dreams on the counter when Gabriel greeted me. The change of surroundings was just as hard on him, and soon, there would be another. "Hey, buddy. Sorry, you've been locked up here all by yourself today." I poured out a few Temptations cat treats into the palm of my hand and knelt down to feed him. "Soon, you'll have your own window you can watch the birds from. I'll be sure to keep the feeders full, so there'll be a lot of action." I scratched behind his ear after he finished the last treat.

"Honey, I'm home." Tim's voice reached my ears before I heard the door close behind him. The bags under his eyes had grown, and the scruff on his face now resembled a homeless man's beard. He set his coffee mug on the table and picked up the file full of magazine clippings. "What's this?" He held up a page. "Oh, I like it." He winked at me as I scurried to retrieve the pile of pictures from his grip.

"Hey, no peeking." I kissed him and pulled it out of his hand. "You look awful."

"Gee, thanks." He rubbed his face. "I thought you'd be turned on by the woodsman look."

"Woodsman? I thought you were going for vagrant."

"Ha-ha... very funny. I guess it's time I shave."

"So... how did it go today?" I'd been waiting all day to hear the details of the case.

"The undercover cop who was watching your building was pulled away to Jimmy's when we got that call. So we think it happened when we were at his place." He stretched his arms out in front of him. "But I really can't say much more."

"Oh, come on..."

"Val, this shit is getting serious. We have the FBI involved now."

"Wow, in little old Lawrenceville?"

"I know, it's crazy... but we found something at every crime scene that ties all five murders together, aside from the clean crime scene and the same kind of gun used... so we definitely have a serial killer on our hands."

"Holy shit... all five... so Seth and Jimmy, too?"

"It looks that way. We just can't figure out why Seth and Jimmy were included in the mix... all the other guys were on the sex offender registry." He scratched his head. "You know, that part makes sense. Those three guys were front-page news, and their addresses were listed online. Plenty of people wanted to kill them, hell, the thought crossed my mind when I heard about Bobby... but..."

"Wait... so what links them all together?"

Tim shook his head. "I really can't say anymore. You know, with the FBI involved, I don't want to..."

"I get it." But I didn't. I wanted to know... needed to know what that link was. It was going to eat away at my sanity now that I knew they were all connected. "But... is it something I could... you know.... guess, and you tell me if I'm close?" I raised my eyebrow in an attempt to look seductive.

"Hmmm... you make it hard to say no..." He bit his bottom lip. "But... I gotta stay strong."

"Fine. I guess I'll drop it... but do you want to talk about it... at least the stuff you can?"

"I don't even know where to start." He rubbed his face with his hands. "It's just so much... you know... a real-life *48 Hours Mystery* that I have to solve." He shook his head.

"Never in all of my years as a detective, did I think I'd have to deal with a murder... let alone five."

"You seriously didn't think you'd have to deal with at least one?"

"This town is lame... nothing ever happens here. Not that I wanted it to. I kind of liked my coffee breaks and simple DUIs."

"I do have to admit, I don't like the idea of you out there in the middle of it all." I opened the refrigerator, took out two beers and handed him one.

"Just what I needed." He twisted off the cap and held it to his lips. "I shouldn't be drinking this... but it sure hits the spot."

"Why can't you have a drink? You're off duty, aren't you?"

"I won't be off duty until we find this guy." He took another sip before setting the empty bottle on the counter.

"That's crazy. What if you never find him?"

He rolled his neck between his shoulders and expelled a puff of air. "I don't even want to think about that. We've got to stop this guy."

"But what if you can't? Is it really that bad? I mean... regular people aren't in danger... just... monsters."

"We don't know that... with Seth and Jimmy in the mix, we don't really know who the targets are."

"It seems like it's just pieces of shit... you know... the people who don't deserve to live anyway..."

"I'm too tired to have this conversation again. You know how I feel." He cracked his knuckles. "I just don't want anyone else to die."

"Fair enough." I took a quick sip of my beer. "So, you guys think Sonya is innocent? I mean, there's no way she could have killed all those guys. Right?"

"We haven't ruled her out a hundred percent yet... but it's highly unlikely it was her. She had the motive to kill Jimmy, but not the others."

"She said she was brought in and questioned about her gun. So, does that mean it was a nine-millimeter used in all of the cases?"

Tim cocked his head. "How do you know that?"

"So, I'm right? Ha... lucky guess. Is that what ties them together?"

"Yeah... but there's more. It's weird. The FBI is checking its database to see if any other areas have reported... shit, Val... you almost got me."

"Ah, I was so close." The more he shared, the more my mind wandered. So far, I knew all five men were shot by a nine-millimeter, and all were dirtbags. What else could it be? I tried to remember some of the cases I'd watched on TV, but nothing came to me. It fascinated me to think about the reason behind it. Was this as simple as a vigilante, or was it deeper than that?

"Don't mention the FBI to anyone yet, okay? I'm not sure they want too many people to know about that. We're hoping with more manpower we'll be able to catch this guy. But, if word gets out, he might be more careful. He's already pretty careful...there hasn't been any real evidence left behind."

I nodded my head as I filed away the rest of the details he let slip out.

"Damn it, you're so easy to talk to... it's hard to stop talking."

"Don't be too hard on yourself, I'm sure you're tired. It's been a long few days."

"It sure has. You know the only thing keeping me going is knowing in just a few short weeks you'll be my wife." He smiled. "And, I'll never have to wake up alone again."

"As you saw, the girls and I did a lot of wedding planning today."

"I saw. That's an impressive file."

I felt my cheeks blush. "Yeah, Norma is really excited. She bought a couple bridal magazines and put the whole thing together. I'll have to bring it to my gram so she can go through it with me." I smiled as I thought about being able to share it with her.

"I can't wait." He bent down to kiss me. "More motivation to get these cases solved... so we can get away for our honeymoon. Wanna do a practice run tonight?" He winked as he unbuttoned his shirt and walked into the bathroom.

The sound of the shower was all it took to entice me to join him. I needed the distraction as much as he did. I was not as scared as I should have been. I was more intrigued. Two jobs done for me. Completing the tasks I planned on carrying out... but who? Who was beating me to the dirty deeds? I needed to know.

CHAPTER TWENTY-ONE

After the last visit with Gram, I couldn't shake the thought that my mom was taking advantage of her. It wasn't new; she used to borrow money from her after my dad left and before she hooked up with Chad. Mom didn't keep it a secret that she was waiting on her inheritance. When I was a kid, it was all she talked about. I couldn't imagine Gram had a lot of money left after all these years of Mom taking it, and now paying for her apartment and nurse at the senior living complex.

I wanted to know what she had made Gram sign. I tried to push it out of my mind, but it wouldn't budge. The worst-case scenarios played on repeat in my head. The most illogical thought of all was that Gram had signed a document granting Mom access to end her life. I knew this didn't exist, but I also knew Mom would be the one to figure out a way to make the impossible happen.

In one of the *Snapped* episodes, I remembered seeing someone use a hidden camera to spy on their lover. I'd never needed anything like this before and had no idea where I'd find one. When I typed *nanny cams* into the search field on Amazon, pages of results came up. I filtered through page after page, unsure of what I was looking for. I knew it had to be simple, and I had to be able to view it on my phone. I ordered the first one meeting those specifications. This wasn't something I wanted Tim to know about, so I had it shipped to the hospital.

When the package arrived, I took the afternoon in my office reading the directions and installing the needed app on my phone. As a practice run, I installed it in the conference room before the ladies arrived to group. There was a setting to record and also watch live. I practiced the live feature before they arrived as I waved at the camera before placing my phone in my sweater pocket.

Lily knocked on the door, reminding me I hadn't unlocked it. "I'm glad you could join us today. How have you been?"

"I almost didn't come." Lily looked down at her feet. "I feel like you all are so close and I'm just the intruder."

"Ah, Lily, I'm sorry it feels like that. You just have to give it time, and I know you'll fit right in. Did you ever go over to Maggie and Norma's? She makes a great cup of tea." I smiled, hoping it would be enough to make her believe me.

"No. It just feels weird... you know. I don't want to force myself on them."

"I get it. I was the same way. It can take a lot to feel comfortable with people we don't know."

"Really? You make it look easy."

"Well... you didn't see me in the beginning. These ladies

are the first friends I've had in over sixteen years. Give it time. There's no rush." I put my hand on Lily's back and gave it a quick pat. "Oh, I'm sorry... I forgot." I cringed as I remembered the bruises covering her body.

"Nah, it's okay. Just my ribs hurt now." She gave me a smile. "You really think they don't mind me being here?"

"I know they don't. They're good people. People you can trust."

Norma and Maggie came through the door, Sonya right behind them. "Oh, it's so nice to see you, Lily." Norma walked over and took the seat next to Lily.

I gave Lily a nod and winked as she smiled back at me. "Aww, that's sweet of you, Norma."

Sonya flopped down next to them, and Maggie sat next to me. "Yeah, it's nice to see you again." Maggie smiled.

"I was just telling Val I feel like an intruder, like I don't belong here."

"Oh, honey, of course you belong here. If we don't have each other's backs, then who will?" Norma patted her knee.

"I was telling Lily it was hard for all of us in the beginning, before we got to know each other." I looked around the circle and remembered how hard it had been for Maggie to open up, and for Sonya to trust us enough to get past her abrasive exterior.

"It's especially difficult when people are so hard to trust." Maggie nodded her head in agreement with herself.

"You know what's funny? Not like ha-ha funny, but funny strange?" Sonya tilted her head.

"What's that, Sonya?" I turned to look at her.

"It seems since joining this group, all my problems disappeared... well, except for the current ones, but you know what I mean."

"What do you mean?" I asked.

"First the old pervert, Donald Brice is found dead... then Jimmy... although I'm not sure how I feel about that yet... but it's like I speak it and it happens."

"Yeah... like Seth." Maggie added.

Norma laughed. "Well, if we can all be so lucky to have a genie grant our wishes for us."

"If it's that easy... I wish Earl would die." Lily blinked her eyes and giggled, triggering laughter from the rest of the group.

"If it were only that easy." I smiled as I saw the ladies bond a little more over the topic. We all had someone we wished we could erase from our lives. I know I have a few.

"Did you see the article in the *Village News*? About the serial killer?" Maggie made eye contact with me.

"I did. Crazy to think about something like that happening here," I said.

"It's a little scary." Maggie bounced her foot as it rested on her crossed leg. "How do we know who's next?"

"I think you're safe. It appears only men need to worry." A nervous laugh spilled out as I tried to remember if that was public knowledge or something I heard from Tim.

"Yeah, only perverts, by the sounds of things." Sonya paused. "Do you think the same person killed Donald?"

"No... he died of natural causes, remember?" My answer came out in an abrupt snap.

Sonya raised her eyebrows. "Whoa. What's up with you?"

"Sorry... I just haven't been able to get much sleep lately... you know with everything going on." I pushed up a half-smile. "And, I guess, I should let you all know I'll be taking some time off. I do want to keep meeting, though, just not here."

"We could meet at our place." Maggie turned to make sure Norma agreed.

"Oh, that would be lovely. Lily, make sure you get our address before we leave today. And, if you tell me what your favorite snack is, I'll be sure to have it waiting for you." Norma's smile pushed up her glasses.

"Thanks, ladies, that was the one piece keeping me from taking time off... I didn't want to go without our meetings, but I knew if I got in the building, I wouldn't be able to leave without getting pulled into something."

"Tim must be exhausted." Norma shook her head. "I don't envy him."

"Yeah, it has taken a toll on him. He said he's never seen anything like this before. He's being so professional, too... I can't get him to spill any information." I laughed. "I can't even get him to talk in his sleep to me."

Norma gave me a smile. "I'm sure it's for the best, dear. You wouldn't want that in your head. I'm sure he knows what he's doing."

"Yeah, I know... I just get curious. I want to know who it could be. And why."

"It does make you wonder, doesn't it?" Norma nodded her head as her eyes went to the clock on the wall. "Oh, heavens, look at the time. I've got to get to my appointment."

The rest of us followed. Not knowing all the details

behind the murders, and not being able to share the things I did know with the ladies made talking about it difficult. I knew it was a lot to process, even for people without a trauma history. But for us, people with trust issues, it made existing in the world that much harder. I hoped for answers, but not before a few more predators met their fate.

CHAPTER TWENTY-TWO

I'd forgotten my nanny cam in the conference room after our group, I didn't realize this until I was ready to visit my gram. I logged onto the app to see if I could replay some of the events from our meeting to make sure it was something I would be able to use at Gram's.

I clicked on the recorded footage and rewound it to the beginning and watched until I saw Lily join me in the room. The picture quality was clear enough to make out who we were, and with the volume up as high as I could get it, I was able to hear our conversation. I muted the phone and watched as the others arrived. It didn't appear anyone knew they were being recorded. No one mentioned it while we were together, and I didn't see anyone make eye contact with the camera. I guess I could call that a success.

Before I left for the day yesterday, I told Jeanine I wouldn't be back for a few weeks, taking her up on the offer to use some of my vacation time. She didn't fight me on it, and I didn't tell her I'd still be running the group. That wasn't something she needed to know, but it was something I needed to do.

I swung by the hospital before I left for my visit. Now with the camera and folder full of my wedding wishes, nothing was stopping me from spending time with Gram. It was a Wednesday morning, so it was doubtful Mom would be there. The idea I would *know* when she was there from now on brought a sinister smile to my face. It was time I was in control of things. I wanted to know what she was up to, but I also wanted to know when the coast was clear.

When I arrived at the senior living complex, I noticed the apple blossoms covering the trees lining the walkway. The sweet aroma was enough to take me back to my childhood. Memories of sitting under the apple tree at Gram's house as I read my newest library book filled my mind. I closed my eyes to savor the memory. What I wouldn't give to go back, just one more day to a simpler time, where the only care I held was whether I'd finish the next chapter before Gram yelled for me to come have lunch. So much had changed since then. I hadn't been that girl in decades.

At the door, I knocked before opening it to find Gram napping in her recliner. "Rise and shine sleepyhead."

"Oh, what a lovely surprise." She took my hand into hers as she looked up at me.

"I brought wedding stuff." I held up the folder and waved it in the air. When I sat on the couch, I looked around the living room to find the best location for the camera. It was hidden in an alarm clock, so it was easy to plug in without too much concern. "I brought you this new clock, too." I pulled it out of my bag. "I think it'll look good right here." I plugged it in as it rested on the third shelf on her bookcase.

"Well, that will help me know what time it is." She laughed. "Thank you, Val. That's sweet of you."

Once back on the couch, I pulled out my phone. "Just a second, Gram, I need to send Tim a message to let him know I made it safe." I opened the app and saw the camera was pointed at Gram, with most of the living room included in the view. Satisfied with the setup, I tucked my phone away. "So, we picked a date... July 15th."

"Oh, that's right around the corner."

"Yeah, we'll probably regret not having a lot of time to plan, but we just wanted to make it official." I smiled, not wanting her to know we were rushing the date to make sure she would be present.

"You found a good one, Val. He's a sweetheart."

"I did get lucky with him. I guess that's what happens when you wait as long as I did to find someone."

We spent the morning going through the pages the ladies and I ripped out of the magazines together days before. We went to her closet and found a pretty purple flowered dress for her to wear, with a matching cardigan. Being with her made me feel like a little girl again. For the few moments we were together; everything was just as it should be. As she made her way back to the living room, pushing a walker to keep her balance, the essence of time slapped me in the face.

The clock was ticking. Hers and mine. "Gram, I've got to tell you something." It was now or never. I had to come clean.

"What is it, dear?" She sat back against her recliner as she listened.

"Well... I didn't want to keep this from you, but I didn't know how to tell you." Guilt and anger were at war with each other inside my chest. I pushed the tears out of my eyes with the sleeve of my sweatshirt.

"It's okay, Valerie. You can tell me."

"I have a..." I inhaled deeply as I searched for the word. "A... son."

"Oh?" She tilted her head. "Well, that's lovely."

"Except, it's not. Well, it wasn't. It is now... but it wasn't lovely. It was awful." I felt my blood boil in my veins as I remembered him being ripped from my arms. "Mom made me give him up for adoption."

"Oh, Valerie." Her hand covered her mouth. "That's why you ran off, isn't it?" She let out a deep sigh. "Your mother is a... real bitch."

I'd never heard her call Mom that before. "She really is." I knew I couldn't tell her the rest, it wasn't something she needed to be kept awake at night with. "But... I found him." The words alone were enough to cover my face with a smile. "You'll get to meet him at the wedding."

Her smile matched mine as a teardrop slid down her cheek. "Oh, that's wonderful, Valerie."

"He's twenty years old now and seems like a sweet young man. He has the best adoptive parents I could have asked for. They'll be at the wedding, too."

Goosebumps covered my limbs. "Having you and he join us is all I could ever ask for."

Gram tilted her head to the side. "You're how old now? Thirty-five? You would have been..."

Shame heated my checks. "I was fifteen." My eyes dropped. "But, it's not what you think... it wasn't..."

"It doesn't matter now. All that matters is you can have him in your life. We all make mistakes, but they don't define us." She gave me a sympathetic smile.

I know she was trying to make me feel better, but I disagreed. Some mistakes do define us. Like Chad. His mistakes, or actually, his actions did define him. They made him a lowlife child molesting creep. Just like Donald Brice, and Jane, and Seth, and Jimmy, and all the other perpetrators roaming the streets. Their actions most certainly defined them. It was their actions alone that ended their lives.

An eye for an eye? Hardly. The life taken from them would never repay what they stole from their victims. It was just a drop in the bucket. I could only hope they would be paying for their sins long after their death.

CHAPTER TWENTY-THREE

The serial killer had taken a few weeks off, allowing Tim to get some much-needed rest, and to enable us to move into our new home. Tim carried the last box of my stuff through the door of the tan ranch-style house we were renting. On a quiet road, ten minutes from town, we would be away from the commotion, but still close enough to run out and grab a gallon of milk.

The large bay window overlooked the giant oak tree that took up much of the front yard, with a single tire swing hanging on one of the thick branches. A black mailbox sat ready to hold our mail as soon as the change address forms took effect. The paved driveway had a basketball hoop near the garage, and I couldn't help imagine the children who had enjoyed it before we moved in.

This was the perfect starter home for a new family. Peaceful and practical, with all of the essentials. The fairy tale ending I had never dared reach for had fallen into my lap.

With the beige curtain brushing my face, I took a step back and looked around at the work we had ahead of us. "Who thought it would be a good idea to host a dinner party tomorrow?"

Tim set the box down and kissed the top of my head. "You did." He laughed. "Don't worry, we can pull it off. Everything should be ready by..." He put his index finger to his chin. "Morning... as long as we don't sleep."

"Ugh." I blew the strand of hair out of my face that had fallen out of my ponytail. "We should cancel it... postpone it, at least."

"Relax, Val. We'll get it done."

"How can you be sure?" I bent down to open the box by my feet.

"Because when you set your mind to something, it happens... that's how. Besides, they know we just moved in, they're not going to expect everything to be unpacked."

"Can we do rent-to-own? I never want to move again." I wiped the sweat off my forehead with my sleeve.

"Well ... there's not enough bedrooms for that ball team..."

"Exactly." I walked over to him and planted a kiss on his lips. "One step at a time, Mr. Philips."

"Hey, I was just pointing out the obvious." His smirk was enough to light my fire. The quicker we got to work, the sooner we could try out our new bedroom.

Since this was the first house for both of us, we didn't have a lot of extra stuff. We had already taken all of our duplicates to the Good Will, so the job ahead was doable. The only motivation I needed to get the job done was knowing my son and his family would be visiting in just a few short hours.

I plugged Tim's phone into the speaker for some music to work by. I still hadn't gotten into the habit of downloading music, I was more a CD kind of girl. With his music app opened, I hit shuffle and went to work. A twangy voice I had heard before started blasting from the speakers. "Whoa... is there something I should know?" I tilted my head and giggled.

"Oh, shit... I forgot that was on there." He unplugged his phone and tapped the screen a few times before setting it back up. "There, that should be better."

Tom Petty started singing. "Wait... why are you listening to *Goodbye Earl?* Don't get me wrong, it's a good song... but it doesn't seem like your style."

His face changed from pink to red. "It's... ah... for work."

"You listen to the Dixie Chicks for work?" I couldn't hold the laughter back.

"Don't you worry your pretty little head about it. Just listen to Tom and get into your groove."

"That's all I get? I need to know more."

He shook his head and left the living room with a box in hand. I couldn't imagine why he would be listening to music for work... and why the Dixie Chicks? I walked over to his phone and opened the music app to see Tim had downloaded the entire *Fly* album. Scrolling deeper into his music library, I also noticed it was the only country music. It still didn't make much sense, but I knew he wouldn't be offering up any information. He'd been pretty tightlipped since the FBI started helping.

After hours of unpacking, the last box was emptied by 11:45pm. I held it upside down. "Oh my god, we did it!"

"See, I told you." Tim reached his arms above his head and stretched. "Now, let's take a shower and get some sleep."

"Can you believe we're getting married in less than a month?" I looked around the house and saw our belongings commingling and saw Gabriel napping on the couch. "And my son will be here tomorrow? Meeting my cat, his namesake." It was the first time it seemed strange to me as I watched Gabriel's black fur rise and fall as he slept. "He's going to think it's weird... isn't he? I mean... it is. Right?"

"Relax, Val." He pulled his t-shirt off over his head. "It's not weird. I think it's sweet."

"You're just saying that so you can get me naked."

"Maybe." He shot me a smile. "But, really, it is sweet. It's not weird. And, how did you know they didn't change his name? If they had given him a new name, we wouldn't even be having this conversation. We'd already be letting the hot water melt our stress away in there." He nodded his head in the direction of the bathroom.

He was right. I was grateful they kept his name, and even more thankful they raised him, letting him know how much he was loved. So what if my cat and son shared a name. It's not like they'd get confused when I called them to dinner. One would be at his food dish, and the other would be at the table.

After a refreshing night of sleep and a day filled with grocery shopping and cooking, we were only minutes away from Gabriel, Beth and Paul arriving. It was a two-hour drive for them, but they insisted they wanted to see where we lived. With the new house, it was the perfect opportunity to have one more meeting before the wedding.

The silver Nissan Pathfinder pulled into the driveway, with the directional signal flashing as Paul put it in park. Gabriel exited the left backdoor and stretched his arms over his head, exposing the band of his boxers and belly when his black t-shirt slid up. I couldn't push back the smile when I imagined him as a little boy. "Hey, Gabriel. Long ride? Huh?" The high pitch in my voice made me blush as I realized he wasn't the child I was addressing.

He flashed me a smile. "Yeah, it wasn't too bad."

"Don't let him fool you, he slept the whole time." Beth joined us in the driveway as Paul opened his door and took his keys out of the ignition. "Rides have always put him to sleep." Beth "Geez, mom." Gabriel ducked down to escape her grooming. "I'm a grown man."

The reality of his words stung me as much as Beth. "But you'll always be my baby." Beth smoothed out her skirt. "Our baby." She smiled as she handed me an enormous wicker gift basket.

"Wow, thank you." My eyes dropped to the bottle of champagne and crystal flutes. "You really shouldn't have."

"Oh, nonsense. It's a housewarming gift." She pulled a thumb drive out of her purse. "This is the real gift." She held my hand at the exchange. "I went through Gabe's baby photos and some of our home videos. We went digital a few years ago... you know, downsizing... so I didn't have any ready to bring, but I thought you could print the ones you wanted."

I couldn't find the words to express the amount of gratitude my heart held. Tears fell onto my sandals, hitting the skin on the top of my exposed feet.

"I knew you'd love them." Beth took the basket and handed it to Paul and wrapped me into a hug. "He's our boy. He always has been."

"Hi, guys." Tim raised the long tongs he had been using at the barbecue. "Do you want to come see the new Webber grill we just got? We're christening it today."

Paul didn't hesitate to take him up on the offer, and Gabe wasn't too far behind, leaving us mothers to talk about all the important things, like first words, first steps, and favorite stuffed animals. Beth and I walked around the yard, stopping at the lilac bush in full bloom. I closed my eyes as I let the sun hit my face as I inhaled the fresh, sweet smell of the purple blossoms.

"You never had any more children?" Beth's question took me out of my moment of bliss.

"No." My eyes fell to my feet. "I didn't want to have any more when I had already had a son out in the world. I didn't want him to think I replaced him, or be upset I gave him away, but kept the others." I shook my head. "It probably doesn't make sense."

"No, of course it does." She gave me a heartfelt smile. "But you shouldn't feel that way. Being a mom is such a gift. One I am thankful for every day."

"Having Gabriel wasn't under the best circumstances. I always felt... I don't know... guilty."

"Oh, you shouldn't feel that way. What you did was a gesture of love. One, I don't think I would ever have been strong enough to do."

"The thing is... I didn't have a choice. I always felt if I had been stronger, I could have fought to keep him. I had this fantasy I could have run away with him, and we would have lived happily ever after."

"Did his father know? Were you going to start a family with him?"

"No... well, he knew, but it's complicated." I closed my eyes and shook out the memories as I contemplated telling Beth the truth. I wasn't sure I wanted Gabriel to know how he was conceived. I didn't want him to think I resented him. I only wanted him to know the love I held for him.

"I think you and Tim would make wonderful parents, and Gabe could finally be a big brother. When he was little, he used to beg us for a sibling. It broke my heart because I knew I'd never be able to grant him that wish." She smiled. "But you can."

"He already is." I pointed to the black face pressed against the glass. "That's my cat, who has been my only constant in my life." I walked over to tap on the glass. "And, you'll never guess his name."

Beth tilted her head and walked over to the window. "Let me think... Sampson?"

"No... Gabriel. I know how crazy that sounds..."

"Oh, it's not crazy, it's sweet." She took my hand. "I probably would have done the same thing."

"It didn't feel strange until I learned he shared his name with Gabriel."

"I don't think it's weird at all, it's just another testament of your love for our boy."

Tim had dinner ready by the time we made it to the backyard with the rest of them. Gabriel looked like he was having a good time. I didn't want to throw myself at him, but I didn't want to ignore him. It was a delicate balance I was still trying to master.

"You'll never guess what Gabe is doing with his summer." Tim's smile couldn't have gotten any bigger.

"Hmmm... I don't even know where to start. Is he going mountain biking cross country?" I squinted my eyes to see if my guess was close.

"No... I think I'd fall off if I tried riding a bike that long." Gabe snickered.

"Oh, I guess you inherited my gracefulness then." I smiled. "I have no idea."

"Tell her... before I do." Tim closed the cover to the grill.

"I signed up for the Police Academy this fall, and Tim offered to let me do some ride-alongs with him this summer."

My eyes met Tim's. "Oh, that's great, Gabe... so that means you'll be staying with us?"

Gabe ran his hand through his hair, the same way Tim does. "Yeah, I hope it's okay."

"Are you kidding me? I think it sounds amazing." I looked back at Beth, who was standing behind me.

"He's always been interested in law enforcement, and on the drive over here, we thought it would be a great opportunity for him. And it would give you all some time together."

"Did you tell him what you've been working on?" With clenched-teeth, I forced a smile at Tim.

"Yeah. It's a once in a lifetime opportunity... well, at least we hope it is."

Beth joined us at the table. "What is this once in a lifetime opportunity you're speaking of?"

"Mom, don't freak out..."

"Whoa... first lesson is never start the conversation like that... a surefire way to make her freak out." Tim looked back at Gabe. "Well, my mother, anyway."

"Well, Tim was telling me the FBI is involved in a case they are working on..."

"The FBI? That can't be good."

"Let me finish." Gabe passed the plate of burgers to Paul, after setting one on his plate. "Tim and the guys are looking for a... ah... how do I put it?"

"Serial killer." Tim blurted out. "But don't you worry. He'll be in good hands. And there hasn't been another murder in a few weeks. They have likely moved on." Tim nonchalantly took a scoop of potato salad.

"Serial killer?" Beth looked to Paul for backup, but his eyes were on his cheeseburger.

"Think about it, though, Mom. What if I'm the one to crack the case? Think about how good it would look on my resume. You always said experience is better than books."

"I don't think that's a direct quote." She sighed. "But, you're old enough to make this decision." She took a drink of water. "And, Tim, I'm sure you know how important Gabe is to me, and Val." She winked at me as she set her glass down.

"I sure do. I wouldn't have offered if I thought he was in danger."

Gabe held up his hand for a high-five from Tim. "Alright!"

Just like that, my son would be living under the same roof

as me, for the very first time. Ever. The joy it brought pushed out any of the apprehension I should be feeling knowing the two men I love will be working together to solve the case I came so close to. Not just once, but twice I was almost in the wrong place at the wrong time. It was too exhilarating to be frightening. And what's the saying? Almost doesn't count? My days of living an almost life were over. My days were all going to count from now on.

CHAPTER TWENTY-FOUR

I took the clean sheets out of the dryer and stuck my nose in the pile. The smell of Snuggle brought me back to my childhood when I spent the night at Gram's. She always made up the bed with fresh, clean sheets. As soon as my head hit the pillow, I was out. I hoped Gabe would enjoy it as much as I did. The sheets were still warm when I made the bed in the guest room.

Gabe would be here next week, and I wanted to make sure he was comfortable. I asked Beth what some of his favorite foods were and stocked the pantry. I even bought him his favorite Pantene shampoo and Axe body wash. He might not be a baby any longer, but I could mother him as much as he would allow. Since he was only fifteen years younger than me, it was a delicate balance between parent and friend. I didn't want to waiver too much one way and not the other. I just wanted to be sure I was everything he needed.

Tim was excited to share our home with him, too. The excitement shone through every conversation. "I'd always wanted a son to follow in my footsteps." I lost count how many times he said that since he found out Gabe would be riding along with him.

The only thing I had been able to get out of Tim was that the FBI was searching their database to see if there had been any murders matching the ones in Lawrenceville. He still wouldn't share what linked them all together, but I was hopeful Gabe might let it slip once he started working with Tim.

After Gabe's room was complete, I pulled out my iPad and entered "serial killers" into the search bar. I had no idea what I was looking for but wanted to learn as much as possible before the guys started talking about work and leaving me out. I took out a notebook and wrote down everything I knew about the cases. I started with the names of the victims, followed by the timeline of the murders. Bobby Green was the last one, and that had been over a month ago. I wrote down murder weapon: nine-millimeter gun. Motive: all pieces of shit... it made me giggle more than it should have. That was all I knew.

I knew three of the five were sex offenders. The rest of the *Village News* readers knew that, too. Seth and Jimmy? I still didn't know how they were tied to this. I spent hours searching their names, looking for something that would have made their existence known to someone who wanted to rid society of predators. I didn't find anything. Granted, I don't have the best technology or even the skill to use what I have efficiently, but there were no hits online connecting Jimmy or Seth to the three known sex offenders. I couldn't even find a parking ticket in their names.

And the thing I couldn't stop thinking about, except, I didn't know what it was. I tried to recall Seth's apartment the day I went to kill him. I couldn't pull anything back to my memory. The image of his dead body slumped over in his recliner was all I could evoke. I closed my eyes tighter as I attempted to retrace my footsteps. My memory wasn't at its fullest potential. Trauma does that to you. Not only does it steal your inner peace, but it also eats away at the memories that linger. At times I was grateful for this weakness, but times like this, it was frustrating. I'd be the last person you'd want to identify a criminal. It always amazes me when someone can recall enough details to get a perfect sketch drawn of the perpetrator. I can barely remember any details.

On Wikipedia, I followed links to a page of unidentified serial killers. If Lawrenceville wasn't their first stop, they were obviously being sought after by another county or state. With the bare minimum information, I wasn't able to find any that looked like they matched. It's just as easy to be someone local, someone that knew them... or their victims.

I wrote Andrew's name on my notebook with a question mark. I wondered how much Sonya talked to him, and if she could have mentioned Seth to him. We were all pretty distraught that day when we discovered he was the one who stole Lexi's heart. Jimmy made sense, though. And if Sonya told him about her past, I can see why he'd want to rid the world of child molesters, especially before their baby was born. But they weren't all child molesters, just all sex offenders.

Sonya was ruled out, but should she have been? It could be possible she was just as involved as Andrew. My mind started running away with different scenarios. I needed to know what the missing piece of information was now more than ever. If it was Andrew and Sonya, I didn't want them getting caught, as long as they weren't planning on hurting anyone else, at least no one who wasn't asking for it.

I know Tim and I disagreed on vigilantes, but I kind of owe this guy a thank you. If it wasn't for him, I'd already be a serial killer. What kind of mother would that make me? And now Gabe was going to be helping. I'd be devastated for him to think of me that way.

When I heard Tim's car pull into the driveway, I clicked out of the Wikipedia page and opened the David's Bridal page and started to scroll through the dresses. I found the one I wanted, I just hadn't taken the time to take my measurements. Tim didn't understand why I didn't want to go try them on, but the idea someone would see my body still made me uneasy. Baby steps. That was the best I could do.

"Day number thirty-seven without a murder." He hung his keys on the key hook and kicked off his shoes. "I call that a success." He came over to kiss me, his eyes on my iPad. "You still haven't got your dress yet? We are in the final stretch countdown."

"You know how well I do with stress." I closed the cover. "I found the one I want... I'll see if Maggie will help get my measurements the next time I'm over there."

"I can do that. It's not like I haven't seen it all before."

"Gross." I wrinkled my nose up. "There are some things you don't need to know."

"Everyone is excited to have some young blood in the

station again. I know he's just a kid, but maybe a new set of eyes will be able to crack this case."

"The FBI will be okay with this?"

"They're pulling out. For now, anyway." He scratched his head. "A case in Upstate New York called them away. And, they've been through all the evidence we have. So, unless we get another murder, they probably won't be back."

"Just like that, Lawrenceville is yesterday's news?"

"Pretty much. I think if the victims were women or at least law-abiding citizens, they would have given it more interest, but I guess you're not the only one who thinks they got what they deserved."

"So, does this mean you can share some of the information you've been withholding from me?" I wiggled my eyebrows at him.

"No, I'm afraid not. Nice try, though."

"Really? How would anyone know?"

"It's a pretty significant piece of information. If leaked it, it could destroy the whole case."

"But who would I tell? I can keep a secret."

"I know, I do trust you, but accidents happen. If this gets out, there could be copycats, or it could get leaked to the news. Just trust me it's for the best I don't share it with you. We won't even be able to share it with Gabe, and he'll be working the case with us."

A heavy sigh expelled from my lips. The plan of getting Gabe to talk was out the window as quickly as I thought it up. "Fine." I crossed my arms. "Can you at least give me a hint?"

"Hmm... you're relentless." He laughed. "Let me think."

He held his chin in his left hand. "Umm... it's interesting... but not gross."

"That's it? Interesting and not gross. Do you have any idea how many things that could be?"

"Things or situations... we think it's this killer's trademark. Like the Boston Strangler's method was strangulation, the BTK killer killed his victims the same way, and Jeffrey Dahmer, well, he ate his. We feel this killer left a trademark, too. An interesting one that we didn't figure out right away, but we feel they intended to leave a message."

"They? Do you think it could be a female?"

"No. We're pretty confident it's a male."

"Hmmm... so a man who owns a nine-millimeter, dislikes predators, and has an interesting trademark... that narrows it down." I rolled my eyes and laughed. "You know this is driving me crazy, right?"

"I see that. Why do you think that is? You know I'll do everything to protect you. I know you've been through a lot, but this guy won't hurt you. I can almost guarantee that."

I'd never be able to tell him. Not about this, or the others. These were secrets I would never be able to speak of, not to Tim, or anyone. "To be honest, I feel safer with him out there."

CHAPTER TWENTY-FIVE

When I pulled up to Norma's for our weekly group, I was surprised to be the first one there. I guessed all the time off was helping me break my bad habits. Norma had three different types of cookies on the table, fresh coffee made and a full pot of tea. "You've outdone yourself again, Norma. It smells amazing in here." I closed my eyes as the smell of freshly baked chocolate chip cookies filled my nose.

"You know I love you girls. It's the least I can do. You all have brought so much joy into my life these last few months." She held her hand to her heart.

"And you to us." I poured myself a cup of tea and sat at the table as Norma joined me. "You know, this is going to sound strange, but you remind me of the mom I never had and always wanted." I cradled the hot cup between my hands. "I've wanted to tell you for a while now... but I didn't want to overstep."

"That means more to me than you'll ever know." The moisture glistened in her eyes as she looked at me.

"You know, if you ever want to talk with me about anything, I'm only a phone call away."

She nodded. "I know, dear."

"Do you ever feel like you want to share with us?" I spun the mug around by the handle before looking at her. "I mean, you've heard all of our tales of horrors, and we haven't been able to help you with yours."

"I've shared so many times, I guess it just doesn't affect me like it used to. I just like your company. You ladies understand the same things I do, and that's really all the help I need." She smiled at me. "Someday, you'll get to where I am and you'll understand."

"You think so?"

"I'm sure of it." She took a drink of coffee as the front door swung open.

Sonya's hands were full of books. She set the stack down on the table, and Norma pushed them away from the food. "I found these on my bookshelf when I was cleaning out the room for the baby."

Norma picked up one of the books and lifted her glasses to read the title. "*Healing the Trauma of Abuse*, well, that sounds like a nice light afternoon read."

Sonya raised her eyebrows, and I couldn't hold back laughter as Norma's joke was lost on poor Sonya. "I figured they might be helpful." Sonya picked up another book. "This one helped me a lot, but not as much as knowing that dirtbag Donald Brice is dead, though. That was the best cure." She choked out a laugh as she tossed the book back on the pile.

"I've been waiting for the day I get news Chad is dead." I covered my mouth. "I've never said that out loud before."

Norma was thumbing through the pages. "It's a natural thought. It doesn't mean anything is wrong with you." She looked up and smiled. "Here, have a cookie." She held up a plate to me and then Sonya.

Sonya puffed out her cheeks and put her hand to her stomach. "Oh, god no. I can't eat anything."

"Morning sickness caught up with you?"

"Yeah, that and this godawful heartburn." Her hand rubbed her throat. "I don't know how much longer I can stand this." She flopped herself onto the couch.

"Oh, honey, I'm afraid you have a ways to go." Norma picked up her mug and motioned for me to follow her to the living room.

Maggie and Lily walked through the front door. Maggie had a solemn look painted on her face. Lily had a stack of papers in her hand, a tissue dabbing her eyes with the other.

"How did it go?" Norma got up to get the plates of cookies.

Lily held up the papers in her hand. "They only granted me the protection order for a year. I have to go through this all over again next year." Her body sank into the plush living room chair.

"At least they granted it." Sonya rolled over to look at her. "When I went to get mine, they told me they didn't think it was necessary... because the dick hadn't physically hit me yet. I was like, so he can stalk me and threaten to kill me all he wants? And the judge said there was nothing he could do until I had proof he caused me harm. It's a fucked-up system." She rolled back over to carry on with her moaning and groaning.

"He *did* hurt Lily. You saw her bruises." I shook my head in Sonya's direction. "I'm sorry you have to deal with this, Lily. It seems like there are always hoops to jump through."

"She did a great job today." Maggie took a cookie off the plate before sitting down. "She was so brave."

"You know the worst part? Filling out that paper." Lily dabbed at her eyes. "The question that made me want to throw up was the one about the 'worst incident' of abuse. I had to relive all of that as I wrote it."

"Do you want to talk about what you wrote?" I turned to Lily.

"Not really. But you can read it if you want. I just don't think I have it in me to utter those words." Lily passed the document to me.

This was the first time I had seen an order of protection. I never had one, I was never able to make Chad pay for anything he did to me, and luckily, I never hooked up with anyone until Tim. I turned the first page. "How much do you want me to read?"

"The first section should be enough for now."

A paragraph had been crossed out. Under the scribble marks was the story she told us at our first time together. I looked up at Lily to see if she was ready. Her eyes were fixated on the flowered mug in her hands.

I read the first line silently before I began. I wasn't sure even I had what it took to read these words out loud. Seeing them written in her handwriting was what tugged at my heartstrings.

The worst incident of abuse was about three years ago when one of Earl's friends made a comment about my body. I didn't react, I knew it was making him mad, so I didn't even look at the other guy. When he left, Earl accused me of having an affair with this guy. He said the only way a guy would think I was worth anything was if he had fucked me. He told me I was worthless, and my only talent was spreading my legs. When I didn't fight back, he assumed what he was saying was true, so he left the room and came back with his rifle. He pointed it at my chest, the gun was pressed into my left breast. I asked him to stop, but he just laughed. He told me he was going to make sure no one ever looked at me again, so he went to pull the trigger. I thought I was going to die, but the gun jammed, or it was out of bullets. He was pissed off, so he took the gun and hit me across the face with it. Then he raped me. He pulled my clothes off and forced himself on me. I didn't fight him, I just laid under him bleeding.

"Oh my god, Lily. That must have been terrifying. I don't even know what to say." I held the papers in my hands, not sure if I should keep reading or hand them back. I found my answer when I looked at the ladies' faces and gave them back to Lily.

"I had forgotten about that time until I sat in the room with the advocate and Maggie and wrote down all of the stuff I could remember." Her focus was on the wall in front of her. "How could I have stayed with him after he did all that to me? And, how do you just forget something like that?"

"It's normal to forget stuff. It's a survival mechanism. There are periods during my abuse I can't remember, not even if I try. It's our body's way of taking care of us. You know, we can only take so much. And don't beat yourself up for not leaving sooner. You left him, and that's all that matters now." The adrenaline pumped through my blood as I thought about what Lily had gone through. I didn't want to think about him ever putting his hands on her again.

"Val's right." Sonya sat up. "There are years of my childhood I can't remember. And I'm not sure I ever want to. I thought I was the only one. I'm glad you shared, it helped me know I'm not all that screwed up."

"I'm just grateful you're safe, Lily." Norma gave Lily a soft smile.

"The more I get to know you, the more I see how strong you really are. Your willingness to share what you went through has already helped each one of us." Maggie looked around the room for confirmation.

"That's true. We get to reclaim our power by sharing our stories. I'm so glad that piece of crap is behind bars." I pushed my hair behind my ear and pulled my legs under me to get comfortable in the chair.

"Yeah... but, he gets out in thirty days." Lily was still not making eye contact.

"How is that possible?" Sonya asked.

"I don't really understand it. The judge said he gets credit for time served, and because this is his first charge of domestic assault, it's a smaller sentence or something like that."

"That's fucken crazy." Sonya crossed her arms. "How is that justice? You had to spill your guts to the judge, and that's the best he could do?" She shook her head.

"Well, at least he got that, I guess." Lily turned her eyes to meet Maggie's.

"That's right, dear. One day at a time. A lot can happen in thirty days." Norma nodded and smiled.

"Yeah, the judge said the order should be enough to protect me. He said," she put her fingers up to make air quotes, "it is a protection order."

"What a dumbass. He does know it's just a piece of paper, right?" Sonya shot a look of disgust in Lily's direction.

"Well, sometimes they're more than that. Sometimes the idea of getting in trouble is enough to keep the abusers away." A heavy sigh I didn't know I was holding escaped. I knew it was just a piece of paper, but I didn't want to take the illusion of protection from Lily. I knew she needed it.

"Earl doesn't want anyone knowing who he really is, so it might be enough to keep him away." Lily shrugged her shoulders. "I guess I'll just have to wait and see."

"We're all here for you. Just a phone call away." Maggie took a bite of the cookie she had been holding.

"That's right, dear. You'll never be alone again." Norma gave her a smile.

I tried to get the image of the story I had just read out of my head, but all I could picture was Earl's naked body, forcing himself on Lily. I didn't know what it was like to be a battered woman, but I knew what it was like to be raped and be taken advantage of. And I knew what fear felt like. I knew all too well what it was like, not knowing what was going to happen next. I knew I had a job to do when Earl was released. At least I'd have time to plan.

CHAPTER TWENTY-SIX

So far, each time I checked the camera at Gram's house, there was nothing to see. She was right when she said Mom didn't come very often. I did see the nurse come and help her with things like she told me. From what I saw, and heard, she seemed like a nice person, and I was glad Gram wasn't always alone. I noticed Gram was sleeping a lot more, but I couldn't blame her, what else did she have to look forward to?

Tim and Gabe walked into the living room as I closed out of the app. "Gabe wants to tell you about his first day with yours truly." Tim pointed to his chest.

"Oh, I can't wait to hear all about it." I put my iPad on the coffee table and gave Gabe my full attention. Gabriel jumped in my lap as I listened.

"I don't know where to start." Gabe's face lit up. "It was awesome."

I raised my eyes and looked at Tim as I pet Gabriel. "Oh? What did you get into today?"

"Tim let me look at all of the crime scene photos. They're going to let me see if I can crack the case." He rubbed his hands together. "I can't wait."

"You got to look at all of the photos? You like that kind of thing?" I tilted my head and he nodded.

"It's awesome."

"Blood and everything?"

"Yeah... it's cool to see the close up of a bullet hole in someone's head. I definitely wanna be a cop now."

"He's not too different from you... well, except he can handle the blood." Tim laughed.

I tossed a throw pillow at Tim. "Very funny, Detective."

"What? It's true, you want to know about everything else. That's not a bad thing. You have the mind for it, just not the stomach." Tim pointed to Gabe. "But this guy, he's got it all. He's going to be a great detective."

"You really think so? A detective? Really?" Gabe's excitement was all over his face.

"I'm glad you had such a great day. Are you boys hungry?"

"I'm starving." Tim rubbed his stomach. "How about we grab a couple pizzas?"

"Sorry, the day got away from me. I've been getting the finishing touches done for the wedding."

"Don't be sorry, I love pizza." Gabe sat next to me and Gabriel on the couch.

I loved having him here, it was like we became a family overnight. It was fun watching Tim and him together. I knew Tim would be a great father, and I didn't want to wait much longer to find out. The wedding was only two weeks away, and then we could start trying for a baby of our own. Tim didn't know of my change of heart, I wanted to surprise him with it on our wedding night. I figured it was the best gift I could possibly give him.

Gabe stayed at the house to shower when Tim went to pick up the pizza. When he was finished, he came back to the living room and joined me in watching an episode of *Snapped*. "You like this stuff, too?"

"I never really did before, but since working with Tim, I can't get enough of it."

"What is it you like so much?"

"I want to know what makes people do the things they do. I want to get inside their head and try to understand the offense from their eyes. I think that's the best way to solve any crime."

"Wow, impressive for your first day." I smiled as I realized what a fine young man he had grown into.

"Well, Tim knows so much. It's a shame his talent is wasted in this crappy little town." He looked up at me. "Ah... I didn't mean..."

"No, you're right. This is a crappy little town. I like the chance of bad things happening here is so rare... well... until the serial killer... but before, it felt like a safe little community. It was just what I needed."

"You ever think about moving?"

"I hadn't, not until I met Tim, but I'd consider it."

"Yeah, I can see what you mean, though. This would be a sweet place to be a detective... you'd have just enough to keep you busy, but enough free time to not be too stressed out."

Gabe nodded as he bent down and scratched Gabriel on the head.

"So, what kind of interesting stuff did you see today?" I settled into the couch and pulled my legs under me.

Gabe laughed. "Tim said you'd try to get information out of me."

I opened my mouth and placed my hand on my heart. "Why would he say such a thing?"

"Well..." He shrugged his shoulders. "That's what you're doing, isn't it?"

"Huh? Good point. I'm just curious. I just want to know who it is and why. I think most people in town feel the same way."

"Yeah. I can see that."

"So, is there anything you can share?"

Gabe scratched his head. "Hmmm... well... all five guys were shot in the head." He turned his head to the side. "Wait, you knew that, right?"

I shook my head.

"Oh, thank god. Umm... it was the same gun... at least the same kind of gun used in each shooting. They all lived alone. And... there wasn't any evidence left at the crime scene... well, except for their trademark."

"Trademark?" I tilted my head to the side.

"Yeah, but don't try to get it out of me, because that's the one piece of evidence they kept from me. It was sealed."

"Really, they wouldn't share that with you?"

"No, that was the stipulation of letting me get involved. They said it could destroy the whole case if that piece of information was leaked."

"And it doesn't bother you?"

"No. I'm just happy I get to be involved at all. Besides, that piece isn't really that important, or at least that's what they said."

"That would drive me nuts... well, it has since Tim told me about it. I've been trying to get him to tell me... but he's keeping it confidential. I can't fault him for being professional... but I can't say it's not frustrating."

"Hmm... why aren't you a detective?"

I laughed. "Because, like Tim said, I can't stand the sight of blood. That's why I'm not a nurse. I wanted to help people, but I knew I couldn't deal with someone bleeding. That wouldn't make me a very good nurse if I passed out on my patient."

"Yeah, that probably would be a deal-breaker." Gabe laughed. "I want to help people, too. I didn't really know what I wanted to do until I heard Tim talk about it when we met."

Tim entered with the pizzas. "Dinner is served." He tilted his head. "She's grilling you for information, isn't she?"

Gabe nodded. "Yup, just like you said."

"Hey... I resent that." I stood up and put my hands on my hips.

"It was only fair to warn him." Tim kissed the top of my head. "Leave the poor guy alone."

"I'm sorry." I placed my hand on my heart. "It won't happen again." I winked at Gabe.

"It'll happen again." Tim pulled me into a hug. "I told you, I'll tell you what I can, but we can't risk sensitive information getting out. It could get the whole case tossed out. So, all this work we're putting in would be for nothing... and all five guys wouldn't get justice."

"That'd be too bad," I mumbled under my breath as I took out the plates.

"Want a beer, man?"

"Whoa... he's not old enough yet. How about a soda?"

"Shit, I'm sorry. What was I thinking?" Tim put his beer back and took out three cans of Pepsi.

"No, it's cool. I don't drink."

"For real?" Tim opened his can and took a sip.

"Well, I don't when my mom's in the same room."

My heart melted when his words met my ears. *His mom.* I was appreciative; he was such a sweet kid. He couldn't have been adopted by better people. All those years of worrying he would hate me was for nothing. I took a bite of pizza to hide my smile.

"So, Gabe. I've got a question... I don't want to put you on the spot... but I was wondering if you'd be my best man?"

"Whoa, really?" Gabe set his drink down on the table and rubbed his hands on his jeans.

Tim nodded his head. "Yeah. I've been thinking about asking you for a while, but I didn't want to make it weird."

"I'd love to. That's going to be so cool." Gabe smiled as he looked at me and then Tim.

Tim caught my attention and shot me a smile. I couldn't hold the emotion in. Quiet, happy tears fell down my cheeks. "I don't even know what to say." I dabbed at my eyes with my harsh paper towel napkin. "I don't think it could get any more perfect."

"Yeah, I thought he was the perfect candidate. When I

thought about the job, I couldn't picture anyone in it, not until I met Gabe. I knew he was the one to fill the suit." Tim laughed.

"And there's your first dad joke." I hung my head and shook it.

"What?" Tim held his hand up in front of his face.

"She's right. That was pretty lame, but we'll let it slide."

"It's going to be a long two weeks now." I pushed my plate away from me as I thought about walking down the aisle and seeing the two men I love waiting for me. It was better than a fairytale.

CHAPTER TWENTY-SEVEN

Knowing Gabe was going to be Tim's best man, the pressure was on to find who would stand next to me. Having Gram be my maid of honor would be the last part of a perfect day. I couldn't think of anyone I'd rather have with me. At our previous visit, we found her the dress she was going to wear. I knew if I gave her time to think about it, she would try to talk her way out of it, so I wouldn't ask her until she arrived at the ceremony.

With that piece settled, I had to find the rest of my wedding party. Tim was going to ask some of the guys from the station and some friends from college. My pool of people to pick from was tiny, but they were each significant. There would be no way I could ask one without the other. I let Tim know he would have to find four groomsmen.

At Norma's house, I handed everyone a card. "Okay, ladies, everyone open these at the same time." I sat down and clenched my teeth. "Alright, ... now."

Norma, Maggie, Lily, and Sonya opened the pink envelope and pulled out a matching card. *Will you be my bridesmaid?*

"Oh my goodness, dear. I'd be honored." Norma smiled and placed her hand on her heart.

"Good timing... my ass won't be too fat by then." Sonya snickered and lifted her butt to the side and slapped it.

"Wow, Val, that's so nice of you." Maggie smiled as she looked at the card.

Lily didn't respond.

"What do you say, Lily?" I bit my fingernail as I waited for her answer.

"It's okay, you don't have to ask me just to be nice." Her eyes did not lift from the card.

"Don't be silly, I want you there. I want you all there. You ladies are my friends, and I couldn't imagine the day without you... all of you... by my side."

"I don't have anything to wear." Lily pulled at the strings on her jean shorts.

"That's okay, it doesn't have to be fancy. Just wear what you're comfortable in. I'm going to ask my gram to be my maid of honor, and she's just wearing a simple dress. Heck, my dress is simple."

"Aww, that's lovely. I bet she was ecstatic when you asked her." Norma's smile kept growing.

"Well, I hope she will when I ask her." I laughed. "I know I didn't give you much time to plan something to wear."

"That's okay, it gives us a reason to go shopping," Sonya said.

"Let's go now. My treat. We could be at the mall in forty-five minutes." I looked around the room to see if everyone was on board with the plan.

"Wow, that sounds like fun." Maggie tapped Lily on the knee. "Shopping always cheers me up, how about you?"

"I don't know... you don't have to..."

"I know I don't have to, I want to. Just like I want *all* of you standing beside me. It would mean the world to me." I stood up. "Who wants to drive?"

"I will." Sonya raised her hand. "I have Andrew's Expedition today, so there'll be plenty of room for us and the bags."

Maggie took Lily's hand and pulled her off the couch. "Come on. It'll be fun."

"Yeah, come on, you're one of us now whether you like it or not." I took her other hand. "Come on."

Sonya elbowed Norma. "Norma, yell shotgun."

Norma cocked her head. "Shotgun?"

"Sorry, ladies, you're stuck in the back." Sonya laughed.

"That's fine with me, it'll give us more time to talk about you." Maggie laughed. "Just kidding, Sonya. You know we love you."

"You forget, I'm the young one, I still have my hearing. I can hear everything." She squinted her eyes and used her finger to draw a circle in the air.

Maggie, Lily, and I climbed into the back of the black Expedition. "Geez, I feel like royalty in this thing. Pretty close to a limo." I jabbed at Maggie as she sat in the middle next to me.

"Yeah, my second job is a chauffeur. I expect tips." Sonya joked as she fastened her seatbelt. "Everybody buckle up." She peered at us in the rearview mirror to make sure we complied. "Just practicing... you know, for when this bun in the oven is out."

"You're going to be a wonderful mother, dear." Norma placed her hand on Sonya's arm.

With the radio on and the hum of the air conditioner, it was too loud to carry on a conversation with the ladies in the front. Maggie, Lily, and I sat in awkward silence until I couldn't stand it any longer. "You know, Lily, I used to feel like you do... or... ah... how it seems like you do. I used to think nobody would want me around, or that I was always in the way. It's an awful feeling... I still struggle with it some-days." I leaned over Maggie to see Lily. "I know it's hard to unlearn all the crap we were told, but it is so worth it." I sat back against my seat.

"She's right. I struggle with that, too." Maggie turned her attention to Lily. "All those years of being told no one loves you, or that you're not worth anything are tough to shake. I hear his voice sometimes, and I have to fight it out of my head." She closed her eyes and shook her head.

"Yeah. That voice can get pretty loud... sometimes it was all I could hear. I used to think it'd never go away, but you know what the trick is?" I laughed. "I know it sounds crazy... but tell it to shut the fuck up. Like, really yell back at it. The first time I did it, I felt like I was losing my mind, but after a while, when that voice entered my head, I'd tell it to shut the fuck up... and it would stop."

"Some days are better than others." Lily turned her head to look out the window. "There are some days I actually feel like my old self." She turned to look at us. "I wasn't always like this."

"Hey, don't feel bad. We've all been there. We might not have gone through the same stuff, but we all know what it's like to be treated like shit by someone. The goal now is to make sure we don't continue where they left off." I nodded as I took inventory of the advice I was giving. "You know, it got to the point where I was probably crueler to myself than they ever were. Sounds bizarre, but I got used to being treated like shit, it was almost like I started to crave it."

"Hmm... that makes sense. When Earl wasn't calling me names, I more than made up for it. I get so mad at myself for letting him destroy me."

"Don't beat yourself up over things you can't change now. I spent more than half of my life wishing things had been different, but you know what? Life is now better than I ever imagined."

"Val's right. Things change so quickly. We have no idea what the future holds. Good things are coming for all of us, I just know it is." Maggie smiled and placed a hand on Lily's knee. "You can't beat yourself up over a lie you had no control over, either. That was something I wished I'd learned sooner."

"What do you mean?" Lily tilted her head.

"Well, like when I met Hank, I never could have imagined he would turn out to be the man he was. The man I fell in love with was... well... just perfect. The image he sold me changed over time and the real Hank was all that was eventually left. Guys like him have that way..."

"Yeah... when I met Earl, I couldn't believe how lucky I was. He had a good job, he was handsome." She paused and laughed. "Well, okay, maybe not handsome, but I was attracted to him. He said all the right things, held the door open for me and paid the bill... it was just what you think about when you imagine the man you'll marry. But, the minute the ink on the wedding certificate dried, it was like a switch flipped." She snapped her fingers. "And just like that, the man I loved turned into a monster. I couldn't even think of what I did to make him change."

"You didn't do anything. Some guys are just... assholes." Maggie smiled and shrugged her shoulders.

"You girls really do know what it's like... you're not just saying things to make me feel better... I can tell." Lily nodded her head. "Thank you for not letting me push you away. It's just that..."

"You don't need to explain... I used to be the queen of pushing people away. Thank you for pushing through the hard stuff and letting us in." I reached over Maggie and took Lily's hand. "We're all like badass superheroes. Maybe we should be shopping for capes, not dresses."

Maggie put her hand on top of ours. "Sounds like a good idea." She winked.

When we arrived at the mall, Sonya led our group to the bathroom. "Hey, no girl's trip is complete without a trip... or two to the bathroom."

A girl's trip... I never thought I'd live to see the day that I'd be spending an afternoon shopping with a group of ladies. Our first stop was to the bridal shop, but upon inspection of the price tags, we found our way to Macy's. The ladies all took matching dresses to the dressing room and modeled them for me. When I saw them, all together, I knew it was the dress I needed them to be immortalized in the wedding photos.

"Oh, my goodness... you're all so..." I pushed the tears out of my eyes. "Beautiful."

"Go get a dress and join us... I want a picture of all of us for my profile." Sonya shoed me in the direction of the women's section. "Go on."

With her encouragement, I found a matching dress in my size and tried it on. When I came out of the changing room, I joined the other ladies. We all stood together in front of the mirrors. It wasn't just the dress that made us match; it was our stories, experiences, and hearts. "It's like our own version of the Sisterhood of the Traveling Pants."

"Umm... I think it was just one pair of pants they all shared... not matching pants..." Sonya laughed. "But, what the hell. They should make a movie about all of us... we're not only beautiful, we're badass superheroes." She winked. "See... I told you I can hear everything. Now, come on, squeeze in together." She snapped a bunch of photos before we all changed back.

I had to get the dress. It wouldn't be my wedding dress, but I needed it to keep the memory of today alive in my heart. These were my sisters and my best friends.

CHAPTER TWENTY-EIGHT

Since Tim and Gabe weren't sharing any information about the case, I had to rely on my own research for any answers. I was at a dead-end on Google. There are only so many times you can click on the same links before you've read all you never knew you wanted to know about serial killers.

The good news for Lawrenceville was the death count had stopped at five. Bobby Green was the last one to be found at least. There had been other sex offenders released from jail, with their mugshot on the front page, but no more murders. The *Village News* loved to keep the community informed, and I can't say I blamed them.

I pulled out my notebook with all of the notes I had taken, and everything led me back to Sonya and Andrew. I know Sonya was cleared, but no one had even talked to Andrew. Why would they? No one else knew he could be a suspect, and I didn't want to give him away if he were. If he killed all of those men for the reason I think he did, then I would be the last person to stop him. The information I was collecting wasn't to implicate him. It was more to find a sense of safety I had been missing since this all started happening.

I called Sonya and invited her to lunch. I suggested we meet in town, but she insisted on coming to my place. I guess she was just as nosey as I was. I fixed a few sandwiches and dumped a bag of chips into a bowl and set it all out on the table. My house may have gotten classier, but I hadn't. I took a step back to admire my attempt at being a hostess. I immediately regretted I wasn't able to talk her out of meeting me here.

I was sitting outside on the front porch when Sonya arrived, Gabriel in my lap, enjoying the hot, July sun with me. When I stood up, I held him in my arms as he squirmed to the ground.

"Hey, Sonya, come on in." I placed Gabriel on the living room floor and stepped back outside while I waited for her.

"This heat is a killer." Sonya used her straw summer hat to fan herself.

"It could be worse... you could be nine months and waddling."

She started to cry. "Waddling. Ugh... does this get any easier?"

"I'd be lying if I said it did, but the reward at the end is going to be so worth it."

"I hope you're right." She sat in the chair closest to the air conditioner. "Can we eat in here?"

"What, you're not up for the grand tour?" I gathered the food from the kitchen and brought it to the coffee table in front of her. "That's Gabriel, not to be confused with the human version, who is at work with Tim." Gabriel rubbed against her bare legs.

She bent down to pet him, but he scurried away. "Even your cat hates me."

"Oh, stop it, the heat has made you go..."

"Insane?" Her top lip quivered.

"No... the hormones and heat are enough to drive anyone crazy." I turned the air to high.

Sonya reached down for a sandwich and started eating before I could give her a plate. So much for worrying about my hostess skills. "This is so good." She took another bite while I slipped a plate in her lap.

"I'm so glad you could make it. I feel like we never have a chance to talk... you know, just the two of us."

"Hmmm, that's true." She took another bite. "Why do you think that is?"

"I think because you and I both have jobs, so it's harder to find the time."

"Yeah... good point. It's nice here." She nodded as she looked around the living room.

"It is. I love it here, it's even better having Gabe staying with us for the summer. He's even going to house and cat sit while we go on our honeymoon."

"Oh... do you think that's a good idea? Party time... I mean... that's what I would do if I had a whole house to myself when I was his age."

"You pretty much are his age... besides, I trust him. He's a good kid, he was raised right. And, he works with the cops, I think he'd be too embarrassed to get caught doing anything wrong in this town."

"I'm just playing with you. I'm sure everything will be fine. It must be so cool having him here."

"It really is." I picked up a sandwich and sat across from her. "So, how are things with you and Andrew?"

"They're good. I told him about the baby before Jimmy was murdered, and he has been by my side ever since."

"He has? I thought you and Jimmy were getting back together before..."

"Yeah, no. I was actually going to get the rest of my stuff. I wanted to get it out of there before I started to show. I didn't want him getting any idea that this was his baby." Her hand rested on the tiny baby bump.

"Really?" I felt my nose scrunch up and couldn't stop the movement before she saw it.

"What? What's that face about?"

"Oh, nothing, I just had an itch." I duplicated the movement with exaggeration to try to redeem myself.

"Huh... well, yeah, really. I had made up my mind that Andrew could give us the best life."

"Why did you act so... upset?"

"Really?" She shook her head. "I found the man I used to love with his head blown off... how was I supposed to act?"

"Sorry. That was stupid of me, of course."

"Yeah, and I had sent him the text threatening to kill him if he didn't answer me, and I'm the one who finds him dead. I guess you could say my head was a little fucked up." She covered her mouth. "Oops... sorry."

"Don't be, he's heard worse." We both laughed and lightened the mood. "I'm glad it's working out with you and Andrew. He seems like a great guy."

"He is. It feels like I don't deserve him... and it's a little boring... knowing I'll be stuck with one guy forever."

"Ah, don't let yourself sabotage it. If he treats you well, cherish him. There are plenty of ways to spice things up." I winked at her.

"Gross." She giggled. "He really is a sweetheart. He's always checking up on me, asks me if he can bring me home anything, rubs my feet, and goes to all the baby appointments with me. I know he'll be a great dad, too."

"Aww, he sounds amazing. Tim and I are talking about having a baby. Maybe they can grow up together and become friends."

"That'd be cool. Too bad you can't be fat and pregnant with me."

"Oh, stop it, you're beautiful. You're glowing."

"I am?"

"Yeah... pregnancy looks great on you." I smiled to soften the next questions. "So, do you tell Andrew everything? Like, is he your go-to person?"

"Go-to? Like my best friend? Hmm... I hadn't really thought about it, but I guess he is."

"That's nice, isn't it? Tim's mine, too. I can tell him everything. Just between us... do you tell him stuff the ladies share in the group?"

Her face turned red. "Ah... no. Do you?"

"Yeah... but I don't use your names. Sometimes it's just too much to keep inside my head. I'd never share who said what... just if something happened to someone, and I have to let it out... before it just drives me over the edge."

"Hmm... I guess I do that, too. I thought it was bad, so I didn't want to tell you."

"It's okay, we all have to have a release somehow. At least Maggie and Norma have each other, so they can talk about everything. You and I need someone to bounce things off of. No judgment here."

"Andrew gets pretty angry when he hears the stuff I share. He said he can't believe there are people out there who treat women like that... especially children."

"Does he know what happened to you... when you were a little girl?"

"Yeah, I told him. We celebrated when the old pervert died. We were just friends then... we didn't even have any benefits." She laughed. "But, yeah, I guess I tell him everything. He's my Tim. We finally won the lottery."

"We sure did... don't you think it was about damn time?"

"Yeah, but some of the best things are worth waiting for."

"That's so true." I reached for my necklace and felt the warm metal between my fingers. "Have you guys talked about the serial killer at all? I can't stop thinking about it... I mean, since he's who killed Jimmy."

"Yeah, it's pretty crazy. Andrew and I did talk about how lucky I was that I didn't walk into something, you know? I could have been killed, too."

"Oh, wow, I didn't even think about it that way. That's scary."

"Yeah. Andrew was happy Jimmy was finally out of the picture, and he wouldn't be interfering with the baby's life. He knew there was a chance the baby wasn't his. He knew Jimmy had... raped me." She looked up at me, the expression had left her face. "Whoever killed Jimmy sure did us a huge favor."

"Don't you think it's weird that the same person killed Seth? I just can't figure that part out."

"What do you mean? Figure it out? There's a serial killer on the loose... I'm more surprised more people haven't been killed." I couldn't read the tone in her voice.

"Yeah, it is strange they just stopped. I'd bet whoever did it, killed Bobby Green when all the cops were at Jimmy's place... because they had a cop guarding his place, and he was still murdered."

"I'm not too scared, though, since everyone getting killed are perverts or assholes. For the first time, men have to be the ones who are afraid, not us girls."

"Hmm... I guess you're right. If you're a piece of shit, you're probably shaking in your boots."

Sonya laughed. "Yeah, what's the saying... Karma's a bitch?"

The meeting with Sonya did answer some of my questions, but I still don't feel I know any more now than I did before. Andrew had the motive to get rid of Jimmy, hell, so did Sonya. That was a given. The others still remained a mystery. Was it possible Andrew could have killed Jimmy and made it look like the serial killer did it? But the trademark piece... the one that is top secret... how would he know about that? The cops weren't talking... unless Andrew has friends on the force. Friends with a bigger mouth than Tim has.

CHAPTER TWENTY-NINE

"I can't believe this is our last meeting... before the wedding." The excitement pushed up my cheeks as I looked around Norma's living room at my friends.

"I can't wait to see you in your dress... you're going to be a beautiful bride." Norma held my hand. "We've got a surprise for you."

"You do? What is it?" I noticed Maggie, Lily, and Sonya had disappeared.

"Surprise!" The three ladies came back in with a cake, balloons, and gifts. "We couldn't let you get married without throwing you a party." Sonya set the gifts she was holding on the coffee table and sat back down in front of the air conditioner.

"I don't even know what to say. I never expected this." A wave of emotions flooded my body. I pushed them away so I could fully enjoy the day.

"From what I could figure, you've never had a party, and we wanted to make sure we celebrated you. You're such a blessing to all of us... without you... we never would have met." Norma stood up to join the other ladies.

"Oh... don't you worry... I talked them into some of the..." Sonya put her fingers up in air quotes... "Normal bridal shower stuff." She ended with an exaggerated wink.

"Oh, god... that sounds... embarrassing..."

The room exploded in laughter. "I tried to tell them." Norma put her hand to her chest and shook her head.

"Oh, come on... you only live once... and what's wrong with a little... risqué stuff? We're all adults?" Sonya pulled out her phone to take a picture of me standing by the cake. When I looked down, I realized it was in the shape of a penis.

"Oh my god. That's..."

"Amazing? I know!" Sonya came over next to me and snapped a selfie with me. She handed me her phone. "Here, take a picture of me with it." She bent down next to the cake and stuck her tongue out.

"You wait until your baby shower." I handed Sonya back her phone.

"What, are you threatening me with a penis cake? Bring it! It would make one hell of a gender reveal story.... unless it's a girl."

"You're a piece of work." Norma came over and gave me a hug. "Were you surprised?"

"Yes... you really pulled this one over on me."

"I made another cake... one you might want your picture taken next to." Lily left the room and returned with an intricately decorated cake, covered with purple flowers.

"You made this? Wow... this is breathtaking. I had no idea you were so talented."

"Before things got bad with Earl, I used to make cakes. It started out just for friends and family, but then people started ordering them. I've always dreamed of starting my own bakery... I was going to call it... Lily Pads."

"You should do it, Lily. I've never seen anything so beautiful. It's like a work of art, I'm going to feel guilty eating it."

"Oh, don't... that's the best part." She smiled. "I forgot how good baking makes me feel. I'm actually good at it."

"Yes, you are. This is amazing." Maggie examined the cake. "Hey, do you think you could make Sammy her cake? I'd love to hire you."

"Really? That would be amazing... but I couldn't charge you. I don't charge my friends."

"Of course you charge your friends... how else are you going to make money?" Sonya stuck her finger into the frosting of the penis cake and snuck a lick.

Norma swatted her hand away. "Look at this one, she can't keep her hands off of it."

"So, we thought it would be fun to go around the room and tell you something we love about you. A way to remind you that you deserve all the love and happiness life has to offer you. So, how it works is, one of us will write it down in this book." Maggie held up a brown leather journal. "And write down what the other person is saying. That way, when things get hard, or you're having a bad day, you can go to this book and have a reminder of how much you are loved and how important you are to all of us."

"Not to be a buzz kill... but why don't we just record it? That way, instead of just reading it, she can watch it?" Sonya shrugged her shoulders as she pulled out her phone.

"That's not a bad idea, but I still want someone to write it in here, too."

"I want to start." Lily sat on the couch and cleared her throat. "Well, I know I don't know you as well as the others, but you've been a good friend. From the first time I met you at the hospital, you treated me with respect, and you actually listened to me. After so many years of never being heard, you heard me, and you didn't break my trust. It would have been so easy for you to tell my mom what had happened, but you respected my wishes. I don't know anyone else who would have done that.

"You also made me feel welcome, even when I tried to fight you on it. No matter how hard I pushed you away, you never stopped showing up. You helped me see I am worth my dreams. And, watching your love story unfold has given me hope that there are good guys out there."

"That's so nice, Lily. I'm so glad you joined our little group." I placed my hand over my heart.

Maggie handed the notebook to Lily. "Okay, I want to go." She rubbed her hands on the front of her shorts. "When I walked into that conference room, I didn't trust anyone. I was scared, and I didn't think I would ever be able to trust any of you. But you made it feel safe. You made Sonya behave." She gave Sonya a quick smile. "And, you made sure I had time to talk. You helped me see I am a good mom and that I didn't screw my girls up. You don't know how good it felt to hear you say that and be able to believe you. If it wasn't for you, Norma and I never would have met, and my girls and I would be lost souls out in the world. Not only are you a great friend, but you help nurture our friendships, too. When you dropped everything to come help me with Lexi... after everything with Seth, I knew you truly cared... when you tell us you'll be there for us, you actually mean it. You are a one in a million kind of person. I hope the rest of your life treats you as good as you deserve." Maggie wiped the tears out of the corners of her eyes and offered to take her job as scribe back.

I put my hand to my heart and gave Maggie a smile. "Thank you, Maggie, I hope the same for you and your girls."

"Guess it's my turn." Sonya uncrossed her legs to get comfortable. "I don't know where to start. You do such a great job of making everyone else comfortable. Even when you shush me, or remind me I need to be... polite... you do it in a place of respect. Just because you have a degree, you never once made me feel like you're superior to me, or any of us. I think it's super cool you were open with us about your past and you trusted us enough to hear all of the details. I don't know what I would have done without you with the whole thing with Jimmy. I know I can be hard to take sometimes, but you never made me feel unwanted or unwelcome. I feel like I could tell you anything, and you'd understand. I hope we can stay friends forever." She winked and rubbed her belly.

"Ah, Sonya, you're not hard to take. Don't be hard on yourself. You're a good person. Don't ever feel bad for being yourself. That's what I love about you." I returned the wink and smiled.

"Okay, okay... enough about me... this is about you. Looks like we saved the best for last." Sonya nudged Norma.

"Oh, dear. I don't know where to start. It's been an absolute blessing having you in my life. That first day, I knew right away you were going to be someone I could trust. You make it easy to feel comfortable, even in the most uncomfortable situations. You have a gift of bringing people together. We're all proof of that. Not only do I think of you as my good friend, I think of you as a daughter." Norma smiled and looked around the room. "I think that about all of you. I'm so blessed to have four beautiful, talented women in my life. Being an old lady, I didn't think I'd find such a strong connection again. I wish nothing but happiness and love for you for the rest of your days. I love you. I love all of you."

"I love you, too, Norma. I love all of you. I'm the lucky one. You girls changed my life. I never thought I'd have friends again, or that I'd let anyone in again... but look at me now. I have you four, Tim, Gabe, and even my gram. My life is complete now, and I owe it to you all. You helped me see I'm not alone, and that good can come from evil."

"Geez, I don't think I can take much more." Sonya walked over to the pile of gifts and handed me a small pink gift bag with tufts of sparkly white tissue peeking out of the top. "Here, open this one."

I pulled out the tissue paper, and a white negligée fell on to my lap. "Oh, my." I held it up as Sonya snapped a picture.

"There's more." She giggled behind the camera.

When I reached in the bag I pulled out the tiny white string. "What is it?"

"Oh, don't act all innocent. Not like you've never seen a G-string before. I wanted to make sure you had something sexy on for your first time as husband and wife."

"Wow, Sonya, great way to turn our feel-good session into

something sleazy." Maggie crossed her arms and pressed her back into the couch.

"Are you being serious?" Sonya lifted her eyes.

"Why don't you give her the white bag." Maggie pointed to the other gift bag on the coffee table.

Sonya handed me the gift. The bag was not as elegantly put together but still looked better than something I could have thrown together. I pulled out the tissue paper, and an even skimpier piece of lingerie came out with it. I turned to look at Maggie. "Ahh... am I missing something?"

Maggie relaxed her body. "No, I figured you didn't need to have underwear."

"Oh, I see what you did there." Sonya nodded her head and pointed to the side of her head. "Great minds."

"Oh, my goodness. You ladies have your mind in the gutter." Norma walked over and picked up a small white box, wrapped in a pink bow, and handed it to me.

I unwrapped the box as Norma watched me. Inside was a teacup, one from the set she always served us tea in. I held the cup and cradled it in my hands. "Oh, Norma, it's perfect."

"I wanted to make sure we could always have tea together, even when we're apart. If you're ever having a bad day and need a little love, just pour yourself a cup of tea, and we can have a drink together."

"Aww, this is probably the sweetest gift I have ever received. But, I don't want to think about not being able to stop over to share a cup with you. You better not be going anywhere."

"Well, you never know what can happen. I just wanted to make sure you were prepared in case. That's all."

"You already saw my gift. Plus, I'm going to make cupcakes to bring to the wedding."

"Thank you, Lily, I can't wait to taste it. It's perfect, everything is. I don't even know what to say. You ladies really know how to make me feel special." I wiped the tears off my cheeks.

We enjoyed the delicious cake and shared silly stories as we let the rest of the day fade around us. I couldn't wait to share the gifts with Tim. It was only a few short days away.

CHAPTER THIRTY

When I arrived at Gram's, she was waiting for me with her purse in her lap. "Oh, Gram, you look beautiful."

"Ah, this?" She used the arms of her chair to push herself up. "I'm so excited the day is finally here." She walked over to me and wrapped her arms around me.

"Me, too. Maybe now I can stop worrying." I gave her my arm to help steady her as we walked out. "Are you sure it's okay I take you?"

"I'm a grown woman, I don't have to report to anyone." She flipped off the TV and stopped by the door. "Oh, wait, would you be able to bring this to the post office for me? The pharmacy sent me someone else's medications."

"Sure." I picked up the small box. "I don't think they can even take it back once it's left the building."

"Ah, let them deal with that."

"We're on a tight schedule today. We have to get to the

Bed and Breakfast so we can meet the other ladies and get our hair done. I booked a spot for you, too."

She ruffled her hair. "Is there something wrong with my curls?"

"No, I just wanted to include you... since you're my maid of honor."

"I'm just teasing." She smiled and continued to look out the window. "It's been ages since I've gotten out of the house, it'll be a real treat."

"Gram? Did you hear what I said?"

"Huh?" She turned to look at me.

"I said since you're my maid of honor." I gave her a quick glance and focused my attention back on the road.

"Oh, my. I guess I missed that. You want me? I'm an old lady... I can barely walk."

"I do. I couldn't think of anyone better to have by my side." I reached over and held out my hand for her to take. "We have a chair set up for you, so you can rest if you need to. Don't worry about anything. I just want you there with me."

"Oh, Valerie, you always were a sweet girl."

When we arrived at the Bed and Breakfast, the grounds were decorated and ready for the ceremony. I pulled my car in front of the double doors where Maggie and Norma were waiting to help Gram into the dressing room. After I parked my car, I looked at the clock and felt nausea creep in as I did the mental countdown in my head. In just three hours, I would be Mrs. Timothy Phillips. I closed my eyes and tried to channel as much calm as I could find. Today was going to be a good day, I wasn't going to let my self-doubt ruin it.

Sonya was out on the lawn waving for me to hurry up.

"Come on, you're going to be late for your own wedding. Get your pretty little ass in here." She gave my butt a slap as I walked by. "You're going to do great, don't you worry."

"How'd you know I was worried?"

"Val, you're going to need a ton of makeup to get some color back on your face. Just relax. Today is your day. Don't let anything take that away from you."

Gram was already getting her hair done when I walked into the dressing room. Norma was sharing a cup of tea with her. "I knew you two would get along."

"We were just sharing stories about our sweet Valerie." Norma stood up to give me a hug. "Only a few more hours as Miss Williamson." She brushed the hair out of my face. "You deserve this... all of this."

My body trembled as I paced the room. "I think I'm going to be sick. I never thought about it as my last day as... me."

"Oh, stop that. You'll still be you. You're just adding a loving, caring, devoted husband. You can be Mrs. Valerie Williamson-Phillips if you want."

"That's awfully close to Wilson Philips. I don't know how I feel about that." I reached for my necklace, only to remember I had taken it off.

"What, you don't want to hold on?" Maggie giggled.

"I see what you did there." Her joke eased some of my nerves. "Okay, I can do this." I rolled my shoulders and shook my hands at my sides.

Lily and Maggie were next to get their hair and makeup done. I slipped out of the room before it was my turn. I asked Gabe to meet me in the gazebo before he started getting ready with the other guys. He was standing with his back to me, admiring the view. The sight of the boy I ached for, all those years, filled my heart. He was a true gift from an unthinkable situation. He was what made me believe there was good in the world.

"It's a beautiful place, isn't it?" I walked through the entrance to stand next to him.

"Yeah, you guys picked a perfect day. This place is amazing."

"We did get lucky with the weather. I'm so thankful you're here. And even more grateful you'll be standing next to Tim. My two favorite guys." I pulled the envelope out of the pocket of my sweatshirt and handed it to him. "I want you to have this."

After he opened it and started to read, the tears hit the paper. He held the half of my necklace in the palm of his hand and squeezed it. "I don't know what to say."

"I wanted you to have the full heart. I don't need my half anymore, because I have you. I wore it every day since the day they took you from me, but I don't need it any longer. Having you in my life completes me and makes my broken heart whole. Now, you can have my whole heart."

He pulled me into a hug and kissed my cheek. "You know, I always knew you loved me. My mom told me I was loved. I just didn't understand how much." He stepped back and pulled a gift from his shirt pocket. "I got you something, too."

My hands shook as I pulled off the black ribbon and unwrapped the box. When I opened the velvet cover, I felt the size of my heart double inside my chest. "Oh, my gosh. I love it." Tears fell onto the silver heart, engraved with the three letters I longed for. *Mom*.

"Turn it over." Gabe brushed a tear out of his eye.

When I flipped the heart over, it was inscribed with three of the most beautiful words I'd ever seen. *Love, your son.* "Oh, Gabe. You don't know what this means to me. I love it. I love you. You've made me the happiest I've ever been."

"I love you, too, Mom."

Gabe and I walked back to the house and parted ways inside. The clock was not slowing down. Sonya and Norma were just leaving to get their dresses on, and I was late for my hair and makeup.

"I told them you'd be late," Sonya said as she pushed me to the beautician's chair. "Come on, Val, you're killing me. You still need to get your dress on."

After all of us were in our dresses, with our hair and makeup complete, I retrieved the bag I had brought with me. Inside the bag, I pulled out five wrapped gifts and handed them out to each of the ladies. "I wanted to give you each something, as a thank you for sharing today with me. I couldn't find anything to truly express what you each mean to me, so just take this as a small token of the love I hold for you."

As they unwrapped their gifts, they each held up their matching bracelet, a silver cuff with the words 'Forever Friends, Always Sisters' engraved on them. I held up my wrist. "I have one, too. These are for whenever we are feeling down or lonely. It'll be a reminder we have each other, no matter where life takes us. We're in it together from now on."

Gram held up her bracelet close to her glasses with her

eyes squinted, she tried to read the engraving on hers. "I can't make out what it says, can you read it to me?"

"It says, '*Forever in my heart, with love, Valerie.*'"

"Aww, honey, it's beautiful." She held out her wrist for me to put her bracelet on.

I drew in some oxygen and looked around the room. "It's show time. I can do this... I can do this."

"Val, you're absolutely stunning." Lily gave me a hug. "You'll do great."

"Break a leg... no wait... don't listen to me." Sonya wrapped her arms around me. "You do clean up well." She took a step back to take another look and gave me a wink. "He's a lucky man."

I held out my foot and shook my white Birkenstocks. "I wore these just so I wouldn't twist my ankle."

"You are as beautiful as your soul is pure." Maggie leaned over and gave me a kiss on the cheek as she walked out with Gram on her arm.

I smiled as I tried to accept her compliment. But she didn't know the dark secrets I held. I didn't want them to haunt me on my wedding day, but it seemed as though there was no escaping them.

Norma walked over and pushed the loose strand of hair behind my ear. "Shake those thoughts out of that pretty little head of yours." She took my hands in hers and kissed my forehead. "Today is about *you*."

As she started to walk out the door to join the other ladies, I grabbed her hand. "Norma, don't go." I squeezed my eyes closed to push the tears back in. "Would you walk me down the aisle? I don't want to go alone."

"Oh, honey, I'd be honored."

The music had started playing, and I knew everyone was waiting for me. As Norma led me to the walkway sprinkled in pink and red rose petals, Tom Petty's *Angel Dream* started playing.

Norma gave my hand a squeeze. "Are you ready, dear?"

I nodded and clutched the bouquet of white and purple roses tight. It was time to walk to the man of my dreams and start living our happily ever after. My white floor-length chiffon dress lightly blew in the slight breeze. I felt like an angel, and for today, I could pretend.

Tim was shaking as he watched me walk toward him. He rubbed his eyes and held his hands together in front of his black tuxedo. His satin, dark purple bowtie matched the handkerchief in his pocket. Norma and I stood at the end of the walkway, where she gave me a kiss on the cheek and found her position next to the other ladies. It was better than any dream I ever had as a little girl about my wedding day. My gram, my son, four of the best friends I could ever ask for, and a man who loved me for *me* and would bend over backward to protect me. There was nothing more I could ask for.

It was all too perfect. Like a fairytale, but I'm old enough to know they don't exist... and if they do, there is always something waiting to steal the joy away. Something was bound to go wrong. It had to. I didn't deserve this much happiness. I reached for my necklace, the one from Gabe, closed my eyes, and shook the self-sabotaging thoughts. Not today. Norma was right, today was *my* day.

I took the steps to join Tim at the altar. He mouthed the words" you're beautiful," as he took my hand. The justice of the peace started talking about love and honesty, and I was lost again in my guilt-ridden thoughts. I wanted to tell Tim everything... but there were some things I knew I never could. I thought about raising a family together and keeping secrets from him. I thought about growing old together, and still, never sharing with him the pieces of me I knew he would despise. *What was I doing?* A cold sweat distracted me as my empty stomach started to gnaw at me.

I grabbed Tim's hand tighter as everything started to spin. I heard Norma whisper. "Don't let them get to you. You are worth being loved." Her voice grounded me and brought me back into my body. I inhaled deeply through my nose and slowly pushed it out my pursed lips, just in time to repeat the words that would bind us in marriage.

"I now pronounce you husband and wife. You may kiss the bride." The small crowd of fifty cheered as Tim bent down to kiss me. When his lips touched mine, I knew everything was going to be alright. I would figure out a way to make it work. I would do my best to never tell another lie to him.

When we walked back down the aisle covered in rose petals, I was able to see the people we shared this day with. Before they were just a blur. These were the people who mattered in our world, and I was grateful to share this memory with them.

Tim and I spent time with the photographer. The wedding party joined us, completing the necessary photos to immortalize the day. When we were finished, it was time to enter the reception tent and start the party. Norma offered to take Gram back home and left before it started. The excitement of the day wore Gram out. I was just glad she stayed long enough to join our family photo. It was one that would make the living room wall.

Tim and I took our seats and continued on with all the traditional parts of the reception. We danced our first dance to *Come to Me* by the Goo Goo Dolls. It wasn't Tom Petty, but it was the perfect song for us. *Because You Loved Me* by Celine Dion started to play, and Gabe tapped Tim on the shoulder.

"Excuse me, can I have this dance?" Tim nodded as he placed my hand in Gabe's.

He wrapped me in a hug and then took a step back. "When I heard this song as a little boy, I always thought about you. I knew if it wasn't for your love, I would never have ended up with the life I had. The only thing missing in it was you, but I always knew we'd be together again."

"Aww, Gabe. That means so much to me. I only wanted the best for you. I'm grateful it worked out the way it did. I had no idea the letter I wrote as a heartbroken fifteen-year-old would have given you so much love and comfort. I guess I was wiser than I knew."

"It must be where I get it from."

"I'll gladly take credit for that, but the real credit goes to Beth and Paul. They are such nice people. I couldn't have hand-picked better parents for you. I guess the angels were watching over you."

"And, you, too. I always asked them to take care of you in my prayers."

"What a sweet boy you were. You're going to make some woman very happy."

When Tim and I were done doing all the things expected of us, we joined Sonya and the ladies at their table. Andrew was Sonya's guest, and I was anxious to talk with him. He didn't look like anything I expected. He looked like he was at least ten years older than Sonya and looked like he just walked off the cover of a GQ magazine. He had a thick mane of grey hair and a goatee to match. His eyes looked like a stormy summer sky. He appeared to be much more sophisticated than I anticipated. He was the total opposite of Jimmy.

"You must be Andrew." I held my hand out for him.

"Yes. Congrats."

"Thanks. It's so good to finally meet you. I've heard so much about you."

He raised his eyebrows and looked at Sonya. "That can't be good." His tone was hard to tell if he was sarcastic or serious.

Sonya sent me daggers and grit her teeth. "Valerie."

"Don't worry, it was all good. You're a great guy. I'm glad you have each other."

"Well, that's a relief." He pretended to wipe the sweat off his forehead.

"She didn't tell me you were funny."

"No, she doesn't appreciate my humor." He took a drink of scotch. "She's told me a lot about you, too. You sound like a pretty great friend."

"Thanks. I knew I liked you." I clicked my beer against his glass. After taking a drink, I had enough liquid courage to continue the conversation. "I'm so glad you've been there for her... you know... since the whole thing with Jimmy." I felt Tim's hand on my back.

Andrew took a slow drink, set his glass down, and furrowed his brows.

"Crazy, though, don't you think... that they found out he was killed by the serial killer." I took another sip of beer and let the cold liquid slide down my throat.

"How so?" He tilted his head, his hand on his hip.

"Just that he's one of the unsolved murders... but the same person killed four other guys. I just think it's... interesting. That's all." I held his gaze until he looked away.

"Yeah, I guess you could say that." He nodded and turned his attention to Tim. "You're a detective, right?"

Tim cleared his throat. "Yup, that's right."

"And? Do you have any leads? Any idea who it could be?"

"I really can't say much about the case. And I really should go mingle with some of the other guests." He extended his hand. "It was great to meet you." Tim stood up and reached for my hand. "Let's go see how my mom's doing."

Frustration kept me from moving. I wanted to keep talking and asking questions. I had a list as long as the table I wanted answers to. I also knew my timing was off. It wasn't the night for it. I stood up and took my husband's hand. "It was very nice to meet you. I look forward to seeing you again."

"What the hell was that, Val?"

"What? I was just making small talk." I shrugged my shoulders and drank the rest of my drink.

"But... it was awkward. You're cut off." He pulled me into a kiss. "Let's get out of here and get some rest before we head out tomorrow."

CHAPTER THIRTY-ONE

"Good morning, Mrs. Philips." Tim rolled over and kissed me.

My hand went to my head. "Ugh. I think I drank too much."

"You think?" With a wink he laughed and pulled me close to him. "That just means we'll have to make it official tonight."

"Oh, man. I'm so sorry. The beers just went down so smoothly... and it helped give me enough nerve to socialize. Did I mention I'm socially awkward?"

"Hmmm... well, not in those words." He brushed the hair off my face. "But it did get a little... uncomfortable with Andrew."

I pulled the blanket over my head. "I really did that, didn't I? He'll probably never want to talk to me again."

"Nah, it wasn't *that* bad. Close, but I think you have a chance to redeem yourself. Don't give it a second thought, just blame the alcohol."

"I'm sorry I embarrassed you."

"Don't ever say that. You could never embarrass me. I'm the luckiest man alive that I get to call you my wife."

I picked up his phone on the nightstand and saw we had slept in. "Shit, we have to get on the road."

"We have some time. You're not excited, are you?"

"Who, me? No... it's just not every day I get to be inches away from the hottest... I mean... my favorite singer of all time."

"I get it... tonight will be just you and Tom Petty, and me and fifty thousand other people." He laughed as he pulled on his jeans.

"You really do make all of my dreams come true."

"That sounds like the slogan to Disney or something. But I don't plan to stop. Get ready for a lifetime of awesomeness."

"I can't wait.... it goes both ways, too. I want to start our family. I can't wait to create a perfect little human with you."

"For real? When are we talking... no rush... well... unless..."

"Well, if we have time, we can start now."

"You don't know how happy this makes me." He held out his fingers and started counting. "So... that means maybe by Easter..."

"Maybe... but it might not be that quick. But I'm up for trying. I stopped taking my pills a couple weeks ago."

"So, you've had this up your sleeve that long and didn't tell me?"

"It was a surprise. Hell, I might already be pregnant. We'll just have to wait and see now."

We piled our luggage into the back of Tim's Touareg and hit the road. New York City was the destination set in the

GPS. I'd never been to the city, and if it were for any other reason, I might have opted for a different destination. It was a six-hour drive unless we hit traffic. Lawrenceville didn't have traffic until the cows escaped from their field. I couldn't focus on the number of people I would be around, or the fear would have paralyzed me.

"Can we make a deal?" Tim rested his hand on my thigh.

"Maybe? What do you have in mind?"

"Don't get mad at me... but... can we not talk about work for the next few days? Yours or mine? I just don't want to have to think about the case or about anything like that. I want this to be our time."

"That's fair. I guess I have been a little... obsessed with the case... I guess I get that way a lot."

"Passionate. You're not obsessed... just passionate. See, it just sounds better."

"Always looking out for me, huh?" I nodded as I looked out the window. "I love that about you."

"Oh, yeah, it's only going to get worse when you get pregnant... then I'll be protecting two... or three of you."

"Three?"

"Yeah... twins." He laughed. "I guess it's not a good time to tell you they run in my family."

"I guess that just means we'd get it over with faster." I didn't want him to know the thought of multiple babies terrified me. I was just getting comfortable with the idea of one... I knew if I fixated on more, I'd change my mind.

Since I wasn't able to ask the questions burning a hole inside my head, we filled the ride with music and talked about our future. It was fun to plan for the days ahead when I had someone I was looking forward to sharing it with.

After we checked into the hotel, we changed into our Tom Petty t-shirts and headed for Madison Square Garden. Tim purchased fan club tickets, and we were able to bypass the line. Inside we made our way to the front of the stage and found our seats; dead center. Tom's microphone would be right in front of me.

The room went dark, and The Wallflowers took the stage. I looked around the stadium as they performed, unable to hear the words they sang as the excitement flooded me. This was my first time in a crowd this size, my first concert... the first time sharing the same air as the man whose music got me through so many difficult times in my life. There was a song for everything; the soundtrack to my life.

When the band was done, the lights came back on, and a crew got the stage ready for Tom Petty and the Heartbreakers. Tim put his arm around me and pulled me close. He bent down to get close to my ear. "Are you having fun?"

I nodded. My eyes unable to leave the stage, in anticipation, I might catch a glimpse of Tom. When the room went dark, the crowd began to scream. My heart danced in my chest as I heard the guitar start to strum. *I Won't Back Down* blasted out of the speakers. A smile spread across my face as I looked up and saw *him* standing there. Maybe it was the exhilaration, but I could have sworn he winked at me. Stuck in a trance, I sang along to every song. Unable to move more than my lips, I soaked up each and every word.

After the final cord filled the stadium, Tom and the band

took a bow, nodding and waving to every corner. As he walked off stage, he blew me a kiss and tossed me a guitar pic.

Tim caught it before it fell to the floor. "Oh, my god, Val. That's awesome."

It was beyond awesome, beyond anything I could have imagined. For the first time in my life, I was able to show my appreciation and he saw me. The adrenaline from the night would be enough to sustain me for the next week. The smile I walked out of the building with permeated my soul. This was something I would never forget.

"I'm not sure how much more of this I can take," I shouted as we waited to exit the parking garage.

"What's that?"

"Everything being so... perfect... magical. I'm afraid I'm going to wake up and find out it's all been a dream."

Tim squeezed my hand. "Did you feel that?"

"Yeah."

"Okay then. There's proof you're not dreaming... and I'll give you something better to prove it once we make it back to the hotel."

And just like that, the storybook ending to a storybook day. The thoughts from the day before started to creep in, but I closed my eyes and pictured Norma reminding me it was my day. Good people can do things they're not proud of and still be good. The problem I was having was believing what I did was bad. It was for the greater good. There was at least one other person out there that could agree with me. The only thing left was for me to figure out who it was.

CHAPTER THIRTY-TWO

My time off from work was coming to an end, after returning from our trip to the city, I had three days left to enjoy the solitude. Having the time off made me realize it may be time for a career change. Tim and I talked about being a stay-at-home mom once we started a family, but I wasn't sure that was the path I wanted to take. The more I worked with the group, the more I had seen how great it felt to work with people who had suffered at the hands of someone else.

Working with the dead and their families was good before. It gave me the chance to not get connected to my clients, but now, I ached for that connection. After hearing what the ladies thought about me, I wanted to be able to offer that to others. If I could turn my suffering into someone else's healing, then all that pain would have been worth something.

With the steam circling out of my coffee mug, I picked up my iPad and slid open the door to the deck. I closed my eyes as the smell of fresh-cut grass filled my nose. The warmth of the sun offered just the right amount of comfort as I sat down in the lawn chair facing the fire pit Tim and Gabe had built. I took a sip of coffee, the bitterness biting my tongue, reminding me I forgot to add the sweetener and cream. I placed the cup in the grass, still wet from the morning dew, and watched it topple over, spilling the black coffee. "I wasn't going to drink it anyway."

I let the serenity and safety of my backyard bring me back to the Zen I had channeled when I first stepped outside. I opened my iPad and adjusted the brightness settings so I could see the screen and logged onto the Indeed app. It'd been a while since I searched for a new job, but it was time. I knew I had to challenge myself in ways that used to be uncomfortable to have my best life.

As always, Lawrenceville didn't have a lot to offer. I toyed with the idea of starting a private practice, but that would require more responsibility than I was up for. I clicked out of the app and closed my eyes, letting the golden rays of the sun encase me. The melody of the birds lulled me to sleep.

My hand on the doorknob, I opened Gram's door, but she wasn't in her recliner. The bracelet I had given her was resting in the middle of her chair. I picked it up to notice the inscription had been scratched off. The clink of the metal echoed throughout the room as it dropped to the floor. "Gram!" I raced down the hall to her bedroom. Her bed was empty. "Gram, where are you?" I pulled open the drawers; they were empty. All of them. Her closet, too. The walls of her apartment began closing in around me, suffocating me. I wasn't able to leave. My mouth opened, but no words came.

A jolt woke me up, my eyes shot open. My heart raced as

the images from the dream wouldn't leave my head. I opened the nanny cam app... Gram's chair was empty. My heart dropped. My eyes glued to the screen, I watched and waited for her to return. The minutes passed like molasses. No movement at all.

I rewound the video feed. A day earlier, the same image was displayed on the screen. Two days, still nothing. Three days... there she was. Not Gram, but Mom. I took a screenshot and zoomed in. This was the first time I'd seen my mother in over sixteen years. Everything remained the same, it looked like she had a way to make time stand still. The hair on the back of my neck stood up.

I returned to the video feed and saw her going through Gram's things. It looked like she was going through her mail... no... her purse. She took something out and brought it under the lamp. It looked like her eyes were squinting... my heart dropped to the pit of my stomach. It had to be the bracelet. The one that tied me to Gram, the one that would let her know I had been around. She put the item in her back pocket and went back to the purse. When she had her wallet, I saw her tear off a check and tucked it into the pile of papers she had already collected.

But where was Gram? What was she doing in Gram's house without her? Gram never left her apartment. I felt the warm liquid turn cold as it fell on my arm. What if she were dead? What if she died, and I didn't get to say goodbye? What if... how would I find out?

I got out of the chair and started pacing the lawn, unable to get out of my own way. I had to go find out. I raced back into the house, grabbed my keys, and got in the car. My hands tapped against the steering wheel as I tried to fight off the tears. The worst-case scenarios played on repeat in my mind. At the stoplight, I knew I couldn't go. I knew I couldn't risk seeing Mom.

I changed the directional signal to turn the other way and followed the road to the only place I knew I could find the comfort I craved. I pounded on the door, no longer able to keep the emotions buried.

The door opened. "Oh, my goodness, Val, what's the matter?" Norma ushered me in and hugged me before I could answer.

"It's... it's..." The sobs wouldn't let me spit the rest of the words out.

"Take a deep breath." She took both of my hands in hers and took one with me. "Now, slow down, dear." She pushed the hair out of my face.

"It's... Gram... I think she's... gone."

"Gone? Why do you think that? What happened?" She led me to the living room and sat next to me on the couch.

"I was checking the app... and she wasn't there... but my mom was. She probably killed her... she probably found out we were seeing each other."

"App? What do you mean?"

"I put a camera in Gram's place, so I could keep an eye on her... I had a dream... nightmare actually, and something told me to check it... but she wasn't there... and then Mom was..."

"But you don't know for sure. Have you called anyone?"

"No, I don't know who to call. I was on my way there, but I knew I couldn't face her... not yet... not alone."

She stood up and got the copy of an old phonebook.

"What's the name of the hospital down there? We can call them to see if maybe she's there."

"Umm... I think it's Saint Mary's."

Norma flipped through the pages and ran her finger down the page. "Oh, here it is." She picked up the phone and dialed the number. "Hello, I'd like to talk with my sister, Marianne Cooper." She winked at me as she waited. "Yes, I'll hold." She handed me the phone. "She's there."

I let go of the tension I had been holding and let my shoulders fall as the weight lifted off. "Gram? It's Val."

"Hi, dear. How did you know I was here?" Her voice was just loud enough for me to make out the words.

"I just had a feeling... are you okay?"

"Oh, I'm going to be fine. I just had a fall."

"A fall?"

"Yes, I must have tripped over something in the night."

"When do you get to go home? I want to come see you."

"I'm not sure yet... your mother thinks I need to go into a home."

"That's ridiculous. You're not going, are you?"

"I'm not sure I have a choice, dear. I don't think it's safe for me at home alone anymore. And... your mom found out about you."

My hair on my neck stood up again, and my breathing increased as the heat of pent up anger released inside me. "Was she..."

"She was surprised. She said she didn't want me talking with you, but I told her it wasn't up to her."

"Gram... was this before or after your fall?"

"Oh, I don't remember... hmm... it might have been before. The nurse is coming back to wash me up, call me later if you want."

"I love you, Gram." I clicked off the phone and handed it back to Norma. My teeth clenched as my pulse played a beat against my neck. The heat from the fury burned as it flared out my nostrils.

"Is everything alright, Val? Is she okay?"

"I hate her." My fists balled at my sides. "I absolutely fucking hate her."

Norma inhaled deeply through her nose and released it through her mouth. "Come on, do it with me."

I tried to match my breathing with hers, but the rage inside me wouldn't budge. "I can't relax this away." I cracked my knuckles and stared straight ahead. "She told Gram to stop talking to me." Tears from my childhood found their way out of my eyes. My heart open and bleeding.

Norma pulled me close to her and started rocking me. "Hush. Hush. Let it out, honey. Let go of that pain."

I gave in and let Norma love the broken child yearning to be released. Her love was the only thing strong enough to quiet the rage. Norma's soft touch on my hair made me remember the times Gram did the same when I was a little girl.

"There, there, sweet, Valerie. Let it all out."

My head burrowed into Norma's arms. "I'd kill the bitch... but I can't, not while her mother is alive. I couldn't watch Gram suffer."

"It's a nice thought, though, isn't it?" Her body vibrated

with laughter. "Get that evil woman out of your mind. Don't let her hurt you any longer. You're in control now, Val. You're powerful. And strong. She can't hurt you anymore."

I nodded and sat up. "You're right. I am in control. She can't keep Gram from me. She is powerless."

CHAPTER THIRTY-THREE

I planned it so my first day back to work would be a group day. I knew it would be just what I needed to get back into the swing of things. After hours of catching up on emails and messages, it was a nice break. The dying didn't have as much appeal to me as they once did. Death wasn't something I chased any longer, it seemed to be something I ran from now. Having people I loved now made me understand the pain of losing people on a level I never understood before. The finality of death was not something I wanted a reminder of.

I sat in the conference room as I waited for the ladies to arrive. The buzz of laughter alerted me Norma, Maggie, and Lily had arrived. "Hey, everybody. I'm so happy to see you."

"Maggie was just telling us a joke... go on, tell her." Lily jabbed Maggie in the side with her elbow.

"Okay... okay... What's the difference between a porcupine and a Corvette?"

"I have no idea?" I titled my head as I waited for the punchline.

"The porcupine has pricks on the outside." Maggie snorted.

I closed my eyes and shook my head. "Oh, my word. Where did you hear that?"

"I saw it on a me-me."

"It's meme." Sonya corrected her as she joined us.

"Oh, good, we're all here. I couldn't wait for you all to get here... today has been brutal." I wiped my forehead with my sleeve. "I really only come here to see you."

"Same." Sonya smiled. "I have some good news."

"What is it?" Maggie sat forward in her seat.

"Andrew and I found out what the baby is."

"And?" Maggie and I asked in unison.

"And, you'll have to wait until we announce it."

"Ugh... you're killing me. I just want to go buy some baby clothes." I crossed my arms and pressed my back against my chair.

"Oh, I'm teasing... it's a... girl!"

"Oh, how sweet." Norma put her hand to her cheek.

"Best of luck." Maggie giggled. "Girls are the hardest."

"I'm excited... I wanted a girl."

"I knew it was a girl. You're too girly to have a boy." Lily nodded and paused. "No offense... I mean, you're beautiful and..."

"None taken, I know... I was kind of scared if it was a boy."

"Looks like a shopping trip is in our future." I rubbed my hands together.

"You want to hear something funny?" Sonya pulled out her phone and started scrolling through it. "I met this girl in a domestic violence support group online. And we got to talking about things... and get this..." She put the phone down. "Her boyfriend was found murdered, too... the same way. A bullet in the head."

"Oh, my." Norma turned to look at Sonya.

"And... she said she goes to a support group, too, and she said there was this old lady in it. So I told her we have one of those, too."

Norma raised her eyebrows and laughed. "Thanks a lot."

"She said her name was Martha... but she sounded so much like you." Sonya turned to look at Norma and picked up her phone. "When she friended me on Facebook, she was looking through my pictures and saw the picture of all of us in our matching dresses... and she said you look just like Martha."

"All of us old ladies look alike. If you've seen one, you've seen them all."

"But... she said Martha was this super awesome person. Always helping the other girls out. She said Martha went missing, and they still haven't found her. Then she said Martha hadn't shared her story before she disappeared. They never knew why she was there ... and then I got to thinking... you've never shared your story."

Norma's rosy cheeks went white and she squinted her eyes. "Not everyone likes to share."

"Sonya, I think you need to drop it," Maggie spoke up.

"One of the group rules is no one has to share. We have to be respectful of that..."

Sonya cut me off. "Yeah, I get it, but don't you think it's strange? Do you have a sister, Norma? I mean, we don't know anything about you."

"Sonya, Maggie was right. Drop it." I looked at Norma and saw she was fidgeting in her seat. "Norma, it's okay, you don't have to share, you never do. We love you just the same."

"Why do you have my picture on Facebook anyway? And, why are you sharing personal information with somebody you don't even know? What else did you tell her? Did you share what these girls told you, too?" Norma stood up and grabbed her purse. "I want you to take my picture down this instant. I didn't give you permission to share it." The door slammed behind her.

"Way to go, Sonya." Maggie got up and chased after Norma.

"Did you... share our stories with that girl?" Lily turned her head to look at Sonya.

"No, I swear. Just the picture. I said we had a cool group, that we became a family. She saw the picture and she assumed it was of our group. That's all."

"It's essential we can all trust each other. I think you should apologize to Norma."

"But what's the big deal? I mean, she hasn't shared... I just think it's strange she knows all of our secrets, but we don't know anything about her. And, why did she get so upset? What's that all about?"

"People react to things differently, just like they heal differently. Maybe Norma doesn't need to talk about her trauma, because being with people who understand what she's been through is healing enough. It's not our place to judge."

"I'm not judging... I was simply asking a question. She's the one who freaked out." Sonya shrugged her shoulders.

"I can see where she's coming from," Lily said. "I never would have shared if I thought it would leave this group. It's scary. Some of our lives are at risk every day, and the not knowing is enough to drive you mad... and then to think the people you thought were safe ended up being unsafe... well, it's a lot."

Sonya's voice increased. "But, I'm not unsafe. I had a question. That's all." She crossed her arms.

"Where is your friend from? Maybe if Norma knew she wasn't going to see her in the grocery store, it might make it better."

"She lives in Maine... Bar Harbor, I think she said." She focused her attention on her phone. "There... the photo is down."

"Thank you. I'm sure she'll appreciate knowing you removed it."

"I didn't do it to be a jerk. I was excited to share it... it was a fun day, I just wanted people to know how awesome you all are." She hung her head.

"It's okay, I know you weren't trying to upset anyone." Norma's reaction was alarming. It was not a side of her I had ever witnessed. Her story was one of those mysteries I wanted to solve, but I didn't want to pry. I figured she may share as time went on, but now, I knew that chance was gone.

"The other part I thought was odd was... her boyfriend was believed to be killed by a serial killer, too. She said this one didn't go after sex offenders... but get this... he went after the guys from the group."

"I'm not following you." I squinted my eyes and rubbed the bridge of my nose to chase away the migraine.

"The guys who had messed with the girls in the group. So, this girl's boyfriend, another lady's husband... the ladies would share, and then the guy would die... there were four in total."

"So, like a genie granting wishes?" Lily wrinkled her nose.

"Kind of. I guess it didn't happen that seamlessly. It wasn't like they mentioned the guy, and then he dropped dead... it just happened over time." Sonya's foot bounced.

"And, did she say if anyone was ever caught?" I asked.

"She said no one ever was. It just kind of dropped out of the news."

"Did she say if anything was linking these guys together... aside from the group?"

"Hmm ... she didn't say. I guess she just assumed it was connection enough."

I shook my head as the new information percolated in my head. "You said she was from Bar Harbor?"

"Yeah, why?"

"No reason."

CHAPTER THIRTY-FOUR

At home, I took out my iPad and typed in *serial killer in Bar Harbor, Maine*, and waited for the results to populate. Nothing matching my search appeared. There were titles of murder mysteries and a few news stories, but nothing fit what I was looking for. I tried again, this time using *murders in Bar Harbor, Maine*.

This search netted better results. The first link I clicked on was a news story about a man that was found shot in the head. There was no mention of him being on the sex offender registry or any other crime for that matter. It said he was found by a neighbor after they noticed an odor. I thought back to the guys killed in Lawrenceville and didn't remember that being the case with any of them. All of the men here were found right away, at least before they started to stink.

The next article was about another guy, found shot in the head at his apartment. Again, there was no mention of this man being a menace to society. I tried to remember the details Sonya shared, to pull up a name or time frame. I'm not sure she mentioned either. I figured all I needed was the town, and I would have been able to Google the rest. No such luck.

I did find the two other murders Sonya's friend had talked about, but they didn't have any more details than the first two. The only name I did remember was Martha. The woman who looked like Norma. I typed *Martha, Bar Harbor, Maine,* to see if I could find a picture of the woman. Without a last name, I wasn't sure what I would find.

On top of the search results, *Martha Newell, 63, of Bar Harbor, Maine, is still missing* got my attention. When I clicked on the story, it brought me to a news article. It said Martha had been missing for three years and was presumed dead. The photo of Martha did resemble Norma. I wondered if maybe she did have a sister she didn't want to talk about. Was that the reason she got so upset?

"What are you doing?" Tim stood behind me before I noticed he was home.

"You scared the crap out of me." I stood up and gave him a kiss. "You're home early, where's Gabe?"

"He's in the car, we wanted to see if you wanted to join us for pizza. We thought we'd go out tonight."

The last time I'd been in that building was when I was with Jane. Somehow, I managed to always get Tim to pick up our orders. "Ah, sure. Let me grab my sweatshirt."

"It's the middle of summer, Val."

"I know... but that place is like the morgue."

"Yum... what a pleasant thought."

I tapped his chest as I walked past him. "You know what I mean."

Gabe was getting out of the car to let me have the front when he saw I was coming.

"Hey, get back in there. You don't have to move for me." I got into the backseat and put my sweatshirt on as the air conditioning gave me goosebumps. "How was your day, guys?"

"I actually got to see Tim in action... we got to go on a high-speed pursuit."

"That sounds dangerous."

"You sound like a mom." Tim looked at me in the rearview mirror.

"It was so much fun. This guy ran a red light, so Tim put his lights and sirens on, but the guy kept on going. We chased the guy through half the town."

"Did you end up catching him?"

"Yeah, the guy ran into a mailbox... you know... one of those big blue things?" Gabe dropped his head, laughed, and slapped his knee. "You should have seen his face."

"Who's? Tim's or the guy?"

"Funny, Val." Tim shook his head. I reached over and ruffled up his hair.

"The guy... he wasn't expecting that mailbox to jump out in front of him." He stopped to laugh. "You know why he was running?"

"Hmm... was he drinking?"

"Nope... he didn't have any pants on."

"What? Why wouldn't he have any pants on?"

"He didn't say... but we had to give him a napkin to get him into the cruiser." Gabe hit his leg again. "A napkin... a fucking napkin."

"Gross... so you had his bare ass in the back of your cruiser?" I stuck out my tongue.

"Yeah... tell me about it... I'm going to have to get the thing detailed now. You never know what you'll see in this town." Tim shook his head. "And now we get to enjoy a pizza that looked like his ass."

"Yuck... I don't think I'm hungry anymore." I shook the image out of my mind and walked into the building with my two guys. The hair on the back of my neck stood up when Tim led us to the booth Jane and I shared. I pulled on his sleeve. "Let's go over there by the window."

They followed me without question. "We haven't been here in ages." Tim picked up the menu.

"Nope, it's been a while." I pulled the menu out of his hands. "Why do you need that thing?"

"Good point. I'll just order our regular. That good for you, Gabe?"

"Yeah, the mushrooms are growing on me... not on my ass yet, though." He slapped the table and started laughing again.

"It sounds like you guys had a lot of fun with that one." I took a drink of water. "I had an interesting day, too."

"Yeah? What happened?" Tim asked.

"Sonya and Norma got into a fight because of a picture Sonya posted on Facebook... and then told Norma she reminded one of her online friends of some woman who disappeared."

"Ah, old people drama." Tim nodded. "See, Gabe, aren't you glad you didn't want to shadow Val? No offense."

"Don't be a smartass." I elbowed him. "The weird thing was this lady said her boyfriend was murdered, the same way

Jimmy was... she said like three other guys were killed the same way."

"Hmm... where are they from?" Tim rolled up the paper from his straw wrapper and flung it at Gabe.

"Bar Harbor, Maine. She said they never found out who did it. Isn't that weird?"

"Yeah... but lots of guys get shot in the head... guys are assholes... they piss a lot of people off... I'm actually surprised more guys don't get shot in the head."

"Come on. It doesn't make you wonder that maybe it's the same guy?"

Tim shook his head. "Nah. The FBI checked its database. They said there were no other cases out there matching ours. It looks like our guy is a one-time killer... well, five-time... but one location."

"Really? You're not curious at all? Four guys shot in the head... all in the same town... and the killer hasn't been caught?"

Tim shook his head. "No. Not at all. There would have been a hit on their database. We're pretty confident our serial killer's trademark would have been used if they were responsible for other murders... and when the Feds did their search, nothing came up."

Gabe scratched his head. "But... it could be the same guy. Maybe these were the first time they started using their calling card."

"Nah. Maybe the Maine cases are drug related. There are thousands of unsolved gang-related crimes."

"And, you guys are confident the Lawrenceville murders

aren't drug related?" I squinted my eyes, waiting for him to say what I already knew.

"Nope. We really think it's personal..." Tim wiped his hands on his napkin. "The vigilante theory is the one that makes the most sense."

"I guess we'll just have to wait and see if he strikes again." I drank the rest of my water and pushed my plate away. I couldn't figure out how the two situations were different, but I couldn't figure out how they were the same, either. And now, it seemed like there were more questions than answers.

CHAPTER THIRTY-FIVE

"Can you meet me at Norma's? It's important. Lily." The message was how I started my day. When I tried calling her back, it went straight to voice mail. This was the first time Lily had called me, and I wasn't sure what I was going to walk into. The tone of her voice didn't sound like this was going to be good.

I tapped Tim on the shoulder and bent down to kiss him. "Hey, I have to go to Norma's, Lily said she needs me to meet her there."

"What time is it?" He didn't lift his head from the pillow.

"It's 7:30. I heard my phone vibrating, and when I saw her name, I had to see what it was. I love you, have a good day at work."

When I arrived at Norma's house, her driveway was already full of cars. I was the last to arrive, even Sonya was there. Maggie met me at the door. "Shh, try to be quiet, the girls are still sleeping."

I rubbed the sleep from my eyes. "What's going on?"

Lily was at the dining room table, a cup of coffee between her hands. Her eyes were bloodshot, and her hair was a mess. Her sweatshirt was inside out, and it looked like she still had her shorts on from bed. She turned her head and gave me a quick nod to acknowledge me before dropping her head again.

"What's wrong, Lily?" I looked to the others to answer for her, but they remained quiet.

"He's getting out today. I found the message late last night." Her body rocked back and forth in the chair. "I didn't have time to prepare... I thought I'd get more notice."

"Have you changed the locks? I can have a locksmith there in a couple hours."

"No, it's no use. I know if he really wants to get to me, he'll find a way. I live in a doublewide, it's not like he wouldn't be able to get in through a window. He'd break it if he had to."

"Lily, why don't you stay here tonight? We can go get some of your things and even leave your car there. That way, he'll have no idea where you are." Norma stood behind her and rubbed her back.

"You sure it's okay? I... don't want to be in the way."

"We'd love to have you here with us, isn't that right Maggie?"

"Of course, we would. Let me go get dressed, and I can follow you in my car. I think the sooner we get your stuff, the better." Maggie looked at the clock on the wall. "It's not 8:oo yet, we'll have time to get there and back here without him knowing."

"Do you have a copy of your protection order?" I looked

around the room to see Sonya sitting in the living room by herself. It appeared she hadn't apologized to Norma yet. I was impressed she even showed up.

"Yeah, it's at the house."

"I need you to make sure you have it with you at all times. I can make you some copies to keep in different places, too. And... make sure the police department has a copy, and I'll let them know to keep an eye out for him."

"I don't think the piece of paper will stop him. At first, I thought it might, but now that he's out, I don't think so. He's going to be pissed I told... I..."

"You're not alone anymore. You have the four of us, and the victim's advocate who are here for you. I'll make sure I keep my phone on at night, so you can call me day or night." I put my hand on hers.

Lily picked up her head. "I don't even know how to function right now. I've never been this afraid before... I mean... I've been scared he was going to kill me... but this time it's different. This time I want to live."

"I understand." Maggie nodded. "Hank's in jail, but I still have nightmares he's going to get out and kill me. It's something I can't put in to words... but I know you know that feeling." She put her hand on Lily's shoulder. "Come on, I think we need to go now. I want to make sure we're back here before..."

"That's a great idea. Sonya, why don't you stay here with Norma and I'll follow behind Maggie? One of us can stay in the car, while the other goes in to help pack." I looked for a reaction from Sonya, but she remained quiet.

The three of us left, leaving an opportunity for Sonya and

Norma to mend what had been shattered. I hoped it would be enough. It didn't feel right with the rift between them. Our unit wasn't a whole without each and every one of us.

I parked in the road, right before Lily's trailer to keep watch. Maggie pulled her car in, right behind Lily, and they went in. It wasn't even 9:00 yet, it was unlikely Earl would have been released yet, but I couldn't shake the lingering uneasy feelings. I was skeptical of every passing car. I squinted to make sure it wasn't him.

I was familiar with the fear the ladies spoke of. It was one that consumed much of my thoughts for the last twenty years. Only recently, I was able to shake it enough to stop looking over my shoulder. Sitting here, the fear returned. It was the unknown and it was being out of control.

When I turned my head to look behind me, I noticed a small brown box on the floor. I reached down to pick it up, making sure my eyes did not leave the road I was guarding. It was the package my gram had asked me to return for her. I picked at the tape to peel open the seam. Inside the box were two bottles of insulin, a package of syringes, and a pack of alcohol wipes. *Jackpot.*

I took this as a sign. There was no question as to what I had to do. Lily needed this as much as I wanted to give it to her. With the box in my hands, the fear evaporated. The tension lifted, and I regained control.

I jumped when Maggie and Lily appeared in front of my car. I fumbled with the box before tossing it in the backseat. Maggie gave me the thumbs up before she got into her car. I waited in the road until she pulled out of the driveway, and I followed them back to Norma's.

Sonya and Norma were sitting on the couch next to each other, each holding a cup of tea and laughing at pictures on Sonya's phone. I gave them a smile and joined them. "What are you looking at?"

"Oh, just some pictures from your wedding." Norma giggled. "You seemed to have had a little too much to drink after the old ladies left."

I felt my cheeks start to burn and pulled the phone out of their hands. "Oh, god, please tell me you didn't post these on Facebook."

"No." Sonya held up her thumb and index finger in front of her nose. "I was this close, though."

I scrolled through the photos and saw the goofy faces I made when Sonya asked me to smile. The ones of me attempting to dance were even worse. I shook my head as the embarrassment settled in. "I can't believe no one stopped me."

"What? Why? You were having fun. Letting loose. Don't be ashamed of that. It was fun." Sonya held her hand out. "Here, let me show you something." She took the phone and hit play and handed it back to me.

She had captured a video of the dance Gabe and I shared. "Oh, Sonya... thank you so much. This is amazing. Can you send me a copy of this?"

"Even better... I saved all of the pictures and videos I took to a thumb drive. I'll bring it to the next meeting."

"She got some great shots." Norma looked up at Sonya and smiled. That was all I needed to know everything was going to be alright.

Lily and Maggie joined us, and Sonya handed them the phone to look through. "I've got to get to work." I looked at the clock to see I was now two hours late and hadn't even called Jeanine to let her know. "Before I go, I want to put together a safety plan. Can someone get some paper so we can write this down?"

Norma picked up a notebook off the coffee table. "I'll be the scribe."

"Can you start with a list of all of the numbers Lily might need? All of ours, the victim's advocate, the domestic violence center, the police department... anyone else you can think of, Lily?"

She shook her head. "No, I think that's a good start. I'll enter them into my phone after, too."

"Great idea. Okay... let's get a list of things we can do to help you feel safe. Any ideas?"

"How about getting a security system installed?" Maggie took her attention away from the phone.

"Oh, that's a great idea." Norma wrote it down. "And the locks, let's get the locks changed."

"Okay, I bet Tim and I could figure out how to do the camera and locks."

"I've been thinking about going to stay with my mom for a while. Now that my bruises have healed, I think going to Florida might be the best thing. Maybe sell the house, too."

"Wow, that's hardcore." Sonya's eyes went wide. "I mean, that's a big decision to make."

"I know, but I've been thinking about it. I actually planned to move before he got out, but time got away from me." Lily dropped her head.

"We could help you. If you want to go stay with your mom, we could pack up your things for you." Maggie took

Lily's hand. "I don't have a good feeling about you staying around here. I got a bad feeling when we were there today... I don't know how to explain it... and I didn't want to scare you... but... I didn't like it at all."

Lily frowned as she shook her head. "I know what you mean. I felt like that all night. I know he wasn't out yet, but just the thought put me on edge. Every sound made my eyes shoot open. I don't know if I'll be able to stay there again."

"Why don't you think about Maggie's offer? We can all help with the house, and you could at least go spend some time with your mom." I noticed Sonya making a gun with her fingers out the corner of my eye.

"I'm just afraid he'd find me there. He knows where she lives, and I don't want to put her life in danger... that's kind of why I haven't gone yet."

"Well, one thing at a time. We can get back together later and add anything else to the plan you can think of. I've got to go, but I'll stop by as soon as I get out of work. Call me if you need me. Is it okay if I let Tim know what's going on?"

Lily nodded. "I'm sorry..."

"No, don't you apologize. We're sisters... and we have your back..." I shut the door behind me. I couldn't stop thinking about how I was going to get my hands on Earl. I knew I needed to find some more information, but I wasn't sure Lily was the person I needed to get it from.

At work, there was no way I could focus on anything else. Earl was the only thought in my head. I logged on to Stephanie Mill's Facebook profile and entered Earl's name in the search bar. His picture was the first one on the list from my last search. This time, I sent him a friend request and proceeded to scroll through his feed.

What I noticed was that he liked beer and women. It didn't seem like it would be too difficult to crack his code. He was simple... but dangerous. I knew I would have to take my time and groom him.

CHAPTER THIRTY-SIX

With no new murders in Lawrenceville, the excitement of the serial killer case lost its appeal to Gabe. "No offense, but this town is kind of... boring." He drank the last of his orange juice before placing his cup in the sink.

I rinsed it out before putting it into the dishwasher. "Yeah, it's a lot like Mayberry here."

"Mayberry?"

"Looks like we have some reruns to watch." I handed him the lunch I made him and placed Tim's on the counter. "Not as exciting as you thought, huh?"

"No... I was really hoping to crack the case, you know?"

"There's still time, isn't there? You have a couple more weeks with Tim. Anything could happen." I said the words I knew he wanted to hear, but I hoped I was wrong. If Andrew is the serial killer, I didn't want him to go to jail. I wanted him to help Sonya raise their baby. And, if Sonya was by chance involved, I definitely didn't want her getting caught.

"I don't know... I mean, they aren't even talking about it anymore."

"Hmm." I looked out the window as I wiped down the counter. "Why don't you come up with a name for him... you know there's the Boston Strangler, the BTK killer, the Zodiac Killer... they were all given names. I think it helped get the media and the community more invested in the case."

"Whoa... you sure know a lot about them. It's a little disturbing.... but... maybe you're right. If I can't catch him, at least I could be the one to name him." He nodded." "Hmmm... what could it be? The Bullet Bandit? The Shooter in the Header?"

I raised my eyebrow and couldn't mask the laugh I tried to hold back. "I think you might want to keep working on it."

"Yeah... you're right." He grabbed Tim's lunch off the counter and handed it to him. "She had a good idea for the case... I'll fill you in on the way."

Tim gave me a kiss. "Oh, she did. I can't wait to hear about it." He turned his head to look at me. I couldn't place the look he gave me, either annoyance or intrigue.

"Yeah, I think she's on to something."

"You're welcome." I snickered as the door shut. "Sorry, I just wanted to spice things up a little for him."

"Geez, I can hardly wait." Tim shook his head. "It has been pretty boring... not the adventure I lured him here with."

"See, I'm just helping."

When Tim and Gabe left, I logged onto Stephanie Mill's Facebook profile and noticed a new notification and a message. Earl accepted my friend request. That confirmed he was released. My hands started to sweat as I clicked on the message. It had to have been him... he was my only 'friend' on there.

When it opened, I saw his round picture at the top of the screen. "Hey, baby. Do I know you? If not, I think we should change that. It's been a long time since I had a sweet piece of ass like yours."

Nausea washed over me as I stared down at the screen. I shook off the chill that traveled down my spine. He was vile. Just the sight of him made the desire to finish the job overwhelm me. *This was going to be easier than I thought.* I just had to play along, make him think I wanted him, and I knew he'd set up a time to meet. I'd just have to dangle the carrot in front of him, and I bet I could complete the job in no time.

Today seemed like a good day as any to call out of work. I hadn't even made it a full week yet, but I knew I wouldn't have what I needed to concentrate. I dialed Jeanine's number and worked on my fake sick voice. It was my lucky day, the call went straight to her voicemail. There would be no need to make up some lame excuse.

With that out of the way, I worked on my response to Earl. I typed out a message and deleted it as soon as I read it. My answer had to be convincing... but not too convincing. This was my only chance to make the connection. "LOL, I'm blushing... we don't know each other yet, but I'd love to change that." I added a couple kissing emojis and hit send. My pulse throbbed in my neck as I waited for him to respond. Minutes passed, and the message was still unread. I looked at the time and realized he was probably hungover and fast asleep.

I grabbed my keys and drove to Norma's. I wanted to check on Lily, but I also needed the comfort that Norma's presence brings. I needed to gather the strength to get this job done, I couldn't let anything get in the way. There was something I wanted to clear up before I began the tedious task ahead.

The door opened before I had a chance to knock. "Good morning, Norma, would you like to go for a ride with me this morning?"

"Okay, let me get my purse and tell the girls."

"Wait, don't you even want to know where we're going?" I put my hands on my hips.

"Oh, honey, I already know."

"You do? How?" I followed her in, waiting in the kitchen as she wrote a note for Maggie and Lily.

"We're going to see your gram."

"How did you know that?"

"I just knew... besides, you're not too hard to figure out." She gave me a wink as she put her purse over her arm.

"It's really that obvious? I'm that easy to read?"

She giggled. "Not too easy. It's only because I love you. Besides, I knew how badly you wanted to see her the other day, and where else would you be going on a Friday morning when you should be working?"

"I can't pull anything over on you... I guess I should be careful."

"Don't you worry, I'll have your back, no matter what."

I stopped at the gas station to fill up and sent Tim a text to let him know of my change of plans, so he wouldn't worry. Mom placed Gram in a rehab center about a half an hour from Lawrenceville in an attempt to create a bigger gap between us, but her plan backfired. She was now even closer to me. Fear had kept me from making the trip, as it did so many years before.

"I don't think I would have been able to find the courage to take this trip without you."

"Oh, I'm sure you would have, but I'm so glad you asked me to come. Your gram's a sweetheart. We had a good visit when I drove her home."

"She is pretty special. You remind me of her." Regret heated my cheeks by my choice of words. "Not because..."

She laughed. "I'm old?"

"No... I wasn't going to say that. I was going to say because of the way you make me feel. You can always fix my bad day." I kept my attention on the road. "You would have made an incredible mother."

"You know, your gram loves you very much. She was heartbroken when you left, but she said she knew in her heart she'd see you again."

I respected her wish to change the subject. It was worth trying to get her to open up, but I expected it to fizzle out. I meant what I said, though. She just had a motherly soul. "It broke mine, too. I hated leaving her... but I felt like I had to."

"She understands now. She loves you, Val. It meant the world to her to be your maid of honor. She said she could die happy now."

"That's what I'm afraid of. I wasted so much time... and now she's going to die." I closed my eyes long enough to push the tears back.

"Oh, Val, she is an old woman. Don't regret what you

can't change. Just cherish the memories you have and make as many new ones as you can."

"Yeah... it's just hard. It's ironic I work with death all the time and I can't even deal with it..."

"Well, it's different when it's someone you love. Your professional and your personal lives are two very different things. Don't beat yourself up, you've overcome so much. You're stronger than you think."

"I just... I don't know what I'll do."

"You'll get that thought out of your head, and you'll enjoy your visit... and every visit and phone call after today. And, when the time comes, you come and find me, and we can cry together."

"Thanks, Norma." I shook away any remaining tears. "What do you think about the whole serial killer thing? Are you worried about him still being on the loose?"

"You know, I haven't given it much thought. I'm not worried, though."

"No? Not at all? I get we're women, and not the target, but isn't it unnerving that we could walk past this guy and not even know it?"

"Nah, there are far better things to spend my time on."

"It's kind of consumed me. It's all I can think about... I just want to know who it is and Tim's not talking..."

"Oh, dear, you shouldn't spend your time thinking about that. Don't let it take any more of your time, and don't let it get between you and your husband."

"I know it's foolish, I just kind of want to know... maybe it's all of those Snapped episodes I watch... it seems like the suspect is always right in front of your nose. But, if the FBI can't figure it out, why should I think I could?"

"Soon, it will be old news, and no one will be thinking about it."

"Maybe... but there are still some unsolved serial killer cases out there... like the Zodiac Killer has never been found, but they're still talking about the case... even still working on it."

"My, my, you really have been obsessing about this." She let out a little laugh. "The Zodiac Killer... the names they come up with are a crime of their own."

"Yeah, some of them are pretty awful, but that's how they get their notoriety."

"You really do need a hobby." She flashed a quick smile. "Let Tim and the guys work on the case... just trust them to do their job. You have so much other stuff to worry about."

"Hmm... yeah... you're right. It's just fascinating... this time the bad guys are the ones being killed, not the inno-cent... well, if you look at it that way."

We arrived at the rehab in less time than I thought. Norma took my hand and led me into the building. I let her take the lead while I stayed in her shadow. They gave us her room number and a quick point and nod to head us in the direction of her room.

Norma knocked on the door while I waited in the hall for her to make sure the room was empty. Gram was alone, watching TV. "Hi, Marianne, I have a visitor for you." Norma pulled me into the room.

"Valerie, what a nice surprise." I felt the joy in her words.

"Hi, Gram. I couldn't wait to see you, how are you feeling?"

"Well, they have me on a lot of pain pills... so... I'm doing pretty good."

"When do you get to go home?"

"I don't think Elaine is going to let me go back home. She's already started packing up my apartment."

Norma put her hand on my back to tame the anger circling me. "She can't do that... she..."

"I'm afraid she can. But don't get upset... it's probably for the best."

"You can come live with Tim and me."

"That's a nice offer... I'll think about it."

"I'll be by to visit more... you're closer now." I took her hand in mine.

"I'd love that, Valerie. But don't you worry about me. I don't hate it here. There are a few cute nurses, too." She winked at Norma.

"I'm glad you're doing so well, Marianne. Would it be okay if I came by to visit, too?"

"That would be lovely. It does get lonely sometimes."

"So, Mom and Chad don't come to visit?"

She shook her head. "No, she only came to sign the paperwork and left. It's further away from her now... so I don't expect to see her again... before I die."

"Gram..."

"What?" She shrugged her shoulders. "I'm old... it's only a matter of time..."

"You're sure you're happy here? Is there anything you want or need?"

"No, dear. I'm fine. Don't you worry about me." She squeezed my hand. "I love you, Valerie. You've always been my special girl." She paused as she searched for the right words. "I know about Gabe... who his father is."

I felt this morning's breakfast burn my throat, and I squeezed my eyes to fight back the tears. "What do you mean?"

"He looks just like him... Chad... I'm so sorry I didn't protect you."

"He looks like Chad? I don't see it."

"Good, and don't you go looking for it, either. I wasn't sure... not until Elaine started giving me hell for seeing you... and then that's when everything clicked."

"Did you tell her... that I found him?"

"No... I don't want her knowing anything about you. She doesn't deserve to know. What she did to you is unforgivable. I don't blame you one bit for taking off."

"I should have told you."

"Nonsense. You did what you had to. I don't hold it against you. You're a good girl, Valerie. I need you to promise me you'll enjoy the rest of your life... don't let anyone steal anything from you ever again."

"She turned into a wonderful woman. You have a lot to be proud of." Norma put her arm around me.

"I am so proud of you. You've overcome so much." She gave me a Cheshire Cat grin. "I met with my lawyer the other day and changed my will." Her smile continued to grow. "I took Elaine's name off and put yours in its place. She won't know until it's too late to change it. I'm leaving everything to you and Tim. That should be enough to make sure you're taken care of for the rest of your life."

"I don't want to think about that..."

"Oh, Valerie. Don't you worry about me. I'll be able to die knowing you'll never have another financial problem. Quit your job, travel, have a family... do whatever it is that will make your heart happy. That's what's important in this life."

"I love you, Gram."

CHAPTER THIRTY-SEVEN

I logged onto my Facebook as soon as I returned home. I had a message waiting for me. When I opened it, I saw Earl had changed his profile picture, and the green dot showed me he was active. My fingers shook as I held my iPad.

"Let's get to know each other."

I started typing my response. My breathing was shallow and every noise forced me to look over my shoulder. Tim could not know. I had to be careful. Everything I wrote, I deleted, just like before. I responded with a wink emoji. It said what I couldn't find the words for.

The little bubbles showed up on the screen, alerting me he was responding. "I'll show you mine... if you show me yours."

I forced a swallow, my tongue blocking my airway. Gross... he can't be serious. I waited to reply... not knowing how to answer. A photo of his penis filled my screen. It took everything I had not to throw up. Why do men think their manhood is attractive? Even if it wasn't his, it would be the last thing I would want a picture of.

"Your turn."

I didn't want to comply, but I didn't want to risk losing his attention. I opened up a browser and searched for pictures of breasts. I took a screenshot of a pair and sent them to him. I waited for his reaction.

"WOW!! I want to taste those beauties."

Repulsed, I sent a smiley face. It was all I had in me. "Where do you live?"

"Lawrenceville. You?"

"Same. Whereabouts?"

"I'm staying with my mom, helping her out."

"That's sweet of you."

"Yup."

"If you live at your mom's, how could we meet?"

"I've got a camp in the woods we could use."

"Ohhh... that sounds nice. Where is it?"

"Down Oak Alley. A friend owes me a favor. Nice and private."

"Perfect. When do you want to get together?"

"Right now."

"No... I can't today... maybe this weekend."

"YES!!!"

I closed out of the app and took a shower. I needed to clean the filth off my skin. I didn't want to touch him, but I knew I would have to. It was the only way. He was eager to meet, and I had to capitalize on the opportunity. As I washed my hair, I played through how the events would take place. It was black. Every time I tried to pull it up in my mind, nothing came. I knew it must be because it felt wrong going behind Tim's back, but it wasn't because I wanted to do it. I had to do it.

When I shut off the blow dryer, I heard Tim and Gabe joking around in the kitchen. They were sharing a pizza, Gabriel at their feet looking for treats. "Go ahead, tell her." Tim nodded his head in my direction.

"Tell me what?" I picked up a slice of pizza and took a bite.

"I came up with the perfect name... wait for it..." He smiled and turned his head to look for Tim's approval. "The Executioner."

"Oh... good one. Did you come up with it on your own?"

"Yeah... every guy died by a shot to the head... so it was like execution style... get it?"

"Yes, that's very clever. Good work."

"But what's even better... Tim had someone interview me."

I turned to look at Tim. "He did?"

"Yeah, I have a friend who owed me a favor... I thought it might be helpful to add interest to the case. I mean, it can't hurt."

"Hmm... sounds like you two had a productive day."

"Yeah, it was one of the best days. Thanks for the great idea." Gabe picked up the last slice and tossed a pepperoni to Gabriel.

"So, you still want to be a cop?" I asked Gabe.

He nodded with his mouth full of pizza. "Uh, huh." He wiped his mouth with his paper towel. "And, they offered me a job here, after police academy."

"Really? And..."

"And I think I'm going to take it. Tim said it'd be okay if I stayed here with you guys until I find a place."

I placed my hand on my heart. "Well, that's the best news I've heard. I'd love to have you stay with us... and no hurry to get your own place. I love... we love having you here."

I went to sleep with a mind and heart full of hope and dread. The future was so bright, but the path to get there was dark. With the darkness comes light. I must remember that. I settled into Tim's arms, knowing I was safe and life was good. If only at that moment, it was enough to fuel me for another day.

My phone woke me up out of a deep sleep. I felt for it on the nightstand, dropping it before I was able to answer it. "Hello?"

"Val... it's Lily... he got to her." Maggie's voice was in a whisper.

"What? How?" I sat up.

"She got a call, and she took off... she said she had to go see a friend, but when she got home, her face was all busted up."

"Where is she now?"

"She's in the shower, getting cleaned up."

"Did you call the cops?"

"No... she doesn't want to... she said he'd kill her."

I thought about my plans for the weekend and knew he couldn't go back to jail. "Okay... are you safe? Does he know where she's staying?"

"She said he didn't follow her."

"Okay... make sure all the doors are locked, windows, too."

Maggie's breathing filled the silence. "But, Val... why did she go see him? I don't get it."

"I don't know... it's hard sometimes to break free. We just have to listen to her wishes and be there for her. She needs to know she can trust you."

Maggie sighed. "I know... it's just hard... I don't want to see her get hurt."

"I know... I don't, either. Are you sure you're okay?"

"Yeah... I just wanted to tell someone... in case..."

"Maggie, just make sure everything is locked up tight. Do you have the pepper spray I gave you?"

"Mhmm."

"Keep that with you at all times. Do you need me to come over?"

"No, not tonight."

Tim continued to snore, the call hadn't woken him. I wouldn't have to tell him. I didn't want him or anyone to know what happened and risk Earl going back to jail. My plan couldn't be carried out if he were in jail. Just two more days.

CHAPTER THIRTY-EIGHT

Gabe went home for the weekend to tell Beth and Paul about the job offer and pick up some of his things. I still couldn't believe he wouldn't be leaving, at least not for long. It would give us more time together, and he may even have a little brother or sister he would be able to get to know. We would be able to be a family.

As Gabe's car was out of sight, Tim handed me my phone when I walked back in the door. I glanced down at the display. "Hi, Maggie, is everything okay?"

"Umm, well... do you think you could come over?"

"Sure. I'll be right there."

I gave Tim a kiss and took the drive to Norma's. It was becoming a drive I could do with my eyes closed. That was the one good thing about Lawrenceville, it only took ten minutes to get from one side of town to the other. Days like today, I was grateful for that.

Maggie opened the door before I could take the keys out

of the ignition. It looked like she hadn't slept, and she was still in her robe. "Hey, thanks for coming."

"What's going on? Is Lily okay?"

"She's inside... she's a mess."

When I entered the house, I saw Lily curled up on the couch with a blanket covering her head. I couldn't see her face, but I heard her crying. "Hey, Lily." I bent down and rubbed her back through the blanket. "Do you want to talk?"

"Not really."

"Okay, well, I'll just sit here until you're ready." I sat on the floor with my back against the coffee table.

Norma came in and handed me a cup of tea, she gave me a half-smile and sat in the chair next to us. She stayed silent as we listened to Lily cry.

"You know, Lily, we're not here to judge you. We just want to make sure you're okay. If being with Earl is what you want, we want to support you." Maggie opened her eyes as wide as she could, and shook her head, shrugging her shoulders in my direction. I held my index finger to my lips. "Remember, you're not in this alone. You have us now."

Lily's sobs quieted and she uncovered her head. Her left eye was swollen shut and purple, a black and blue shadowed her nose, falling onto her cheek. I coughed to hide the gasp, wanting to escape. "I had to go..."

"It's okay, Lily."

"He said if I didn't go, he'd kill my new friends. I didn't want him to find you and hurt you. I figured he wouldn't want to come after any of you if he got to me."

"How did he find you?" Maggie asked.

"He sent me a text... I forgot to get a new number."

"Where did you go to see him?" I got up from the floor and joined Lily on the couch.

"I walked to his mom's house... it's only a couple streets over. When he sent me those messages, I just got so scared... he said he knew where I was, and if I didn't go to him, he'd find me."

"Did his mom see you?" I asked as I tried to replay the timeline of our conversation over in my head.

"No, she was sleeping. She's hard of hearing, so I don't think she even heard anything. He covered my mouth while he raped me, so I couldn't scream."

"Oh my god, Lily, he raped you, too?" Tears filled Maggie's eyes.

"I didn't want to tell you last night... you were already so upset. I felt so stupid for going to him... it's just that... I didn't know what else to do." She hung her head.

Disgust and shame took turns slapping me when I thought about the photo I sent Earl earlier in the night. It was the perfect storm to turn Lily into his sex slave. I shook my head to push the guilt away. "Lily, it's not stupid. You were afraid... you did what you thought you had to do to protect your friends." I looked over at Norma, she was just staring ahead, sipping her tea. I couldn't tell if she was upset or just not awake after a sleepless night.

"I am stupid... I should have gotten a new number or at least blocked his number. I could have called the cops. I could have told one of you... but I didn't do any of that."

"That's not stupid... do you know how many times it takes

to break free from an abusive asshole like Earl?" I looked to see her shake her head no. "Seven. Seven times. What you did last night was normal, not stupid."

"Seven times? Really?"

"Yeah... it's not easy to break free. All those old habits are hard to break. When you're used to being treated like a piece of shit, it's hard to accept there is anything else out there. But, Lily... you deserve so much more. You're beautiful and funny and talented. You're the best baker I've ever met... you have such big dreams... and you deserve them... you deserve to be happy and loved... and you deserve to be safe."

Lily pushed the tears off the unbruised cheek and flinched with pain as her sleeve brushed against her face. "I don't even love him... it's just that I don't love myself, either."

"Oh, don't I know what that's like." I brushed my tears away with the sleeve of my sweatshirt. "But you know what... I love you, Lily... we all do... and we'll love you enough for you, too, until you're able to see who we see when we look at you." I looked up at Norma and Maggie. "You know how I know this? Because that's what these ladies did for me. They showed me I was worth loving. It's not easy... but you know what... life has gotten so much better since I started loving myself."

"I'm really sorry I..."

"You don't have to be sorry. Val's right, we do love you and we won't stop." Maggie sat on her hands to keep from fidgeting. "It just hurt me to see you in so much pain, and I was afraid he might have followed you back here."

"I just wasn't thinking... but he fell asleep after he was done with me. I waited until I knew he was out cold before I snuck out. I lied about who I was staying with. I didn't want to put any of you in danger."

"That was smart." I nodded. "See, you're resourceful, too."

"I just can't go to the police..."

"That's okay... I understand. You know him best, and you know what will keep you safe. Sometimes the things we do don't make sense to anyone else, but all that matters is we know why we do what we do. It's almost like a landmine... we know where not to step to survive, but if someone else came in, and they took a wrong step... everything is blown to hell."

"That makes a lot of sense, Val. I never knew how to put it into words before... but that's true. Sometimes it felt safer to get the beatings because at least I knew what to expect. When the cops get involved, I lose control of the situation, and even though they're there to help, I know when they leave, it's going to be ten times worse."

"I'm glad you're safe, dear." Norma broke her silence but still didn't make eye contact with any of us.

I wondered if Norma knew what Lily had gone through. If maybe her story had pieces of Lily's in it. I couldn't tell if that was it or if she was upset about what had happened. It was evident the abuse would escalate. It was only a matter of time before Lily wouldn't be walking back home. She wouldn't be walking at all.

I had to hold Earl off until Sunday. It would be the only day Tim wouldn't notice me missing. I only needed a couple hours, and it would be over. Lily would be safe, and she could start living. She'd never be free as long as she was under his spell. With each passing minute, I was looking forward to breaking it.

When I got home, I couldn't tell Tim any of what we talked about. I hated the secrets, but it would be the last one; it had to be. I didn't want to bring a baby into these unsafe situations. Even now, there was a slight chance I could already be pregnant. I just couldn't take the test until Monday. Nothing could get in the way of this... there was no choice this time.

I brought my tote bag into the bedroom while Tim was out mowing the lawn. Inside Tim's closet, I dug out one of his ugliest ties and pushed it under the files in my bag. I slipped my iPad in and stood on the back deck. "Hey... Tim..." I waved my arm to get his attention. "Hey, I have to go into work and finish some things up... I should never take Fridays off." I blew him a kiss and drove to the hospital.

I walked down to the basement, past the morgue. It used to be the most peaceful place in the whole hospital, now all it does is make me sad. I never let myself think about anyone that I knew dying, but now, the stakes were higher. Gram was ready. I've seen that look on others before. As I unlocked my office door, I shook the thought out of my mind. Not today... not now. One thing at a time.

At my desk, I placed the bag on top as I opened my drawer. I pushed the files to the front and took out the box I put there for safekeeping. I unwrapped the package and held up the bottles. Still in the boxes. Novolin. For the life of me, I couldn't recall what I used on Donald Brice, or even how much it took.

I opened the boxes and placed the bottles in my tote bag, along with the syringes. I opened my iPad to research the insulin I had... before I hit enter to complete the search, I placed my finger on the delete button. This was something I couldn't have on my search history. I'd have to chance it, and hope it was enough to do the job. It worked last time.

When I opened the Facebook app, another message was waiting. Earl sent it after I went to bed last night, but before Lily went over. "Hey, baby, don't you want to help a horny old guy out?" The messages increased in vulgarity as the night went on. If I had answered him, and got the job done last night, he never would have gotten to Lily. She never would have been put in that situation.

Just one more day. I had to make sure he didn't get to Lily again. "Hey there. I can't wait to satisfy all of your desires." I tossed the iPad onto the desk and sat back in my chair. My body sank into it as I thought about the plan. There was more apprehension than the others this time... something didn't feel right.

I rolled my shoulders to push some of it away. This had to work, there was no other option. Maybe it was because I was worried about Gram or lying to Tim that made it feel different this time. Whatever it was, I had to push it aside. This would all be over in less than thirty-six hours.

The ping alerting me of a message pulled me back into the room. Earl had responded. "All of my desires? Oh, boy!"

The fact he could pretend he did nothing wrong last night illuminated the monster he was. People like him are a hazard to society. He probably didn't even think he did anything wrong... I was sure he'd spin it, so it was all on Lily. I had to respond without letting my hatred show. "Tomorrow night." I followed it up with a wink emoji.

"You better believe it. I'm rock hard waiting for you."

Oh, please, no. The picture of his penis appeared. An emoji was all I could stomach. Thank goodness they were there to do the flirting.

"You like that, huh?"

He repulsed me. It was way past disgust. I fought back the urge to vomit and replied. "Uh, huh."

"Meet me at the cabin tomorrow at 8."

"Address?"

"Oak Alley, cabin 2."

"How will I know you're there?"

"My blue pickup will be out front. Follow the first road in, it's at the end of the road."

"Mmm... I can't wait. See you at 8pm. Make sure you save it all for me. I don't want to find out you've been sharing."

"It's all yours baby."

"I can hardly wait." And I meant it.

CHAPTER THIRTY-NINE

I called Tim to let him know I'd be later than I thought before I left my office. I needed to make sure Lily was alright and try to convince her to stay away from Earl. I also needed Norma to calm my nerves. I sent Sonya a text, asking her to meet us there before I picked up some ice cream.

With my arms full of grocery bags, I used my foot to knock on the door. "Oh my, look at you. What on Earth?" Norma took a couple of bags to ease my load.

"I hope you don't mind. I thought we could all use a little girl time. Sonya's on her way, too."

"Of course not, you're always welcome here, all of you girls are." She set the bags on the counter. "My goodness, did you buy out the whole store?"

I laughed. "No... I just didn't know what everyone liked, so I got an... assortment."

"I guess." She opened the bags and started taking out the cartons of ice cream.

"And, I figured what we didn't eat the girls would take care of."

Norma reached into the cabinet and took out five bowls and set them on the counter. While she was getting everything ready, I walked into the living room and found Maggie and Lily watching Lifetime movies. "What are you guys doing? Sad movies? Ugh... I've got something better than that, come on out to the kitchen."

The front door swung open. "Did someone say ice cream?" The tank top Sonya had on accentuated the cute little baby bump.

"I knew that would get you here." I couldn't help myself, I had to rub her belly. "Aww... you're so cute."

"Blech... I feel like a whale."

"Stop that. You're beautiful. Pregnancy looks good on you." I handed her a bowl.

"This is fun, what a great idea." Maggie took a bowl and handed one to Lily.

"I thought it'd do us good to have a little fun."

"You got whipped cream, too? You thought of everything... I haven't had a sundae in ages." Lily held the can over her tower of ice cream and sprayed.

"I haven't, either." I laughed. "I figured we could eat away our worries."

We found our place around Norma's table after we had our ice cream and all the fixings. "It's funny how we all have our own spot."

"Creatures of habit." Norma pushed the spoon into her mouth. "Mmm... what a treat."

"I don't want to be a buzz kill, but... do you have a gun,

Lily?" Sonya set her spoon down. "I brought mine... in case you want to borrow it."

"I don't know anything about guns." The smile left Lily's face. "Only how it feels to be terrified of them."

"I was afraid of them at first, too... but Andrew has been working with me, showing me things."

"Andrew has a gun?" I titled my head as I listened to their conversation.

"Yeah, he's got a few of them... we have matching nine-millimeters... his and hers." She laughed.

"He's got the same gun as you?" My wheels started turning.

"Yeah, only his isn't pink."

"Is he pretty good with it?" I let the ice cream melt in my mouth as I thought back to my list.

"Yeah, he's like a pro or something." She held up her hands in the shape of a gun. "Pow."

I shook my head and gave her a smirk. "Pow? I'm sure it doesn't sound so innocent when you pull the actual trigger."

"Well, no... it's pretty loud... but one of his guns has this thing that makes it quiet... it's a quieter... or something..."

"A silencer?" Norma pushed her spoon around the melted ice cream.

"Yeah, that's it. I don't know if he's supposed to have it or not... he told me not to tell anyone about that gun."

Everything began to add up. No one ever heard a gunshot at any of the murders, at least, no one reported hearing one. A silencer would have given the murderer a chance to do the crime and flee. No one would even suspect anything. And,

Andrew looks like a regular guy. I'm sure if he walked past you in the hall, you wouldn't even remember seeing him. I felt my head nodding. "Hmmm."

"What?" Sonya stopped her story and looked at me.

"Nothing."

"You said... hmmm... you're not going to tell Tim about the gun, are you... Andrew will be so mad at me... I promised him I wouldn't say anything."

"Relax... I was just enjoying my ice cream." I shoved a spoon in my mouth. "Mmmm."

"So anyway... I can leave my gun here if you'd like. I can show you how to use it."

"No, I don't think that's necessary." Norma got up from the table and started cleaning up our mess.

Sonya leaned over to Lily and whispered. "Just let me know if you want it."

Lily nodded. "Thanks."

"What are your plans this evening?" I turned my attention to Lily.

"Maggie and I are going to binge-watch the Lifetime movie marathon. We're just going to hang out together."

"Yeah, we've got the air on and the blinds closed. We're not going to leave the couch for anything... except to go to the bathroom. Do you want to join us?" Maggie looked at Sonya and me.

"It does sound like a lot of fun... but I told Tim I'd spend some time with him since Gabe's gone for the weekend."

Sonya winked. "Hubba hubba."

"Oh my god, what are you, five?" I brushed the hair out of

my face. "We have decided to try for a baby... so I guess this is as good a time as any."

"Aww, Val, that's exciting." Maggie bit her fingernail.

"Yeah... and slightly terrifying... but I think it's time."

"That's wonderful news, Val." Norma rejoined us at the table. "Your babies can grow up together."

"And mine can babysit." Maggie laughed. "What I really mean is, I can babysit... any time."

"Thanks, Maggie, you'll be the best Auntie ever. These babies are going to be lucky to have so many aunts. I couldn't think of anyone better to share my baby with. I love you ladies."

The visit did just what I needed. Sonya, Maggie, Lily, and Norma each offered something different to the mix. And, seeing how much better Lily was feeling, I had all I needed to complete the plan. The thought of him getting to her before I get to him was the fuel to my fire and gave me the courage I had been lacking. The countdown was on.

Tim was in the shower when I arrived home. It gave me enough time to pull out my notebook and read over all of my notes. I added the new information about Andrew and the nine-millimeter with the silencer. It all added up to Andrew. He had the motive and the means. And he wasn't someone the cops had on their radar. The murders stopped after the FBI got involved.

I tried to think if I had shared that piece of information in the group. If Sonya knew, she would have told Andrew. I probably would have told him, too. I still couldn't understand the other guys, though. Aside from being sex offenders, they weren't connected to Sonya. At least not that I knew. But it had to be him. Who else could it be? I wrote Andrew's name down on the paper and circled it. Andrew was the Executioner.

CHAPTER FORTY

"Thank you for being so great with Gabe. I know you're the reason he took that job."

"He's a great kid. He's smart and driven, like his mom." He kissed the top of my head.

"You think I'm driven?" My eyes went to the ceiling fan as it spun around above us. "I wouldn't say that..."

"I would. You know what you want and you go after it. You don't give up until you have what you want."

"Hmm... I'd say that description fits you more than me."

He pulled me close. "Yeah... I'm glad I didn't stop chasing you. But... you were worth the wait."

"I'm glad you didn't give up." I pressed my face into his chest. "What would make you stop loving me?"

"What?" He moved my hair out of my face. "Why would you ask such a thing? Nothing could make me stop loving you."

"Not even if I really screwed up?"

"Val, there's nothing you could do to make me stop loving

you. I'm afraid you're stuck with me... forever. You know... until death do us part." He gave me a tight squeeze. "What's going on? Is there something you want to talk about?"

I closed my eyes tight. "No... I was just checking. I just don't want you to ever be disappointed in me."

"Not a chance. Whatever happens in life, I'll be by your side. No matter what."

"You promise?"

"Yes."

"Say it... say you promise."

"Val, I promise I'll never leave you. I'll be by your side, by our kids' side, until my last breath."

"Good. I promise, too."

The warmth of his arms gave me the protection I needed. Thoughts of Gram came in waves. I didn't want to get the call. I'd been on the other end of that call more times than I can count. I'm not ready for that pain. Not now, not when life was being created. Mine, and the baby we were trying for.

Thoughts of Earl pushed out the pain of losing Gram. I know what Tim said, but he didn't know why. I wanted to believe him, but it was too much to ask of him. There were pieces of me he didn't know.... he'd never know. The shame of that weighed as heavy as the pain of losing him. I sold him a version of myself that didn't exist. I couldn't expect him to keep his word when I never kept mine.

Then there was Mom and Chad. Even after all of these years, she was still out to make my life miserable. I hated myself for not turning Chad in for raping me. If I had, perhaps my life could have been easier.

I didn't care about the money Gram was leaving behind,

but I knew Mom did. It was all Mom ever talked about when I was a kid. "Wait until your gram dies... life will be so much better." I didn't believe her, because it wasn't Gram's money I loved, it was Gram. When she found out about the will, I knew she'd show up on my doorstep. Not to offer an apology, but to try to change history. To make me see things the way she wants me to. The thought that Mom might get to see her grandchild was enough to make me want to learn how to shoot a gun. I'd stop at nothing to protect my child, unlike her.

"Val, you okay?" Tim's voice pulled me out of my racing thoughts.

"I'm fine." A sigh filled the silence I wasn't able to. "I'm just thinking."

"About what?"

"Our future.... I'm just thinking about our baby... well... when we have one. I just hope I'll be a good mom... but I know one thing... I'll do way better than my mom."

"You're going to be a great mom. Look at how great you are with Gabriel... both of them." He laughed. "The reason Gabe is so great is because you were able to let him know how important he was to you... you were just a kid yourself, but you knew how to show him love. All a kid needs is love. And I know you have so much to give."

"You think so?"

"I know so. Stop beating yourself up, Val. You're the sweetest, most caring woman I've ever met. Try to let go of that doubt and enjoy this time we have."

"About that... I think I'm going to give my notice at the

hospital. I think I want to be an advocate and help women who've been hurt."

"Like at the domestic violence center?"

"Well, kind of. I was thinking about doing my own thing, though. I think being at the center scares some ladies away. I just want to help the ones who aren't going to go get help... you know... maybe the ones who haven't left yet and just need to talk to someone."

"Hmm... that sounds like something you'd be great at. That's exciting, Val."

"I never would have found out how much I love that kind of thing if it wasn't for you. Without your love and support, I'd be stuck in the morgue for the rest of my life."

"Now, isn't that a lovely thought."

"Ha-ha. I'm done with death... I'm ready to join the living." Well, almost.

CHAPTER FORTY-ONE

"I've got to run out to do a few errands. I should be back in a couple hours, do you need anything?" It was the best excuse I could think of to keep me from lying to my new husband.

"Yeah, I could use some creamer for my coffee. I think we're almost out." Tim got up from his recliner and stretched. "Let me come with you." He looked down at his watch and grabbed his keys.

My stomach flipped. "I, ah... have to stop at Norma's, too. We might be awhile. You're welcome to join me if you want."

"Hmmm, so we might not be back in time for the game?" His head turned to the TV and then back to me.

"Most likely not." I mustered up a laugh. "But it's fine if you just want to stay here." I picked up my keys and my purse and gave him a kiss. "I'll bring you back some snacks."

"You're too good to me." He walked me to the door and kissed me goodbye. "You're sure it's okay?"

"Positive." I hated I had to lie. I despise liars, and here I am, lying to my sweet husband. The thought of what I was going to do next was enough to put me over the edge, but I had to. Lily's life depended on me.

I drove to the hospital to grab my supplies and change into the provocative top I shoved into my purse. There was enough cleavage to complete the look I was going for with the top two buttons undone. I zipped up my jacket to cover myself and headed back to my car. I opened my tote bag and found Tim's tie, the bottle of insulin, and the syringes. I took out one of the needles and injected it into the vile, pulling it back until it was full. I repeated this with three more and placed them back in my bag. In the rearview mirror, I fixed my hair and put on the lipstick Sonya had given me, puckering my lips at my reflection.

I took a deep breath, closed my eyes, and reminded myself why I was doing this. Lily needs this. On the drive over, I half wished Andrew would beat me to the job, like the last two. Earl hadn't made the front page for what he did to Lily, I don't even think he made the news at all. Bobby Green was the last murder to take place in Lawrenceville. I think once Jimmy was out of the picture, his job was done. Bobby was just to keep the attention off of him. I knew this one would be left to me.

From the stories Lily had shared, I was a little nervous. Something didn't sit right in my gut. I tried to brush that feeling aside, blaming it on the guilt I felt for the white lie I had to tell Tim. The long, winding dirt road that took me to the cabin had no lights illuminating the road. Just the light of the full moon lit the way. When I arrived at Earl's place, I pulled my car in as close as possible to try and hide it from the view of passing cars. The camp was set back into the trees. A quick look around satisfied any fear of being found. There was no one around.

When I picked up my cell phone, I saw there was no service. Tim wouldn't be able to reach me. The pregame had already started, and if tonight was like any other night, nothing would be able to pull his attention away from the TV. I took one last look in the mirror, tossed my hair off my shoulders, and removed my coat. I unbuttoned one more button for good measure. *This was for Lily.*

Earl met me at the door. "Well, look at you. You're as hot as the pictures you sent. I was a little afraid you'd be ugly, or a fat cow like some of the other girls I've talked to." He licked his lips and bit his bottom lip. "Mmmm. Mmmm. Mmmm." His hand went to his groin. "Calm down, boy." He laughed as I walked in.

"Hi there." I winked as I slipped inside, making sure to rub against him as I entered. "So, you want to get to know each other a little more, or get straight to business?"

"Well, hell, that don't sound like there's even an option, Stephanie. I don't think I want to waste any time talking when I've got such a fine piece of ass right here at my disposal."

Little did he know he would be the one being disposed of. "You want to play a little game?" I pulled out the tie and held it up for him.

"What in the hell is that for?" He cocked his head.

"I want to tie you up and have my way with you. How does that sound?" I unbuttoned another button and ran my fingers down my chest, licking my lips as I held eye contact with him.

He unbuttoned his jeans and let them fall around his ankles. "Why tie me up, when I'll just give it to you?" He held his erect penis in his hand. "Come on over here. I want to feel those pretty little lips of yours wrapped around it."

Repulsed by the sight, I fought back the urge to dry heave. "I really want to tie you up with this thing. It... turns me on. Don't you want to make me wet?"

"Oh fuck, I guess you talked me into it." He took my hand and led me down the hall to the bedroom.

I set my tote bag down and pushed him onto the bed. "Come on, big boy, put your hands over your head." With his arms stretched out above his head, I wrapped the tie around his wrists and tied it to a slat on the headboard, giving it one last pull to get it as tight as possible.

"Hmmm... so you like it rough?"

"I guess you could say that."

"Well, go on, get to work." His nude body was eager to be touched.

I retrieved my tote bag. "Just a minute."

"Come on, Stephanie, you're going to give me blue balls if you don't start doing something."

I pulled out the first syringe and took off the cover. I held it over him as I flicked the side with my finger. "Where do you want this one?"

"What the fuck are you doing, you stupid bitch?" He started to wiggle his hands to break free.

When I got closer to him, before I could inject him with the needle, he kicked at me, causing me to lose my balance. I tumbled onto the floor by the side of the bed. Once I was back on my feet, I saw he was free. *Fuck.* My heart started pounding so loud, I couldn't hear anything over the blood pumping against my ears. Everything went into slow motion. My first thought was to cover my body, so I grabbed my shirt and slipped it on. I felt for my keys in my jeans pocket... they weren't there. I must have put them in my tote bag. By the time I realized where they were, Earl had a hold of my shirt.

"What the fuck do you think you're doing? Who the fuck are you? You stupid whore."

I tried to take my shirt off, to slip away from him, but it was too late. His hands were tight around my neck, my body pressed up against the wall.

"I said, who the fuck are you?" With his eyes bulging out of his head, his spit covered my face. His grip became tighter, and everything started to fade to black. I thought about Tim and Gabe and the girls from group. I finally had the life I always wanted, and it was going to be extinguished before I had the chance to live it.

Everything around me went black. In the blackness, I saw a bright white light. Someone was walking toward me. I didn't know who it was, but a sense of peace washed over me. All of my worries were replaced with warmth, and the purest love I'd ever felt encased me. I began to make my way to the glow of the light. I was drawn to it like a moth to a lamp. "No, Valerie, keep fighting. It's not your time yet."

The light slowly started to drift away until the darkness returned. When I opened my eyes, I was free. Earl no longer had his hand around my throat. I placed my hand on my neck to soothe the pain his hands had caused. I gasped when I looked down.

Earl's body was on the floor in front of me. He had what looked like a gunshot wound to the head. I took a step to the side to get away from him, unsure if he could get up and come after me. I turned my attention away from Earl and scanned the room to see who was in the cabin with me. In the doorway, a familiar face smiled back at me. "Don't worry, dear, The Executioner is here."

"Norma?" Relief and shock swam around inside my stomach. The warmth of the love I had felt moments before returned. "How... how did you know I was here?"

"Oh, honey. This isn't my first rodeo." She made her way over to me and helped button up my blouse. "Let's get you cleaned up and get all your stuff out of here." She wiped the tears off my face.

"You saved my life. I thought he was going to kill me." The tears she cleaned off my face returned.

"I'd never let that happen. I love you, Val." She took my hand in hers and squeezed it.

"But how did you know I'd be here?"

"I've been following you. We're a lot more alike than you know."

"Following me?"

"I know about Donald Brice. I saw what you did to him." She brushed the hair out of my face. "I wanted to give you the satisfaction of completing the job. But I didn't want you to get a taste for it."

I swallowed hard to remove the lump in my throat. "You knew?"

"I knew about your plans for Seth and Jimmy, too. I just couldn't let you take those risks."

"How?"

"Like I said, you and I are a lot alike. I saw the way those stories affected you. The same way they always have me. I knew you wanted to protect those girls and the only way you knew how was to eliminate the problem." Norma continued to talk as she helped me gather my things. "I didn't want you to fall into the life I have. You're young and have your whole life ahead of you. I knew the job needed to be done, so I just got there before you could."

"Wait... you're the..."

She giggled. "The Executioner? That's a silly name if you ask me."

"So... you killed... them all?"

"I don't like to talk shop. Let's get out of here." She took a CD from her purse and tossed it next to Earl's body.

"What's that?" I bent down and saw a copy of *Fly* by the Dixie Chicks.

"That's my trademark." She winked. "And, for the first time, I actually have an Earl to dedicate that song to. Good-bye, and good riddance, Earl."

"But why? What made you want to... kill?"

"Oh, honey, that's a story for another day."

ACKNOWLEDGMENTS

Many thanks to the people who helped Confidentiality come to life:

Victoria Cooper for the amazing cover. Her work can be found at Facebook.com/VictoriaCooperArt.

Proofreading by the Page: Samantha Wiley, Rachel Pugh, and Anne Dailey for editing and proofreading.

Jill Nichols, Debbie Russell, Michele Avery, and Caitlyn Page for beta reading.

To the victims of domestic violence who become survivors; I believe you. You are stronger than you think. You are not alone. Never stop believing in yourself. You are worth so much more. Take time to love yourself first; you won't regret it.

Thank you to the readers. Without you, my characters would never have any fun! Your honest feedback is always appreciated and helps improve my craft. Reviews help other readers as much as they help me. Please consider leaving one.

If you or someone you know is struggling, please know there is help.

Domestic Violence Hotline

www.thehotline.org

1-800-799-7233

National Suicide Prevention Lifeline

www.suicidepreventionlifeline.org

1-800-273-8255

Child Abuse Hotline

1-800-4-A-CHILD

National Alliance on Mental Illness (NAMI)

www.nami.org

1-800-950-NAMI (6264)

ABOUT THE AUTHOR

Jessica Aiken-Hall, author of her award-winning memoir, *The Monster That Ate My Mommy* lives in New Hampshire with her husband, three children, and three dogs. She is a survivor of child abuse and domestic violence and is a fierce advocate. Her mission is to help others share their story.

She has a master's degree in Mental Health Counseling, with over a decade of experience as a social worker. She is also a Reiki Master and focuses her attention on healing.

When she is not writing, she enjoys listening to Tom Petty, walking along the beach, looking at the moon, and watching murder shows.

To follow what she's doing next check out http://www.jessicaaikenhall.com.

www.ingramcontent.com/pod-product-compliance
Lightning Source LLC
Chambersburg PA
CBHW021641110726
47902CB00007B/1782